# THE
# BOOK
*of*
# STORY
# BEGINNINGS

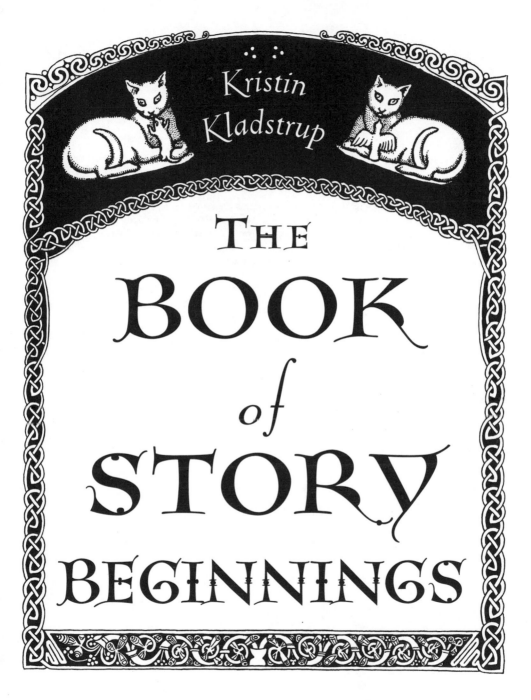

Kristin
Kladstrup

# THE
# BOOK
## of
# STORY
# BEGINNINGS

 **CANDLEWICK PRESS**
CAMBRIDGE, MASSACHUSETTS

Copyright © 2006 by Kristin Kladstrup

First edition 2006

Library of Congress Cataloging-in-Publication Data
Kladstrup, Kristin.
The book of story beginnings / Kristin Kladstrup.
p.   cm.
Summary: After moving with her parents to Iowa, twelve-year-old Lucy
discovers a mysterious notebook that can bring stories to life and which
has a link to the 1914 disappearance of her great uncle.
ISBN-10 0-7636-2609-0
ISBN-13 978-0-7636-2609-9
[1. Authorship—Fiction. 2. Storytelling—Fiction. 3. Magic—Fiction.
4. Space and time—Fiction.]
I. Title.
PZ7.K6767Boo 2006
[Fic]—dc22   2005054262

Printed in the United States of America

This book was typeset in Sabon.

Candlewick Press
2067 Massachusetts Avenue
Cambridge, MA 02140

visit us at www.candlewick.com

*For my family:*
*John and Tommy*
*and Rob*

# ❧ CONTENTS ❧

| | | |
|---|---|---:|
| | JUNE 1914 | 1 |
| 1 | THE LETTER FROM AUNT LAVONNE | 6 |
| 2 | THE BRICK | 16 |
| 3 | THE ROWBOAT | 23 |
| 4 | THE COMPOSITION BOOKS | 34 |
| 5 | A GOOD IDEA FOR A STORY | 45 |
| 6 | IN THE ATTIC | 61 |
| 7 | FROM FAR AWAY IN TIME | 75 |
| 8 | A CAT'S LIFE | 87 |
| 9 | A TERRIBLE MIDDLE | 100 |
| 10 | A BETTER BEGINNING | 114 |
| 11 | THE TRANSFORMING POTION | 128 |
| 12 | AUNT LAVONNE'S NOTES | 144 |
| 13 | THE BROKEN MOON | 158 |
| 14 | CAPTAIN MACK | 171 |

| 15 | EXTREME THIRST | 190 |
| 16 | A RARE BIRD | 204 |
| 17 | THE WAYS OF ROYALTY | 217 |
| 18 | FELLOW SORCERERS | 235 |
| 19 | THE KING'S FAMILIAR | 249 |
| 20 | DIPLOMACY | 264 |
| 21 | A BIRD'S-EYE VIEW | 274 |
| 22 | THE TRAVELING TALISMAN | 283 |
| 23 | THE WRONG ENDING | 296 |
| 24 | KINGS AND QUEENS | 305 |
| 25 | THE BIRD TRADERS | 313 |
| 26 | A SHIP'S CAT | 324 |
| 27 | THINKING ABOUT TIME | 337 |
| 28 | CHOOSING | 350 |

# June 1914

He was up late reading *Treasure Island* for the hundredth time when the story idea came to him. Like all of his ideas, it was only the beginning of a story. But a beginning was better than nothing at all, so he climbed out of bed—quietly, because the rest of his family was asleep and he didn't want to wake them.

*Treasure Island* was a book he had read so often that he hardly needed to look at the well-worn copy that Pa and Ma had given him for Christmas two years before. He needed only to open it and dream of adventure. That was how the story beginning had come to him, like a dream—the words falling into place like notes of music from Ma's fiddle. He held them in his mind carefully, not wanting to forget them before he had time to write them down.

He sat at his old worn desk—there were ink stains all over it—and drew out a secret book from the bottom of a drawer filled with papers. It wasn't the five-cent composition book in which he kept his journal. That was where he wrote down his thoughts and observations on everything that mattered and didn't matter. The secret book was one he had found in the attic among Ma's things—secret things maybe, for the trunk had been locked, and perhaps he oughtn't to have used the key he'd found in Ma's room.

As he had done many times since finding the book, he looked at the words on its title page: *The Book of Story Beginnings*. There was a verse beneath the title. It made him shiver a bit because it was so wonderful. Almost like a story beginning itself:

Beware, you writers who write within;
Be mindful of stories that you begin;
For every story that has a beginning
May have a middle and an end.

Know this, too, before you write:
Though day must always lead to night,
Not all beginnings make good tales;
Some succeed, while others fail.

Let this book its judgment lend
On whether and how your beginning ends.

And there were story beginnings inside, one written by some unknown writer—who knew how long ago (after all, the book was *old*)—and two that he had already written himself. There were blank pages as well, waiting for more story beginnings.

Quickly he began writing—it was as if the pencil were moving of its own accord, making a pattern of words across the page:

*Once upon a time, there was a boy who lived in a farmhouse high on a hill in the middle of nowhere. Below the hill lay endless fields of corn and more corn, divided by long, dull roads that went on forever before they came to anywhere that was somewhere. The boy liked to imagine that his house was surrounded by the sea and that he could sail forth from his home to find adventure. Such thoughts seemed no more than a dream to him. Then one night, as he sat alone in his room, he had a feeling that something strange had happened outside. When he went to look, he saw that his dream had come true. His house on the hill was surrounded by a great black sea. And in the moonlight, he saw a little boat waiting for him on the shore.*

He stopped to read over his words. He was the boy, of course. The house was his own house in Iowa. The rest was all wishful thinking. He rolled the pencil between his fingers, wondering whether he ought to revise or whether he ought to go on. And then he stopped, holding his head up, listening. What sound was that he heard? Not the familiar, dark sounds of a summer night—crickets and frogs, corn rustling, and cattle lowing down below the barns. No—there was a deeper sound, a sound like sighing. He turned to the window just as a cold wind ruffled the lace curtain. It was a rough, wet breeze that smelled of salt.

He pulled on his trousers and stepped out into the hall. He could see the moon through the large front window at the end of the hall as he crept down the stairs. And then, through the glass-paneled front door of the house, he saw two moons—one in the starlit sky and its reflection in the water below, where it rippled in shimmering stripes across the waves. He opened the door, hardly noticing it was there, and walked outside.

Like the boy in his story beginning, he had never seen the sea before. How could he possibly have imagined it, so cold and dark and immense? He couldn't have imagined the smell of the sea. He couldn't have imagined the way it didn't stop at the boundary between water and air. The sea was *in* the air. But he *had* imagined the rowboat, and there it was at the end of the gravel path, tied up to one of the cement urns that Ma used for geraniums.

Was it real? Were the sea and the boat real? He stood there a minute, debating the matter. *The Book of Story Beginnings* was still in his hand, and he thought of the inscription inside. The *warning*, he thought, and for the first time, he shivered for a different reason. *Beware*, the book had said. But surely the time for being careful was past. He had already written the beginning. The story—if it *was* real—had already begun.

# CHAPTER ONE

## THE LETTER FROM AUNT LAVONNE

On most afternoons, Lucy Martin sat on the dusty, sagging sofa near the front window of the first-floor apartment where she lived with her parents, waiting for her father to come home from work. She could always hear him, jogging up the cement steps outside, singing a song he liked to sing:

> "*Can she make a cherry pie, Billy Boy, Billy Boy?*
> *Can she make a cherry pie, charming Billy?*
> *She can make a cherry pie*
> *Quick as a cat can wink her eye;*
> *Sheeeeeeee's . . .*"

Her father always timed his singing so he could hold this note while he fiddled with the lock on the outside front door. He held the note while his keys jingled at the inside front door. He held the note, taking intermittent breaths to replenish his oxygen supply, for the two steps from the inside front door to the door of their apartment. On most days, Lucy had already opened this last door so that she could let her own voice slide into the last line of the song with him:

"*. . . a young thing and cannot leave her mother.*"

But today was not most days, and Lucy didn't get up from the sofa when she heard her father coming up the steps. She didn't rush to the door, and she didn't join in the last line of the song. She didn't even look around as her father came into the apartment. She stared out the window, listening to him sort through the mail and check the answering machine in the front hall. She heard him walk across the floor and felt the other end of the sofa sink as he sat down.

"I guess your mother told you the news," he said.

The news was that he had lost his job. He was a chemistry professor, and the university wasn't giving him tenure, which meant that they didn't want him back to teach in the fall. No matter how you looked at it, this was bad news, for it meant they would not have enough money to live on.

But there had been other news as well—news that Lucy's mother had tried to present as good news. They were moving to Iowa.

It was because of Aunt Lavonne that they were moving. Aunt Lavonne was Lucy's father's aunt, which made her Lucy's great-aunt. She had died only a month ago. Lucy had known this fact already because her father had flown out to Iowa for the funeral. What she hadn't known until that morning was that Aunt Lavonne had given them her house.

"She left it to your father in her will," Lucy's mother had explained. "And we're going to live there."

"But *this* is our home!" Lucy had protested.

Home wasn't merely the apartment where she had lived all her life. Home was the city, her neighborhood, everything she knew. Lucy thought of school—where she was getting A's in everything except gym, where she had finally, after years of being too shy, found a best friend. She thought of youth orchestra, where she had just made it into the first violin section. She thought of the movie theater near their apartment that showed old films. She thought of the used bookstore down the street. The owner knew her by name and always set aside books he thought she would like. Everything that Lucy loved—everything that meant *home*—paraded through her mind.

"Why?" she had asked her mother. "Why do we have to move?"

"It's a wonderful opportunity for us," her mother had explained. "It's going to be cheaper to live in Aunt Lavonne's house. We won't have to pay rent. And I can do my work there just as well as here." She was an editor who worked at home. People were always sending her manuscripts for scientific books and magazine articles to read and revise. The books and articles were dull and technical, full of words like *pyrolysis, mutase,* and *stoichiometric.* Lucy always wondered how her mother could stand to work on them. After all, her mother had wanted to be a writer once upon a time. She had actually written stories. But writing stories didn't make money. Editing articles and books for scientists did.

"What about Dad?" Lucy had asked.

"Oh, I expect he can find some sort of job in Iowa. There's a community college nearby. He might try for a teaching position there."

"What I meant was, does he want to move?" It seemed to Lucy that if money was the reason they were moving to Iowa (and it clearly was), then it was obvious that her mother was behind the decision. Lucy's mother was always worried about money.

Now Lucy asked her father, "Why do we have to move?" Her voice came out angry because she was trying not to cry.

"Oh, Lucy." Her father frowned, not because he was angry but because he never knew what to say when somebody cried. "Maybe it'll be all right once you get used to it," he said. "You've always wanted to go to Iowa."

Lucy began pulling the stuffing out of a small hole in the padded arm of the sofa. She supposed she ought to be glad her father wasn't going on about how they needed to save money. And he wasn't doing what her mother had done, which was to list all the advantages of living in Iowa—having a house to themselves, meeting new children, making new friends. Lucy's mother had made moving sound like the beginning of a whole new life, not the end of the one they already had. But Lucy didn't feel glad. "I wanted to visit Iowa—not move there," she told her father.

He was fumbling in his jacket pockets and pulled out a handful of papers. "I've got something to show you," he told Lucy as he unfolded them.

"What is it?"

"A letter from Aunt Lavonne."

"But she's dead."

"I got this a few days after she died. She must have written it before."

In spite of herself, Lucy felt a prickle of interest. A letter from someone who had died sounded much more important than an ordinary sort of letter. "What's it about?" she asked.

"Oscar." Lucy's father looked at her over the top of his horn-rimmed glasses. "And you."

"Me!" Lucy stopped pulling the stuffing out of the sofa. "Oscar and me?"

Of all the stories Lucy's father had told her about Aunt Lavonne—and there were many because her father and his brother Byron had grown up in the town where Aunt Lavonne lived—Lucy's favorite by far was the story of Oscar.

Oscar was Aunt Lavonne's older brother. He had disappeared when he was fourteen years old, way back in 1914, when Aunt Lavonne was a little girl and people drove around in Model T's. Aunt Lavonne had woken up one summer night and found an ocean surrounding their house in Iowa. That was the most interesting part of the story, for there shouldn't have been an ocean—there weren't oceans in Iowa—and Aunt Lavonne's house stood on a hill overlooking the Missouri River valley. But there the ocean had been, according to Aunt Lavonne, with waves rolling right up the front lawn. Oscar had been pushing a rowboat into the surf. She had run outside to stop him. She had called out to him, but he hadn't listened. He had rowed out to sea, and nobody had ever seen him again.

Unfortunately, the sea around the house had vanished. Nobody had believed Aunt Lavonne's account of what had happened, not even when Oscar's rowboat came back a month later. Lucy really loved that part of the story—how one morning when the family was sitting at the table having breakfast, the hired girl had come in from gathering eggs, wondering why in heaven's name there was a rowboat sitting on the front lawn. Lavonne was sure it was the boat Oscar had rowed away in, but her parents hadn't listened. They believed that Oscar had run away. Eventually, they decided that he must have met with some sort of accident, that he must have died.

Lucy's father handed her the letter. "You'll see where she mentions you. She wanted us to come visit. I thought maybe we could go this summer, after classes ended. But now . . ."

Looking up at him, Lucy saw a sad expression on her father's face. Then she began to read:

*Dear Shel,*

*I've just counted the years since we last saw each other. Would you believe I counted ten? I'm sure you'll agree that it's about time you come for a visit!*

*When you come (notice that I say* when, *not* if*), I have something exciting to show you. It's a new book about alchemy. New to me, that is, for I'm quite sure the book is much older than I dare to guess. I've never seen anything quite like it, Shel. The parts I've been able to translate have got me to thinking about a dream I had recently.*

*You will remember, of course, that I told you Oscar said something to me across the water that night he disappeared, something I couldn't quite hear. Well, a few nights ago, I dreamed it all again. I dreamed I was a girl, and I dreamed of that night. Only this time, I did* hear what *Oscar said, Shel. As clear as anything, I heard him say, "Lucy will explain!"*

*In the dream, I called out, "Explain what? What will she explain?" But then Oscar was gone, and all I saw was the sea.*

*The next thing I knew, I was lying awake in my bed, an old woman once more. I lay there for a while wondering what it meant. How could Lucy be involved? What was it that she could explain?*

*Those questions have led me back to Oscar's old composition books. I've been reading them again, even though I practically have them committed to memory by now. But that's just it. Maybe they're too familiar to me. I wonder if new eyes are needed—Lucy's eyes, perhaps. Oh, I know it sounds crazy. But please write when you can, Shel, and let me know what you think.*

*Love to you and Jean and Lucy,*

*Lavonne*

The story of Oscar's disappearance had always made Lucy feel shivery—*magical*. Now, finishing the letter, she got that same shivery feeling all over again. Aunt Lavonne had dreamed about her! What was it Oscar had said in the dream? *Lucy will explain!*

She looked down at the letter, letting her eyes brush over the words. "What does she mean, a book about alchemy?"

"I've told you how she got involved in that sort of thing," said her father.

"You mean magic," said Lucy. One of the most intriguing things about Aunt Lavonne (in Lucy's opinion, at least) was that she had believed in magic. She had devoted her life to the study of it, reading every book she could find about spells, incantations, astrology, numerology, potions, and alchemy.

"She always insisted that something magical had happened to Oscar," said her father, shaking his head. "She never gave up on that belief."

Lucy could tell that her father didn't think anything magical had happened. She felt a rush of compassion for Aunt Lavonne. How awful to have nobody believe you!

She looked down at the letter. "What does she mean by 'Oscar's composition books'?" she asked.

"Oscar wanted to be a writer. He wrote all the time. Aunt Lavonne had notebooks filled with his writings. Sort of a journal, really."

"Could there be some kind of clue in them?"

"It's hard to believe Aunt Lavonne would have missed something like that. She wasn't exaggerating when she said she had those notebooks memorized."

"But she was too familiar with them. That's what she says. Maybe there's something there and she just couldn't see it. It's like she says; it needs new eyes," said Lucy. *My eyes,* she thought. And for the first time that day, going to Iowa didn't sound so bad after all.

# Chapter Two

## The Brick

Lucy woke up suddenly. The station wagon was slowing down. The sun was much lower in the sky than she remembered, and it took her a moment to understand that she had been asleep. As the car stopped, then turned onto another highway, she asked, "Are we almost there?"

Compared to how quickly they had packed up their belongings and moved out of their apartment, driving to their new home seemed to be taking forever. They had been on the road for three days, and Lucy was tired of sitting in the back of the station wagon along with all the boxes that hadn't fit into the rented trailer that was rattling behind the car.

In the front seat, her parents were having a conversation about Lucy's uncle Byron and aunt Helen and whether they would have dinner ready. Lucy's father was sure they would. Her mother didn't want them to make a fuss. "Are we almost there?" Lucy asked again, louder this time.

"Not far now," said her father. "Look at the hills out the window. They're called bluffs."

The bluffs made Lucy think of their new house, which she knew was built on top of a hill. Of course, it wasn't a new house at all. Aunt Lavonne's grandfather had built it in the 1800s. His family had lived there. And then Aunt Lavonne, with her parents and Oscar and her little brother, Morris, who had grown up to be Lucy's father's father. Lucy had seen a photograph of the house before, a large brick house with a wide porch in front, a house for families, a house that even had a name. People had been calling it *The Brick* for over a hundred years.

Were she and her parents the sort of family who belonged in The Brick? Lucy looked at her father and mother and wondered. Her parents were so different from each other that they reminded her of a bedtime story her father used to tell, about a king who loved cats and a queen who loved birds. The king loved his cats so much and the queen loved her birds so much that they couldn't get along with each other. They fought all the time. The story was really just the beginning of a story, because Lucy would always ask what happened next, and her father would shake his head and say, "I don't know. Not a very pretty situation, was it?"

That was how it was with her parents, who always seemed to disagree more than they agreed. Sometimes it was hard to remember they had fallen in love once upon a time. *The Brick,* thought Lucy. *Our house, The Brick.* It sounded funny.

Looking down the highway, she saw a town that looked the same as all the others she had already seen—a small cluster of houses, stores, grain elevators, and a tall water tower. The car slowed as it passed through the town. Then, just outside it, Lucy saw a sign that said MARTIN: 8 MILES.

"That's it!" she cried. The town near their new house was named after Lucy's family. Aunt Lavonne's grandfather had been one of the founders of the town. Lucy liked being connected to history. She liked sharing her last name with the town. It made her feel that she and her parents might just possibly belong there.

Looking out the window, Lucy saw cedar trees gripping the sides of the hills and cottonwood trees shimmering in the valleys. She glimpsed cattle grazing around a small pond. The station wagon rolled downhill, crossed over a little creek that had etched itself into the land, and began to climb again. At last it came up over a rise, and Lucy saw that the farmland to the west was completely flat. "That's the Missouri River valley," said her father.

The station wagon curved north, following the edge of the bluffs, climbing even higher. Down below the road, Lucy saw several large white barns grouped together. A white farmhouse stood nearby. "That's Helen and Byron's place," said her father. "See that mailbox up ahead? That's us."

As the car slowed, Lucy saw the name *Martin* stenciled on the mailbox. Then, as her father turned onto a long gravel driveway, she rolled down her window and leaned out of the car to get her first look at The Brick.

The house was set back from the highway, and in the light from the setting sun, its bricks looked almost pink. Two tall spruce trees grew close to the left side of a long white front porch. Lilac bushes, their purple blooms weighing down their branches, leaned into the other end of the porch. Five tall windows looked out over a balcony on the porch roof. Without knowing how she knew, Lucy was sure that the two on the left would be her windows.

Her father stopped the car beside the spruce trees just as two people came around from the back of the house: a man who looked like a shorter, sturdier version of Lucy's father, and a smiling woman with dark, graying hair cut short.

"It's Byron and Helen!" Her father threw open the car door.

In the bustle of chattering and introducing that followed, Lucy found herself held at arm's length, hugged, then held at arm's length again as Aunt Helen exclaimed, "Look at you! How old are you now? Twelve? My goodness! You're practically grown up."

Meanwhile, Uncle Byron was quietly herding everyone toward the back door of the house. "The table's all set, and I've got a casserole warmed up in the oven," said Aunt Helen as they came into the kitchen. "I know you folks must be hungry." Then Aunt Helen noticed that Lucy was poking her head through a tall doorway leading from the kitchen. "Goodness! It looks to me as if Lucy is too excited to eat right away," she said with a laugh.

"Can I go look around?" said Lucy.

"Of course, dear. It's your house."

*Our house.* Lucy passed through a dining room, then another room filled with old furniture: tables with curly legs and clawed feet, a faded red velvet couch, and an enormous leather chair. There were lace curtains at the windows. In any other house, the room would have been a living room. In this house, it was clearly a *parlor*, Lucy thought.

"I made up Lavonne's bed for you, dear," she heard Aunt Helen's voice call. "I thought you'd like her room. It's upstairs at the front of the house. Not the room with the big bed—I made that one up for your parents. It's the other room."

The front stairs were in a hallway just outside the parlor. There was a glass-paneled front door at one end of the hallway and a grandfather clock at the other, and two doors in between. One of these was closed. Peeking in the other door, Lucy saw a few chairs and a baby grand piano. Then she hurried up the stairs, admiring their threadbare magenta carpeting. It made her think of the plush seats in an old movie theater.

Upstairs, she found Aunt Lavonne's room. *My room*, thought Lucy. She was sure it was the one she had chosen from outside. The wallpaper was old-fashioned, with faded vines twisting around faded tree branches. Between the two windows that faced west stood a spindle bed, much higher than her old bed. There was a tall wooden dresser and a funny little vanity table. Lucy looked at herself in its folding mirrors. She made her brown eyes and round face serious, like a face in an old photograph. She let her long, dark brown hair fall over her shoulders, just like an old-fashioned girl might do. Only her T-shirt and jeans looked out of place in the room. Aunt Lavonne must have worn dresses when she was a girl.

Seeing the remains of the sunset reflected in the mirror, Lucy turned and moved to the window. The plains were growing dark, and she saw the gleaming silver threads of a four-lane highway cutting across them. Except for the highway, which couldn't have been there in 1914, she might have been looking back in time. She wondered if Lavonne had been looking out this very window when she had seen Oscar standing at the edge of a great, magical sea.

Lucy closed her eyes, picturing the sea in her mind. She imagined Oscar standing beside the rowboat, turning around to look at Lavonne. No—he wasn't looking at Lavonne. He was looking at *her,* as if to say once again, "Lucy will explain!"

# CHAPTER THREE

## THE ROWBOAT

When Lucy came downstairs the next morning, Uncle Byron was sitting at the table having coffee with her parents. Aunt Helen was standing at the stove pouring pancake batter onto a griddle. There were sausages sizzling in a pan. "I came up to cook breakfast for you and your folks," Aunt Helen told Lucy.

"I love this kitchen," said Lucy's mother, looking around with pleasure. "Look how old it is. It reminds me of my grandmother's kitchen when I was a girl." The walls of the kitchen were pale green and the floor was polished wood. The cabinets were so tall that there was a little stepladder under one of the windows so you could reach the top shelves.

"Lavonne liked old things. I'm just glad she replaced the coal stove," said Aunt Helen. "Now, who gets the first pancakes?"

They ate in comfortable silence for a while. Aunt Helen hovered between the stove and the table, making sure everyone had enough to eat. Then Lucy noticed that she was looking at Uncle Byron and wagging her head toward Lucy's father.

Uncle Byron set down his coffee. "Bill Parker says they're looking for someone to teach a chemistry class at the community college over in Onawa this summer," he said, wiping his mouth with his napkin. "Thought you might be interested, Shel."

Her father put down his fork. "It's good of you to think of us, Byron. But Jean and I have talked it over. I think I'll be taking the summer off."

"I bet this summer position could lead to something in the fall," said Aunt Helen. "You never know. The college would be so lucky to have you, Shel."

"What I really want is to take some time off from teaching chemistry. Maybe try my hand at something else."

"I don't mean to interfere, Shel, but jobs around here are few and far between," said Uncle Byron.

"I think we'll be all right," said Lucy's father.

Lucy noticed that her mother was cutting her pancakes into precise, even pieces. She didn't look very happy. Lucy wondered if her parents really had "talked it over," as her father had said.

"What kind of job would you get, Dad?" she asked. She had a hard time picturing him doing anything but teaching chemistry. Could he raise cattle, like Uncle Byron?

Her father smiled, then winked at her. "Oh, I don't know, Lucy. Maybe I'll take up alchemy, like Aunt Lavonne."

"What?" said Aunt Helen, a blank look on her face.

"Just a joke, Helen," said Lucy's father. "But I did think I'd take a look at her laboratory up in the attic— maybe read over her notes. I haven't been up there in years. Byron and I used to help her out with her experiments when we were boys. Remember, Byron?"

"I remember you and Aunt Lavonne nearly blowing the roof off the house," said Uncle Byron.

Lucy's father laughed. "I hope I know a little more about chemistry now."

"What's alchemy got to do with chemistry?" asked Lucy. "I thought it was all about making gold out of lead."

"There's a little bit more to it than that," said her father. "The alchemists experimented with all sorts of chemicals. Their work is pretty interesting, especially from a historical point of view."

"I never did understand what Lavonne was doing up there in the attic. Now you tell me she was making gold!" said Aunt Helen.

The laughter that followed this comment made Lucy want to defend Aunt Lavonne. "She was trying to find out what happened to Oscar."

"Oh, poor Lavonne!" said Aunt Helen. "I think she believed that ridiculous story about her brother sailing away in a rowboat right up until the day she died. Sometimes I wonder if she wasn't a bit touched in the head."

Lucy gave her father a questioning look. Wasn't he going to defend Aunt Lavonne?

Instead, he cleared his throat and said, "What a fine breakfast this has been, Helen. Thank you! And now I think Lucy and I had better start unloading that trailer."

Outside, Lucy sat on the front porch while her father talked with Uncle Byron. At last she heard Uncle Byron's pickup truck start, then watched it roll out the gravel driveway. Her father came around the corner of the house and sat down beside her.

"How could you let Aunt Helen say all those things about Aunt Lavonne?" she asked.

"Oh, Lucy. She didn't mean any harm."

"Was Aunt Lavonne crazy? Touched in the head, like she says?"

"Of course not."

"But how could it have happened the way Aunt Lavonne said?" Lucy looked out across the front lawn. Last night at sunset, it had been easy to imagine a magical ocean appearing around the house. In the light of day, the wide expanse of land beyond the crest of their hill looked perfectly ordinary. "Maybe she just dreamed the whole thing."

"Probably," said her father.

Lucy didn't like that answer. "Maybe she didn't dream it," she argued. "Just because you can't explain something doesn't mean it didn't happen."

"You sound like Lavonne," said her father. "She used to say that some things simply defied explanation."

"Well, something happened to Oscar, and I want to find out what," said Lucy. "Dad, why did Aunt Lavonne study alchemy?"

"Good question. For one thing, the alchemists believed there was a strong connection between the human spirit and the natural world. The work of changing a base metal like lead into gold was supposed to mirror a person's journey to greater understanding. And I think some alchemists thought that the chemical reactions they were observing were in some way influenced by their own thoughts and desires."

"Sort of like magic," said Lucy.

"Sort of, I guess. At least that's what Lavonne thought."

"Sort of like making an ocean appear where there isn't one," said Lucy.

"Maybe," said her father, smiling. "Come on. I want to show you something."

They walked around the house, past the spruce trees, past the back door. Lucy heard the clink and murmur of Aunt Helen and her mother washing dishes and talking.

"Look there, Lucy," said her father, pointing to a crowd of bushes growing up against the porch screen. "Gooseberry bushes. Lavonne used to make jam every summer."

"That's what you wanted to show me?"

"No." Her father strode past the bushes. "I want to show you the smokehouse."

"The smokehouse?"

"Well, it used to be the smokehouse back in the 1800s. They used it to preserve meat. By the time Byron and I were kids, it was just a storage shed. We used to play in it."

The smokehouse, a small square building made of the same brick as the main house, stood in a grove of elm trees not far from the back porch. A chimney poked up from its pointed roof. Lucy's father pushed open a green door with a black knob. He stepped over the threshold, and Lucy followed. The wooden floor creaked under their weight. Lucy brushed a cobweb away from her face with a shudder.

There was another door in the wall on their right. Her father pushed it open, and a stripe of bright morning sun poured across the floor.

"Dad! It's the boat! Oscar's boat!" Lucy cried.

Along the far wall, a small rowboat lay tilted on its side. A pair of oars was propped against it.

Together, they laid the boat flat on the floor. Lucy climbed in and sat down on one of the two seats. Her father handed her the oars, and Lucy rubbed her hands down the length of them. She thought of Oscar holding the oars in his hands, pulling them through water that shouldn't have been there. Was that a faint smell of the sea coming up from the old boards beneath her feet? "This must be the real boat, Dad," she said. "It smells like it's been on the ocean."

"Your Aunt Lavonne thought the same thing. She used to say—"

Lucy never found out what Aunt Lavonne used to say, because at that moment she gave a shriek and leaped out of the boat. Something had brushed against her arm. Something alive.

"What is it?" she gasped.

Two golden eyes flashed from the shadowy corner. In the dim light, Lucy saw the outline of a cat. It stared back at her, then jumped down and strolled over to rub against her father's leg.

"Just a farm cat," said her father.

"What's it doing here?"

"Farm cats hang around farms, killing rats and mice."

"I thought it might be a rat."

"I could tell."

The cat followed them as they left the smokehouse. In the full light of day, he turned out to be a large gray tabby.

Lucy's mother waved from the kitchen window, then came outside to meet them. "Did you find a pet, Lucy?" she asked.

"I guess so," said Lucy.

"That cat for a pet?" said Aunt Helen, joining Lucy's mother on the porch. "Why, he's just a stray. Showed up a couple of months ago. You never saw such a scrawny-looking thing. I must say he looks better now. Must be the milk I keep leaving out for him down at our house. He's all over the place, that cat. If you let him inside, Jean, he'll rip the furniture to shreds!"

"Well, the furniture's so old it can't matter." Lucy's mother opened the door. "Look at him! He wants to come in," she said as the cat darted past her ankles into the kitchen. "I love cats," she confided to Aunt Helen. "Sometimes I think I must have been a cat in another life. But we've lived in an apartment for so long. No pets! Lucy's never even had a goldfish."

When Lucy went to look for the cat, she found him in her bedroom, sniffing delicately at a suitcase. As she approached, he darted under the bed. She leaned down to coax him out, and he ran out the other side of the bed into the hallway.

This time she was quick enough to see him disappear into the room just down the hall. Oscar's room — her father had said so last night, only she had been too tired to look at it.

She ignored the cat as she came through the door. Instead, she wandered over to the dresser to look at the photographs displayed on top of it. Some were new — Lucy's school photo from last year, a picture of Uncle Byron and Aunt Helen and their two grown-up boys. Lucy picked up an old photograph in a tarnished silver frame. A young woman in a white lace dress was holding a chubby baby in her lap. Standing on either side of her were a tall boy wearing a jacket and tie and a girl with a big white bow in her hair. It must be Oscar and Lavonne, Lucy realized. And the baby must be Morris, her own grandfather. The photograph must have been taken just before Oscar disappeared.

Oscar had light brown hair. Lucy studied his long, solemn face, as if she might find some hint that he knew what was about to happen to him. Then she looked around the room. Perhaps Oscar's composition books were here. She scanned the titles on a bookshelf that stood against one wall. She ignored the newer-looking books. Those surely couldn't have belonged to Oscar. But some of the older ones—perhaps he had read those. Lucy recognized *Huckleberry Finn* and *Treasure Island*. She opened the cover of *Treasure Island* and read the inscription on the flyleaf:

*A Merry Christmas to Oscar, 1912*
*With Love from Ma and Pa*

She felt a ruffle of excitement and an almost un-bearable eagerness. "Where are Oscar's composition books?" she said, sitting back on her heels and looking at the cat.

At that very moment, she heard her father calling. "Lucy! Let's unload that trailer!"

"As if you would know!" Lucy said to the cat.

Of course, looking at the cat, crouched like a sphinx in the sunlight pouring through the window, you'd never believe he didn't know, she thought. Cats always managed to look as though they knew something.

"What does a composition book look like, anyway?" she wondered aloud. Then she hurried downstairs to help her father.

# Chapter Four

## The Composition Books

After only a few days in The Brick, Lucy's mother claimed she needed to "get working and start earning some money again." She set up an office in a small room behind the room with the baby grand piano—behind the *music parlor*, which was what you were supposed to call that room. Soon she had sequestered herself and was busily marking up a manuscript that had arrived by overnight mail the day after they arrived.

Lucy's father had already found the book about alchemy that Aunt Lavonne had described in her letter. He spent much of his time in the attic looking at her notes about it.

When her father wasn't in the attic, Lucy helped him with unpacking. While she worked, she thought about Oscar and his composition books. According to her father, a composition book was just a notebook with blank paper inside, not much different than a modern-day spiral-bound notebook—only there weren't spiral bindings in Oscar's time. After a week of poking around the house, however, Lucy still hadn't found anything resembling a composition book.

One afternoon, Aunt Helen and Uncle Byron took everyone on a tour of Martin. By the time they got back, it was nearly suppertime, and Lucy's parents invited Helen and Byron to stay for frozen pizza. Lucy's father and Uncle Byron wandered off to the kitchen to turn on the oven and talk. To Lucy's dismay, her mother suggested that she play the violin for Aunt Helen.

Lucy considered protesting. It wasn't that she minded playing the violin. She played well enough to enjoy it. She just didn't care much for people listening. On the other hand, she knew she couldn't avoid playing without looking childish, so she gave in without a fuss and played.

She was putting her violin back into its case when her mother asked why Aunt Lavonne had so little piano music. Other than a few old standbys—"Für Elise" and *The Well-Tempered Clavier*—sitting on the piano, they hadn't found any other pieces.

"Don't tell me Lucy plays the piano, too!" exclaimed Aunt Helen.

"Actually, I like playing myself," said Lucy's mother. "Lucy's never learned because we've never had a piano before."

"Lavonne loved to play," said Aunt Helen. "She kept her music over in the window seat."

As her mother and Aunt Helen left the room, Lucy wandered over to look at the window seat. Why hadn't she noticed before that it opened? Raising the hinged lid curiously, she saw a jumbled pile of piano pieces—Beethoven sonatas, Chopin waltzes, and old sheet music titles like "Ramona" and "Heliotrope Bouquet." To her surprise, she also found some violin music. She lifted a stack of yellowed pages.

And then she saw the book that lay beneath the pages. It took a moment for the words on the cover to sink in:

Harrison's

Quality

Composition Book

Property of **Oscar Martin**

As she pulled out the book, she found another composition book beneath the first. And then another, and another, and another. The last one fell open as she held it, and Lucy saw that only the first few pages were written on. Looking quickly through the other notebooks, she saw that their pages were full. Lucy gathered the notebooks into a stack and jumped to her feet. "Dad!" she called. "Dad!"

She almost ran into her father in the front hall. "The pizza's ready," he said.

"No!"

Her father raised his eyebrows in surprise.

"I've found the composition books! Please don't make me eat dinner right now," Lucy begged.

"Oh, go on." Smiling, her father waved her up the stairs. Lucy took them two at a time.

She slowed as she passed the door of Oscar's room. She should read the notebooks there, she decided. After all, they contained Oscar's thoughts.

As she entered, she saw that the smokehouse cat was occupying the bed. "Get down, Walter," she said, using the name her mother had chosen. It was the name of some famous actor, but the cat didn't seem to care that it was now his name. Lucy sat down next to him and opened the notebook on the top of the stack.

The first entry was dated June 15, 1912. Lucy opened the second notebook and found that it began in December 1912. The third notebook began in September 1913, the fourth in January 1914, and the fifth in June 1914. There was only one entry in the fifth notebook.

Oscar's last entry, Lucy thought. She resisted the temptation to read it. She wanted to read the journal entries in order. Opening the first notebook, she began:

June 15, 1912
Today I bought this notebook at Sunderlund's Store. Keeping a journal is important for a writer, which is what I want to be, so I have made a solemn vow to write every day. My friend Earl says it is foolish to think I will write every day. He wanted me to buy fishhooks.

Seeing how nothing much happened today, I will describe my family. Besides me, there are my pa and ma; my sister, Lavonne; and my brother, Morris. Pa grows corn and raises cattle on our farm. He wants me to do the same someday. He doesn't think much of my plans for becoming a writer. Ma likes to play the violin and read books. Lavonne is younger than I am—only eight years old and bothersome. Morris is just a baby, so he is bothersome mostly at night. That's all I can think of to write about. Nothing much ever happens around here.

Lucy grinned. Oscar's journal sounded like the diary she had tried to keep during the past year. She could never figure out what to say, so her diary was peppered with comments like "Well, nothing happened today, *again*."

As she read on, she discovered that Oscar liked to read, just as she did. And he liked school. He was a good student, though he did seem to get into trouble frequently. *Earl and I are talented at getting into scrapes,* he wrote. Lucy, who hardly ever got into trouble, decided that Oscar's life was more interesting than her own. And his family seemed happier than hers; she could tell they belonged in The Brick.

Then she came to the last entry in the second notebook:

August 2, 1913
One of the horses got hurt this morning, so Pa came home early. Ma was in the music parlor playing her violin. The breakfast dishes were still

on the table, and Pa yelled at Ma for leaving the mess. Nothing gets her more riled than being interrupted when she is playing music. She told him it was none of his business how she keeps house. Pa just laughed at her. It wasn't a nice laugh. He said was that what she called it, keeping house? He said it was more like keeping a pigsty! Then they went at each other hammer and tongs, shouting all sorts of hurtful things. Lavonne and I were upstairs with Morris and heard everything. Did they think we wouldn't hear? Finally Ma said, "Either you leave this house, George Martin, or I will!" The glass in the front door broke when Pa slammed it behind him. Now he is staying up at Uncle Ned's. Ma looks as if she will break in half. I wish . . .

The entry ended abruptly. Quickly, anxiously, Lucy grabbed the third notebook to see what had happened next. But the next entry was dated September 15, 1913, and Oscar described an outing to the county fair. Pa and Ma must have made up after their quarrel, because Oscar wrote about Ma blushing when Pa told her she looked like a cross between a princess and a bluebird in her new dress.

It was getting dark and Lucy had to turn on a lamp. She continued reading, only vaguely aware of certain sounds—the back door creaking as Aunt Helen and Uncle Byron left, their voices fading, car doors opening and slamming, and the pickup truck grinding down the driveway. Not long after, her father tiptoed in with a peanut butter and jelly sandwich and a glass of milk. He was gone before she had time to come out of her haze of reading.

Later, she heard her parents coming upstairs and going into their room. She guessed that her father must have convinced her mother that Lucy was involved in something so important that she couldn't be interrupted, not even to go to bed. Or maybe he had told her Lucy had fallen asleep in Oscar's room. At any rate, nobody bothered her, and she kept reading.

May 2, 1914

It was damp this morning. "Mushroom hunting weather," Pa said at breakfast, so we all went to the North Pasture. We searched for hours around the rotting logs and stumps in the woods there, and now we have a bag full of mushrooms. They are morels—very ugly, all wrinkled and poisonous-looking. But they will taste just fine tomorrow when Ma dips them in butter and bread crumbs and fries them in a pan!

The best part of the mushroom hunt came at the end of the day. Pa made a bonfire so we could toast bread and cheese over the coals. Then, when the stars came out, Ma took out her fiddle. We all quieted down while she tuned the strings, and I got the funniest feeling. I felt as if I was looking at everyone from far away in space, or maybe even in time. They all looked so beautiful sitting in the darkness of the woods under the stars. Their faces were pink and warm and happy in the firelight. I felt perfectly happy and perfectly sad all at the same time, and tears came into my eyes.

Luckily, before anybody noticed what a sop I was, Ma started to play songs that we could sing. She played "Buffalo Gals," "Home Sweet Home," and Pa's favorite, "Billy Boy." We always hold the note on the word *she* in the line that goes, "*She's* a young thing and cannot leave her mother." That makes us all laugh.

"Billy Boy"! thought Lucy. The very same song she liked to sing with her father. She felt a strange, warm sort of feeling. She felt suddenly as if she knew Oscar, as if she were part of his family. She imagined herself traveling back in time, stealing through the dark woods toward the warm fire and their happy music. As she approached, everyone would turn to welcome her. . . .

She was losing herself in this reverie—almost drifting off to sleep, as a matter of fact—when her mind began to picture how everyone must have reacted when Oscar vanished. She could see Ma distraught, Pa troubled. And she could imagine how Lavonne must have felt. *Forlorn*—that was how you would feel if you lost your brother.

Lucy had to pull herself back to the present. It was like swimming up from a great depth to the surface of a lake. As she sat up and stretched, it occurred to her that it had been quite some time since her parents had gone to bed. Even Walter had disappeared, gone off for a nightly prowl.

Tired though she was, Lucy opened the last notebook to its first and only entry:

June 5, 1914
I have decided to keep a notebook of story ideas. Not stories about my family, which are easy to write. My story ideas are strange ones that are hard to write about. I don't even talk about them,

except sometimes to Lavonne. She lurks around me so much I can't *not* tell her what I think about. Besides, she likes my stories. They are like fairy tales, I suppose, full of kings and queens and adventures. Ma says people think fairy tales are simple stories but they are not. I guess I agree. My trouble is I have no talent for thinking up plots. The best I can do is come up with a good beginning. My book of story ideas is really just a book of story beginnings. Still and all, that is something.

If Lucy hadn't been so tired, she might have been disappointed. All that reading, and not a single clue. But she was half-asleep, and at the moment, she didn't care. She left the composition books in a heap on the floor, then shuffled down the hall to her room, pulled off her jeans, and slid into bed.

It wasn't until she was almost completely asleep that she thought of something that might be important: If Oscar had begun a notebook of story ideas, where was it?

# Chapter Five

## A Good Idea for a Story

I read them!" Lucy announced the next morning. She dropped the stack of composition books on the kitchen table and slid into a chair.

Her father was studying a recipe card. There was a can of soup, a box of rice, a carton of eggs, a head of broccoli, and part of a ham on the counter. "You don't know anything about boiling eggs, do you?" he asked Lucy.

"Are you cooking, Dad?"

"Your aunt Helen left this recipe. She said it was easy to throw together, so I thought I'd give it a whirl."

"I didn't know you could cook." Lucy took a bowl out of the dish drainer on the counter. She poured some cereal from a box on the table.

"I'm a chemist, Lucy. Chemistry and cooking are practically the same thing."

"I guess you ought to be able to figure out how to boil an egg, then."

"You're absolutely right," said her father. "It's all a matter of timing, I imagine." He picked up an egg and weighed it in his hand. "About sixty grams, I'd say. The shell is fragile, not impermeable to the water as it heats. Let's give it ten minutes."

"Dad—I read the composition books last night."

"I wonder where your mother keeps the pans."

"Aunt Helen puts them in the bottom cupboard next to the refrigerator. Mom hasn't cooked since we got here. Did you hear what I said?"

"You read the composition books. Did you find anything?"

"Not exactly—maybe—I don't know." Lucy wondered what it was that she had found. A boy who wanted to be a writer. And a family who had picnics under the stars. She felt as if she had lost something. After all, that family now lived only in the pages of an old diary.

"Dad, did you know that Oscar's mother played the violin?" she asked.

"I did. It's his mother's violin that you play."

"You never told me that! I thought the violin belonged to Grandpa Morris!"

"Well, it did. He got it from his mother. She taught Morris to play when he was a boy." Lucy's father found the saucepan and filled it with water. He dropped in three eggs and set the pan on the stove.

Lucy thought about the familiar feel of her violin in her hands, the bow drawing across the strings, producing notes that seemed to stretch over time. "Dad, is Oscar why you like to sing 'Billy Boy'?" she asked.

"Is Oscar *what*?" Her father lit the gas with a match.

"In Oscar's diary, he talks about everybody singing 'Billy Boy.' It was his father's favorite song."

"Whose father's favorite song?"

"Oscar's. Are you even listening to me?"

Her father looked up from staring into the pot of water. "Lucy, I'm sorry," he apologized. "I guess cooking isn't quite like chemistry."

"Why *are* you cooking?"

"Oh, your mother's so busy. I thought I could help— do something, anyway. Now that I'm not working, I mean." Her father sat down at the table, looking a little depressed, and Lucy thought about how her mother had been disappearing into her new office more and more over the past few days. Just this morning she had been on the phone with someone. Lucy had heard, "I can get it to you by Friday, not Wednesday," over the busy sound of papers being shuffled.

"So, what did you find in Oscar's diary?" asked her father.

"Nothing really, I guess. Only that he sounds like someone I'd like to know."

"No clues?"

"No—except for one thing. Oscar says he started a book of story ideas."

"He wanted to be a writer."

"I know. But where is the book of story ideas? Did Aunt Lavonne ever show it to you?"

"I don't think so. Lavonne used to tell me about his stories, but I got the impression he'd told them to her directly."

"Maybe she never saw it!"

"Well, she would have read about it in his diary, the same way you did."

"But maybe she didn't think it was important. I mean, she did say she thought there might be something she missed in the diaries. Maybe she missed the fact that Oscar says he started a book of story ideas."

Lucy opened the fifth composition book to Oscar's final diary entry.

Her father read the entry, then looked thoughtful. "Maybe you're right. Though if such a book really existed—if it were anywhere in this house—Lavonne would have found it, even if she wasn't looking for it."

"I guess it doesn't really make much difference." Lucy felt deflated. "A book of story ideas isn't really a clue."

"On the other hand, maybe she didn't think that last entry was important. Or maybe the book isn't in the house at all."

"What do you mean?"

"Maybe Oscar took it with him."

"That helps a lot," Lucy said. "The only clue disappearing with the mystery."

"Has it been ten minutes yet?" Her father jumped up to look at the pot on the stove.

Lucy decided that her father was probably right. If Oscar's book of story ideas was somewhere in the house, Aunt Lavonne would have found it already. The book had probably sailed away with Oscar and that was that.

On the other hand, there was another possibility. Maybe Oscar was secretive about his writing. Maybe he had hidden the book of story ideas from the prying eyes of his eleven-year-old sister, Lavonne. Maybe the book was so well hidden that Aunt Lavonne had never found it.

Where could it be? Lucy thought first of the window seats. She hadn't noticed that the one in the music parlor opened until yesterday. Maybe there were others.

As it turned out, there were three. But they were filled with ordinary items like sewing supplies and blankets. Of course the book wouldn't be in the window seats, thought Lucy, or Aunt Lavonne would have found it already.

She tried knocking on walls, like Nancy Drew looking for a secret compartment. She actually started to enjoy herself until her mother's voice came through the wall. "What are you doing, Lucy?" Before Lucy could even answer, her mother snapped, "Never mind! I don't care what you're doing. Just stop it!"

She thought of the attic. In stories, important things were always hidden in the attic. But Aunt Lavonne had spent much of her life working in the attic of The Brick. It seemed unlikely that she would have missed something hidden there.

She thought about the cellar, a place so musty that her father had decided against using it for storage. Which was fine with Lucy, who didn't like dark, dank cellars. She would just as soon exhaust all other possibilities first.

That left the kitchen, which was the only room whose closets and cupboards she and her father hadn't explored completely during all their unpacking. It seemed an unlikely hiding place. It was too ordinary — not as mysterious as the attic or the cellar. But perhaps that was something in its favor. After all, if Oscar's goal had been to hide something, he might very well have chosen a place where no one would think to look.

She headed for the back stairs that led from the storeroom on the second floor to the kitchen below. She was halfway down the stairs when she stopped.

She could hear her parents talking. In fact, because the door at the bottom opened right into the kitchen, she could hear every word they said. Just at this moment, they weren't talking about anything much. Her mother was complaining that she didn't have time to eat right now. She was too busy working on something that somebody in Boston wanted yesterday and was upset that he wouldn't get until next week. And there was something else that somebody in New York wanted tomorrow and was upset that he wouldn't get until Friday. Lucy's father made sympathetic noises, and her mother added that it was all just one big headache, and she wished people would figure out that work took time.

Although their conversation might have seemed perfectly normal to the casual observer, Lucy knew from the tone of her mother's voice that it wasn't going to end up that way. It was going to end up as a fight. And a fight always meant that the day was going to be ruined.

Maybe she could distract them from the treacherous conversation just long enough to head off the inevitable argument. She hesitated, wondering whether she was already too late or whether she ought to come bounding into the kitchen with some exciting piece of news.

But she couldn't think of anything particularly exciting, and the thought of trying to make something up was tiring somehow. She moved silently back upstairs.

She drifted into the hallway, not sure what to do or where to go. She didn't much feel like searching anymore. Finally, she went down the front stairs. She stood at the door of the music parlor, trying to pretend that she was Lavonne. She pretended that Ma was standing there, playing her violin for everyone.

As far as pretending went, it wasn't very successful. It bordered on wishing and it made Lucy feel rather lonely, so she turned away and opened the front door to go outside.

Something brushed past her leg—Walter. He gamboled down the length of the porch and slipped into the lilac bushes at the far end.

"Hey!" Lucy followed him around the side of the house, reaching the backyard just as Walter disappeared inside the smokehouse.

"Walter?" she said into the dark patch of the open door. She stepped into the smokehouse and opened the other door to let in more light.

Walter was perched on the rowboat, watching her. Lucy climbed into the rowboat. She pretended she was Oscar, getting ready to shove off from land. She picked up the oars and fitted them into the oarlocks. "Did you have your book of story ideas with you, Oscar?" she murmured as she pretended to row through dark, black waters.

And it was then that she noticed something—right under Walter's tail.

The sides of the boat came to a point at the front of the boat. The *bow,* Lucy reminded herself. Not that she knew much about boats, but she had figured out *bow* and *stern* and *port* and *starboard* from books and movies. Walter was sitting on a triangular piece of wood nailed across the bow. Beneath this piece of wood was a rectangular piece of wood that was shoved vertically into the space formed by the triangular piece of wood and the sides and floor of the boat. When Lucy knocked on the rectangular piece of wood, she heard a hollow noise.

"A secret compartment!" she whispered. She kicked at the wood, causing Walter to shoot out of the boat and through the open door of the smokehouse.

When she kicked at the wood again, it fell inward. She pulled it aside, feeling eagerly inside the dark space behind it.

There was nothing there. She felt again and again just to make certain until at last she scraped her finger on a splinter of wood. Tears of pain and frustration blurred her vision.

A scratching noise overhead made her look up. She saw Walter's eyes peering out of a hole in the wooden ceiling of the smokehouse.

"How did you get up there?" Lucy wiped her eyes, feeling oddly grateful to Walter for distracting her. She balanced herself on the starboard side of the boat, grabbed one side of the hole, and stood on tiptoe.

There was a hole in a corner of the roof where some shingles had fallen off. Some animal—a squirrel perhaps—had gnawed away part of the board underneath, leaving just enough room for Walter to squeeze from the roof into the tiny attic of the smokehouse.

Lucy could barely make out a lump sitting next to Walter. *A dead animal!* was her first thought. Then she chided herself for being stupid. After all, a dead animal would smell terribly, and Walter wouldn't be sitting so calmly next to it. She reached out and brushed her hand against the lump. It was made of a coarse material.

When she tugged at the lump, it was lighter than she expected. She lost her balance and tumbled backward into the boat with the lump on top of her.

Lucy knew what the lump was now. It was a burlap bag. She turned it this way and that, feeling through the cloth, searching for an opening, feeling the interesting shapes inside. These fell out all of a sudden: a rope, a tin can, an ancient-looking stub of a pencil, and a large rubbery cloth. The last turned out to be a dirty gray slicker—the kind of coat that a person would wear on a boat in bad weather, Lucy thought. She shook it, feeling in its pockets until she found what she was looking for. Her hand closed around its cool leather cover and she pulled it out.

The book was much older than Oscar's composition books. Lucy wondered where he had found it. There was no title on the cover, which was embossed with an intricate design of interwoven branches and flowers.

She opened the book and turned it so that light from the doorway fell across the ornate lettering on the first page.

# The Book of Story Beginnings

Beware, you writers who write within;
Be mindful of stories that you begin;
For every story that has a beginning
May have a middle and an end.

Know this, too, before you write:
Though day must always lead to night,
Not all beginnings make good tales;
Some succeed, while others fail.

Let this book its judgment lend
On whether and how your beginning ends.

Lucy felt the smallest of thrills, like a feather brushing over her neck. What a wonderful poem, she thought. It made her want to turn the page.

When she did, she saw that the next four pages were filled with cramped, old-fashioned writing. There were four paragraphs, the first written in faded black ink, in a foreign language Lucy didn't recognize. She wondered whether Oscar had written it. The handwriting didn't look anything like what she had seen in his journals.

The next paragraphs were written in pencil, and Lucy was sure that Oscar had written them. Could he have used the pencil in the burlap bag? Lucy picked it up and held it in her hand as she began to read:

> There was once a country ruled by a king and queen who loved different things. The king loved cats and the queen loved birds. And just as cats and birds never get along, so it was that the king and queen never got along. And everyone in the country suffered as a result. In short, it was not a very pretty situation.

How strange, Lucy thought, that the same story her father used to tell her was here in Oscar's book. Then again, Oscar had written in his journal that Lavonne liked his stories. Perhaps he had told this one to her before his disappearance. I bet Aunt Lavonne told the story to my dad, thought Lucy.

There was a soft thud beside her. It was Walter jumping down from the ceiling. Lucy went on reading.

*Once upon a time, there was a ship of orphans. Excepting the captain, all the crew from the first mate down to the cabin boy were orphans. These children were bound to their captain, who stomped about the deck from morning till night, ordering them about and making their lives hard. For the most part, the crew were accepting of their lot, climbing the rigging like pirates, shouting gaily to each other as they swabbed the deck, and generally loving the life of the sea. But one of them, a young girl with long, tangled curls, dreamed of other things—of lords and ladies, of kings and queens. She dreamed of escape.*

It was a bit frustrating, thought Lucy, to read only the beginning of a story. A picture came into your mind, an expectation of things to come, and then *nothing*. She read on:

*Once upon a time, there was a boy who lived in a farmhouse high on a hill in the middle of no-where. Below the hill lay endless fields of corn and more corn, divided by long, dull roads that went on forever before they came to anywhere that was somewhere. The boy liked to imagine that his house was surrounded by the sea and that he could sail forth from his home to find adventure. Such thoughts seemed no more than a dream to him. Then one night, as he sat alone in his room, he had a feeling that something strange had happened outside. When he went to look, he saw that his dream had come true. His house on the hill was surrounded by a great black sea. And in the moonlight, he saw a little boat waiting for him on the shore.*

"Oh!" Lucy breathed in sharply. She could imagine Oscar floating in the rowboat in the middle of the sea, wrapped up for warmth in the rain slicker, watching the sun rise. *The Book of Story Beginnings* was open on his knee, and the pencil was scribbling down what had just happened to him. "Maybe Oscar told Lavonne the first story idea, but I bet he never told her this one," Lucy told Walter. "He did take *The Book of Story Beginnings* with him after all. Only it came back with the boat."

But if that were true, how had the book and the rain slicker and everything else ended up in the space above the smokehouse ceiling? And most of all, what had happened to Oscar?

Lucy wondered about the first paragraph in *The Book of Story Beginnings*—the paragraph written in a foreign language. Could it yield some sort of clue? She thought of her father, who knew Greek, Latin, and German. If you gave him a dictionary and enough time, he could maneuver his way through almost any language.

She stuffed the raincoat and the rope back in the bag and left them in the boat. Taking the book and the pencil, she moved to the door. Her eyes blinked in the bright sunlight as she headed for the house.

# Chapter Six

## In the Attic

As Lucy crossed the yard, she could hear her mother's voice through the open window. By the time she reached the screen porch door, she could hear her father's voice as well, softer than her mother's, less strident, but still tense and almost as terrible. Her prediction had come true: her parents were arguing.

She stepped into a space between the house and a gooseberry bush to listen.

"Shel, I never said it was okay for you to just stop working," her mother was saying. "All I said was that if that's what you wanted to do, I couldn't stop you."

"A little time off, Jean. That's all I ask."

"And what are we supposed to do if you can't find a job?"

"I'll find a job, Jean."

"I'm just trying to get the bills paid, Shel. Meanwhile, you're up there playing around in the attic, trying to turn lead into gold."

"Come on, Jean! That isn't fair."

Why was it, Lucy wondered, that whenever her parents argued, they used each other's names over and over again?

Her father was saying something else—she couldn't tell what. When he was really angry, his voice always got very quiet. Then, suddenly, the door from the kitchen to the screen porch flew open. The screen porch door banged open as well. Lucy shrank back into the prickly branches of the gooseberry bush as her father strode past, down the walk and around the house. She heard the car door open and slam, the engine sputter to life, and the wheels spin on the gravel drive. It was odd, she thought, how even the car sounded mad.

She heard her mother bang a pot in the kitchen sink. She heard a choked sob. Then the sound of crying grew faint as her mother left the room.

Lucy waited, then pulled herself free from the gooseberry bush. Its thorns scratched her, leaving ruby stripes on her arms. She walked around the house to the front porch and sat down on the top step. Walter came near and pushed against her back, then sprang away when she tried to pet him. And because the warmth of a purring cat sitting next to her was just what she needed right then, Lucy's eyes filled with tears.

"If I could wish . . ." she whispered, wiping her eyes with her hands. "What would I wish?" It was something she had said to herself since she was small.

She wished her mother would stop worrying about money. She wished her father *could* turn lead into gold. Looking down, she saw *The Book of Story Beginnings* in her lap. She opened it to the first blank page. Then, using the pencil she had found in the burlap bag, she began to write: *Once upon a time, there was a girl whose father was . . .* She almost wrote *an alchemist,* then changed her mind.

> *Once upon a time, there was a girl whose father was a magician.*

Lucy leaned her head over the book, watching the pencil twitch expectantly in her hand, almost as if it were waiting for another sentence to propel it across the page. What should she write next? Perhaps she should describe the magician's extraordinary powers.

Just then, however, something perfectly ordinary happened. Uncle Byron came up the driveway in his pickup truck. "Hello, Lucy," he called.

She leaned forward to hide *The Book of Story Beginnings,* even though Uncle Byron was not the sort of person who would care about what she was writing in a book, even if he noticed that she was writing something.

"I'm going down to the barn to load cattle onto some trucks, Lucy. Want to come watch?"

"All right." Lucy wasn't sure how to say no.

"Why don't you let your mom and dad know where you're going."

"My dad's not here. Just a second, and I'll tell my mom." Lucy opened the front door and hurried up the stairs. She ran to her room and shoved *The Book of Story Beginnings* in the first place that occurred to her: under the afghan at the foot of her bed.

"Mom!"

Her mother poked her head out of the bathroom. Her eyes were red from crying, Lucy noticed.

"Mom, I'm going with Uncle Byron to watch him load cattle."

"All right." Her mother looked surprised, then almost pleased. "Do you want some lunch before you go?"

"Uncle Byron's waiting ouside." Lucy was already halfway downstairs. "I'm fine!" she called back.

Lucy spent the afternoon watching her uncle and two farm hands force great, lumbering steers onto trucks headed for a slaughterhouse. When the men were finished, Uncle Byron invited Lucy over for supper. "We'll give your folks a call to let them know where you are," he said.

During supper, Lucy waited for a lull in the conversation, then said, "Uncle Byron, I was wondering about something I found in the smokehouse."

"The smokehouse! You mean that boat, eh?"

"No, not the boat. I found a bag."

"A bag?" Uncle Byron took a sip of his iced tea.

"What was in it, dear?" asked Aunt Helen.

"Well, just some old things, really. A raincoat, a tin can, a rope—nothing much."

Uncle Byron frowned. "That sounds like that junk they found in the boat."

Lucy's heartbeat quickened. "You mean they found it after Oscar disappeared?"

"That's right," said Uncle Byron. "My dad told me his pa found some things stowed in the front of the boat. You didn't find them there, did you?"

"No. They were in a space above the smokehouse ceiling."

"Well, I'll be!" said Uncle Byron. "I guess somebody must have put them up there."

"Did Aunt Lavonne know about the things? Did she ever see them?" Lucy asked.

"I couldn't say, Lucy. I just assumed that junk got thrown away years ago."

I bet Aunt Lavonne didn't see them, thought Lucy. I bet she never even knew about *The Book of Story Beginnings*.

Had she found a clue at last? Lucy couldn't wait to talk to her father.

After supper, when Uncle Byron drove her back to The Brick, Lucy could see a light on in the attic. Her father was home. She waved goodbye to her uncle and hurried inside.

Her mother stopped her at the top of the stairs. "How did you like loading cattle?"

"Fine! Is Dad in the attic?"

"Yes—but before you go another step, you need a bath."

"Can't it wait?"

"Lucy, you smell like a barn."

"Mom, please!"

"And as near as I can tell, you didn't get to bed last night until the wee hours of the morning. I know you too well, Lucy Lavonne Martin. If you go up to the attic now, you'll be there for hours. Bath first—and wash your hair. Then you can say good night to your father."

Lucy took the world's fastest bath. Even so, by the time it was over, the sky outside was getting dark. She pulled on her nightgown. She checked beneath the afghan on her bed. *The Book of Story Beginnings* was still there.

"Comb your hair!" called her mother.

Lucy groaned, then began the laborious process of untangling her long, wet hair. She heard her mother go downstairs, and then it was quiet.

It was so quiet that Lucy didn't really hear the soft, sighing sound at first. And when she did hear it, she didn't understand what it was. She stood there listening, wondering whether the sound came from somewhere inside the house. It was only when she attached the sound to a memory—the memory of the ocean at Rockport one summer, of waves brushing against the shore—that she ran to her window.

And there it was: a great sea surrounding the house, the water lit with a reddish glow from the sun sinking beneath the waves. Lucy could see the shadows of the waves, smaller in the distance, then much larger as they splashed against the front lawn.

"Dad," she whispered.

The ladderlike stairs to the attic were in a closet near Oscar's old room. "Dad!" Lucy called as she entered the closet.

He didn't answer, but she could hear him humming as he worked. She began climbing the stairs. She was so excited that she slipped as she scrambled up the last few steps. She pulled herself through the trapdoor in the attic floor.

Her father looked up from the worktable. "Lucy!"

"Dad—did you see? Out the window?"

"I have something to show you!"

"But Dad—"

"Watch this, Lucy!"

There was a cage sitting on her father's worktable. Inside it was a white mouse. Gently, Lucy's father took the mouse in his hand. He stared at it intently.

Lucy watched him raise a tiny blue bottle over the mouse's head. She saw a drop of bright blue liquid form at the mouth of the bottle. As the drop fell, her father said, "Salamander!"

And the next thing she knew, her father was holding a damp, wriggling salamander. "Did you see that, Lucy? Did you see?" he said.

"Where did you get a mouse? Or a salamander? Which is it?" A series of stupid questions came out of Lucy's mouth. She was too dumbfounded to know what else to say.

"It's a mouse," said her father. "It was the funniest thing. I went up to Sioux City this afternoon. I was walking down the street and I saw a pet store. Don't ask me why, but I went inside. I took one look at this little fellow and thought, Maybe what I need is a familiar!"

"A *what*?"

"A familiar—it's something I read in that book Lavonne mentioned in her letter. There are several chapters about magic—about the importance of having a familiar if you want to perform magic. There's some really crazy stuff in that book!" Her father laughed. "Anyway, I said to myself, Why not? And I bought him. Honestly, I don't know what came over me!"

"How did you change him into a salamander?" said Lucy. "And what's that blue stuff in the bottle?"

"Oh, that! It's a transforming potion—something Lavonne was working on before she died. I've been reading her notes. She came up with a theory based on something she found in that crazy book. *Very* interesting stuff there, if you can get beyond the mystical language. It's almost impossible to figure out what these old alchemists were talking about. They use symbols for everything," said her father. "What Lavonne's theory boils down to is that the imagination has a potential for bringing about a transformation. And that potential is capable of being activated by language. The potion becomes a catalyst for the interaction between imagination and language. So when I imagined the mouse as a salamander and said the word *salamander*—well, you saw what happened!"

Her father beamed ecstatically—first at Lucy, then at the salamander, then at Lucy again. He was so excited that Lucy felt like she was standing next to a giant sparkler.

"Dad—I think . . ." She wanted her father to look at her, to listen to her—only she wasn't quite sure what she would say.

"Just look! I can change it back again!" Her father poured a drop of liquid onto the salamander's head. "I don't have to say anything this time—the potion also works as an antidote for transformations. There! You see? Mouse again!"

"Dad—don't you think he'd rather just be a mouse?" Lucy wondered how many times her father had used the transforming potion. Could a mouse get dizzy?

"Did you look out the window?" asked her father. He put the mouse back in the cage and pulled Lucy over to a window at one end of the attic. Ordinarily, the view from that window showed the line of bluffs bending toward the east. The hill on which The Brick stood plunged down into a grove of oak trees. But there were no trees there now. Instead, the sea curved around the hill. Its shore turned south when it met the bluffs again.

"Watch this!" Lucy's father poured a drop of liquid onto the end of the nearest object he could grab—a pencil—and leaned out the window. He was careful at first to make sure that the liquid didn't fall off the pencil. Then, with a flick of his wrist, he tossed the pencil through the air, and suddenly there was land again. "Would you look at that!" he exclaimed.

Then he did it all again, only this time he grabbed a glass stirring rod, and as he threw it, he said, "Sea!"

Lucy blinked, startled by a rush of cold sea air. She stared out the window in disbelief.

"The sea will stay there for as long as I'm here, until I decide to change it back," said Lucy's father. "It's my imagination that makes it happen. The astonishing thing is that *you* can see it as well."

"Dad!" Lucy was surprised to hear how sharp her own voice had become.

Her father's eyes were gleaming. "I wonder if I can transform myself," he said.

"Dad—please—" Lucy had a terrifying feeling of acceleration, as if her father had forgotten that he was supposed to be driving their car, and the car was careening down a steep slope. She watched—half in fear, half in fascination—as her father lifted the bottle to his lips.

"What do I want to be?" he mused. Then his face lit up, and he took a sip. "Bird!" he said.

Lucy opened her mouth, but nothing came out. She watched her father's eyes widen. She saw him grip the table. The bottle fell with a dull clink to the floor.

And then her father was gone. A bird was sitting on the table—a big black bird—an enormous crow with a purple sheen to its feathers. It cocked its head and looked at Lucy, blinking a shiny black eye.

Lucy stepped cautiously toward the bird.

At that moment, however, a terrible thing happened. There was a flash of gray at Lucy's feet. Suddenly there was an explosion of fur and feathers, a ruckus of yowling and flapping and squawking and her own voice crying, "Walter! No!"

The flapping headed for the end of the attic. Both Walter and Lucy dashed toward the window as her father flew out into the night.

"Dad!" Lucy cried as the black bird circled once in the darkening sky. She watched it settle momentarily in a spruce tree. She cried out again as the bird flapped its wings, lifted itself from the tree, and headed out across the water. Then Lucy watched, aghast, as the ocean pulled itself away from the lawn. It rose up in a great wave behind the bird, falling away from the hills as it disappeared in the distance. In less than a minute, her father was gone. And with her father went the sea.

Lucy turned from the window. For a moment, she was not completely sure of herself. After all, it might be a dream. Something that seemed so impossible should be a dream.

Then she saw Walter crouched on the floor, lapping at a pool of bright blue potion dripping out of the bottle that had fallen from the table. And suddenly, a sob forced itself out of her throat. Because no matter how impossible it might seem, she didn't believe it was a dream. If it was a dream, then her entire day had been a dream. If her entire day had been a dream, then her entire life was a dream. And Lucy was too sensible to believe that.

"Get away, you stupid cat!" She knelt down, shoving Walter aside. Lucy watched in horror as the potion dripped down between the floorboards. She could see it there, quivering, too thick to soak into the wood.

"Stupid, *stupid* cat!" Lucy shoved the stopper into the bottle. She set it down on the floor and pushed her hands into her eyes, trying not to cry, trying to think what she should do.

When her hands came away, she froze.

Precisely where Walter's cat feet had been resting only a moment before stood a pair of dirty human feet. Rising from the feet was a pair of legs wearing sand-colored knickers.

Trembling, Lucy rose to her feet, her eyes traveling upward to meet the stern gaze of a boy whose long, solemn face she recognized immediately. She recognized it because she had seen it before in a photograph.

"Who are you, and what are you doing in our attic?" said Oscar.

# CHAPTER SEVEN
## FROM FAR AWAY IN TIME

What are you doing in our attic?" Oscar said again.

Lucy was wondering the same thing about him.

"Who are you?" said Oscar.

That was one advantage she had over Oscar. She knew who he was. "I—I'm Lucy."

"How did I get here?" Oscar murmured, looking around the attic and pushing the palm of his hand against his brow. "I was dreaming. I was dreaming I was a cat! This is a dream."

"I wish it was a dream," said Lucy.

"I know you." Oscar studied Lucy closely. "You're that girl. There's a man and a woman, too."

"Those are my parents."

"Nobody ever had a dream like this one. I was a cat—I don't think a real cat could be more of a cat than I was. I thought like a cat. I ate like a cat. I hunted mice, right here in my own house. . . ."

"It's not a dream."

At that moment, Lucy heard a creaking. Her mother's voice came floating up the attic stairs. "Shel? Lucy?"

Lucy hurried to the trapdoor. In the dim light below, her mother's face looked cross. "What was all that racket?" said her mother.

"It's nothing, Mom. Dad dropped something."

"Lucy, I want you in bed."

"I'll be right down."

"Now!" Her mother's foot was poised on the bottom step.

"Don't come up!" said Lucy. "I'll come down."

"Say good night, Lucy. Shel—I'm counting on you to send her down." Her mother disappeared, just as Oscar came over and looked through the trapdoor.

"That's the woman who fed me in my dream," he said.

Lucy felt like screaming, but she whispered for fear her mother would hear. "Look, Oscar. I know this must seem like a dream to you, but as far as I know, it's not.

Something very strange has happened. Something terrible, actually. And I don't know what to do about it, and now I've got to go to bed."

"If it's not a dream, how do you know my name? You've never met me before."

Lucy thought that if she ever found herself in a strange place and couldn't figure out how she had got there, she would not waste everyone's time trying to convince herself that it was all a dream. "Believe me! I can explain how I know who you are," she told Oscar. "But for now, please listen to me. I've got to go to bed or my mother will be up here faster than anything and I don't know what I'll tell her."

She glanced around the attic. The worktable was a mess. Black feathers, scattered papers, and a rack of shattered test tubes lay on the floor. The window was still open. Maybe he'll come back, Lucy thought. He's got to come back.

"Please stay here, Oscar," she pleaded as she started down the stairs. "Just for a bit. I'll go down and pretend to go to bed. When my mother's asleep, I swear I'll come back."

But she might just as well have been a flickering face in the dream Oscar had convinced himself he was having. Lucy watched as he gingerly touched a metal lamp that was clamped to the worktable. As she went down the steps, she saw his hand curling around her father's scientific calculator.

Lucy climbed into bed, leaving the door to the hallway open so that she could watch the crack of light under her mother's door. Was her mother waiting for her father to come down?

What if her father didn't come back?

No! Her father would return, and she would use the potion to change him back. Then panic gripped her. What if Walter—what if Oscar had drunk all the potion?

Then she heard a small thud across the hall. She recognized the sound; her mother had dozed off, and her book had fallen to the floor. Now her mother was groping for the switch on the lamp beside her bed. Lucy could picture it in her mind.

Sure enough, the crack of light under her mother's door went out. Lucy hesitated, trying to decide all over again what to do.

Then, in the tense silence, she heard the grandfather clock downstairs begin to strike. As if this were some kind of signal, the stairs in the attic closet gave a creak. This creak was followed by another and another as someone made his way down the steps.

Maybe it was her father, Lucy thought. Soon he would come down the hall into her parents' room. Or maybe he would stop in the bathroom to brush his teeth.

She waited, listening to a door squeak on its hinges. It was the door to Oscar's room. She could imagine Oscar standing there, staring at the shapes of the furniture jutting out in the darkness. Did he know about electric lights?

She heard footsteps padding down the front stairs, then climbed out of bed and groped around on the floor for the T-shirt and dirty jeans she had thrown down earlier. She dressed quickly, then tiptoed out into the hall and down the stairs.

Lucy passed from one darkened room to another. With all the antiques in the house, Oscar might be fooled into thinking that his family was fast asleep upstairs. On the other hand, her mother's computer monitor was still turned on in her office. A green dot traveled tirelessly from the top of the screen to the bottom, from side to side, like a little eye darting about curiously in the dark. In the kitchen, Lucy found the refrigerator door ajar. It was an old-fashioned refrigerator. It was easy enough to open, but you had to know the trick of slamming it hard to get the latch on the side to snap shut. The refrigerator probably wouldn't be old-fashioned to Oscar, thought Lucy as she closed the door. She imagined his face filled with wonder as its cold light poured out at him, as he stared at the jugs of milk and juice, at Aunt Helen's half-eaten casseroles and desserts.

It was after she had passed back through the dining room and the front parlor that Lucy found Oscar at last. Through the moonlit rectangle of the screen door, she could see him sitting on the steps of the front porch, hunched over with his knees and arms drawn in close, as if he were trying to make himself as small as possible. He was gazing at the silvery grass of the front lawn and the moonlit plain beyond. The four-lane highway that couldn't have been there in 1914 stood out like a scratch on the land.

Lucy hesitated, then pushed open the screen door and quietly crossed the porch. She sat down, waiting for Oscar to acknowledge her presence. When he didn't, she worried. Should she say something? What should she say?

She sat there waiting, listening to the enormous noise that filled the night air—millions of crickets whispering the same sound over and over and over. If you didn't listen for it, you might not notice it. But it was always there, never stopping, never slowing. It was like a clock.

"It's just time, isn't it?" Oscar said suddenly.

"Time?" said Lucy, startled. She thought he meant the crickets.

"Some time has passed since I was here last. That's all."

Lucy started to speak, but Oscar continued. "I knew it wasn't really a dream. I think I knew it right away. I just didn't want to believe it. But I'm no fool. Anybody can see that things have changed around here. What did you say your name was?" he asked without pause.

"It's Lucy." She added cautiously, "Lucy Martin."

A look of something between pain and fear flickered across Oscar's face. Then, sounding brave, he said, "Well, Lucy Martin—suppose you tell me what the date is today."

"June something. I think the sixteenth."

"I mean, what *year*," said Oscar.

When Lucy told him, softly, for fear of what he would say, he looked at her as if he hadn't understood. "That's impossible," he said.

At that moment, a pickup roared by on the road in front of the house. Its windows were open, and Lucy and Oscar were hit by a blast of music—the wail of an electric guitar and the throb of an electric bass. Lucy glanced at Oscar when it was over. He looked pale.

"Oscar, what happened to you?" she asked. "Where have you been?"

"No!" Oscar's voice was harsh. "You tell me. Who are you? How did you know my name? Where is my family?"

"I'll tell you what I know," said Lucy. "What do you remember?"

"I remember a lot of things."

"What's the last thing you remember about being here—at The Brick? Before tonight, I mean. Do you remember leaving in the rowboat?"

"How do you know about that?" Oscar said.

"My father told me," said Lucy. "We're sort of related to you."

"Related *how*? I've never met you in my life! What are you talking about?"

Oscar sounded so furious, Lucy was sure he must hate her. "Please, Oscar! I—I'll try to explain," she stammered. "Just let me try."

Oscar leaned forward, his arms on his knees. He stared out at the front lawn again. "All right then," he said. "Try."

"My—my father told me what happened. That's how I know. He said that after you left in the boat, your sister ran inside to get your parents. But when everyone came back out, you were gone. So was the sea. There was only land—like there is now."

Lucy went on with the story she had heard from her father. Oscar frowned when she told him no one believed Lavonne's story. When she got to the part about finding the boat on the front lawn, he looked surprised.

"How did it get there?" he wondered aloud. "They must have believed Lavonne then."

"But they didn't. Everyone was sure you had run away."

"Run away! They ought to know I'd never do that. Ma knows I'd never—" Oscar stopped midsentence, a look of horror on his face. "Ma," he whispered. "Where is she? Where's Pa? Are they—they aren't *dead,* are they?"

Up until that moment, when Lucy had tried to fathom what it must be like for Oscar to find himself suddenly in the future, she had thought of him being astounded by modern inventions: televisions, refrigerators, computers. Then there was all the history that he would be amazed to learn: world wars, atomic bombs, rockets going to the moon. But what did all that matter to him? His parents were dead. For Oscar, it was as if they had just died. For a moment, Lucy didn't dare look at him.

When she stole a glance at last, she saw that his face was buried in his arms.

Lucy remembered what Oscar had written in his journal, about the picnic in the woods and Ma playing the fiddle. About feeling as though he were looking at his family from far away in time. She wanted to tell Oscar that she understood what he'd meant when he'd written about how beautiful they were, and how seeing them made him feel perfectly happy and perfectly sad at the same time. And now they were dead. "I'm sorry," she whispered.

"How—when did my mother die?" Oscar asked in a calm, terrible voice.

"I—I don't know."

"And my father?"

"I don't know."

"And my brother and sister?"

Lucy felt a pang of guilt for not having asked her father more about Oscar's family. "Morris was my grandfather. I think he died before I was born."

Oscar raised his head and looked at her. "Your grandfather," he said. "What does that make you? My *niece*?"

"I think you're my great-uncle. Lavonne was my father's aunt."

"And I suppose *she* died twenty years ago." Oscar's voice was cold, his face stern.

"Well, no. She died this spring. She's the reason we're here. She left the house to my father in her will."

The stern look dropped from Oscar's face. "Was she an old lady?" he asked in a faltering voice.

Lucy nodded.

"I saw her! She was lying in a bedroom upstairs, and I was on the porch roof looking in the window. She looked at me. She didn't say a word. She didn't even move. But I think she wanted me to come inside."

"How do you know?"

"I don't know exactly. It's hard to explain." Oscar frowned. "When you're a cat, most of the time you're thinking about cat things. Little movements in the grass, cupboards that aren't quite closed, patches of sunlight on rocks, narrow places at the backs of closets—you're always noticing those things. You can't help yourself. It's boring if you think about it, but you don't think about it because you're a cat. All the same, you know things when you're a cat."

"Like what people are thinking?"

"No—not exactly," said Oscar. "But sometimes you know what people want. You don't always care; but you know what they want. And I guess I knew when I looked in that window that the old woman wanted me to come inside. Only I didn't know it was Lavonne."

"What did you do?"

"I got spooked. A woman came into the room. She's been here a lot. She lives in the big white farmhouse down by the barns."

"Aunt Helen!"

"I guess that must be right. Your aunt Helen came in, and I got spooked and ran away."

"Did you ever see Aunt Lavonne again?"

"No." Oscar's voice sounded hollow.

"She must have died soon after that," Lucy said, catching herself too late, wishing she hadn't been so blunt.

But Oscar didn't say anything. He was staring into the darkness, and Lucy was sure he was thinking about his family, far away in time.

The thought of Oscar's family made her think of her own family, of her father. Where was he? Would he ever come back?

"What am I going to do?" said Oscar, his voice filled with despair.

Lucy looked at him. "What happened to you?" she asked.

"What?" said Oscar.

"All this time—where were you? Tell me," Lucy insisted. "Maybe we'll think of what to do."

# CHAPTER EIGHT

## A CAT'S LIFE

First you saw the sea, didn't you?" Lucy prompted.

"Yes—well, not exactly. I heard it first. I was in my room. I was writing." Oscar looked rueful. "I shouldn't have been—I never should have been writing."

"But what happened?" asked Lucy.

"I heard something queer outside," said Oscar.

"It was the sea!" said Lucy.

"I threw on my trousers over my nightshirt and went outdoors to have a look."

"And then you saw the sea!"

"I was sure I was dreaming. I went down to the shore and found a boat tied up to one of Ma's cement urns. A perfect little rowboat—not as big as the one over at Norby's Pond, but just the right size for me. I started to untie it."

"And then Aunt Lavonne came," Lucy said.

"She didn't want me to get in the boat. But I didn't listen."

"Then you climbed in," said Lucy.

"That's right. And I shoved myself away from shore with one of the oars. I could tell Lavonne was scared, so I hollered—"

"Lucy will explain!" Lucy interrupted. She was thinking of Aunt Lavonne's dream.

"What?" said Oscar.

"Isn't that what you said?"

"Why would I say that?" Oscar looked puzzled.

Of course he wouldn't have said those words, Lucy realized. Not back in 1914! Yet she wondered if Aunt Lavonne's dream wasn't a little bit true. Oscar was here, and she was going to find out what had happened to him. Lucy will explain, she thought. "What *did* you say?" she asked Oscar.

"I think I just told her to go back to bed. She ran into the house and I kept on rowing—and getting shivers up and down my arms because, for a dream, it was all so real. The air was cold and wet—it smelled like the sea. The moon was glittering on the water. I should have known it wasn't a dream!"

"But you didn't know," said Lucy. "How could you know?"

Oscar didn't answer her. After a moment, he continued. "I fancied I was pretty good with boats. My friend Earl and I were always messing about on the pond at his farm. So I rowed along the path the moon made on the water. Pretty soon, though, I was so far from shore I could barely see our house. I turned around and tried to row back to shore, but I couldn't because the current was pulling me out to sea. That's when I stopped telling myself how real everything seemed. Just a bad dream, I told myself. Nothing to worry about. Dreams are scary sometimes. I started pinching myself, trying to wake up."

"Could you see the house?"

Oscar shook his head. "Too far out. And it was getting dark. There were black clouds coming in, covering the moon. The wind picked up, and the boat started to rock. Waves were coming over the sides. I pulled in the oars and tried to bail out the water with my hands.

"Then the boat climbed way up in the air on a wave, turning and turning. Lightning flashed. The boat was going to dive back down. Right then, I was so scared I didn't even think about it being a bad dream. It just *was*," said Oscar. "The boat came down and I got hurled into the bow—I thought I'd broken my wrist.

But the good thing was that I knocked loose a piece of wood under the bow. There was a hollow place there, with a raincoat inside and an old tin can."

"The tin can was for bailing!" said Lucy.

"That's right. I pulled on the coat and started bailing. It was raining by then, rain like I'd never seen. What with that and the waves, I could barely keep up. I was sure the boat was going to capsize and I was going to drown. I kept thinking about something Earl used to say—that if you dream of your own death, you'll die in your sleep and never wake up," said Oscar. "But finally the rain let up, and the wind died down. I could see stars here and there. I bailed out as much water as I could and hunkered down in the boat.

"I watched the stars and wondered whether I was dreaming and whether I would wake up. Only—" Oscar looked at Lucy. "Now that things were all right again, I didn't want to. There I was, lost in the middle of the ocean, and I didn't want to wake up." He shook his head. "I didn't want to wake up because I was in the middle of an *adventure*. I was *happy* about it!"

"Then what happened?" asked Lucy.

"I fell asleep. And when I woke up, the stars were gone and the sky was light gray. It was dawn. I sat up and looked around and saw an island."

"An island!"

"Yes, and you can bet I was glad to see it, too—a hump of land poking up out of the water, and close enough to get to, even if I did have to row lopsided because of my wrist.

"And all the while I was thinking how lucky I was," said Oscar. "The island was just like Treasure Island— a long beach and towering cliffs and mountains. I rowed in close enough and got out, sure I was going to find pirates or something. I waded through the water, pulling the boat behind me, dragging it up on the beach. I danced around on the sand, crazy with glee." Oscar sounded disgusted with himself.

"I pulled the boat farther up the shore. I shoved the raincoat and the bailing can back under the bow and jammed the piece of wood back in place. 'Everything shipshape,' I remember saying out loud. I remember feeling kind of smug that I'd thought of exactly the right thing to say. I headed down the beach singing, 'Fifteen men on a dead man's chest.'"

"Yo, ho, ho, and a bottle of rum," Lucy finished. "Then what happened?"

"I found a stream coming down onto the beach. I followed it up into the forest a ways, until the water was clear and clean. I lay down flat and took a long drink. I could see my face grinning back at me from the water. Then I raised my head and saw all the cats."

"Cats!" said Lucy.

"There must have been a hundred of them," said Oscar. "They were all around me, poking their whiskers in my face, kneading me with their paws. Some of them tried to lie on top of me before I could scramble to my feet. And they were all meowing. It was loud.

"Every time I'd move, I'd trip or step on a tail. But I found I could sort of stumble upstream. The cats followed along the banks.

"Finally, I splashed around a bend in the river. I had to duck under some vines. The stream opened out in a pool—almost a pond, really. And there on a big rock at the far end sat a man dangling his bare feet in the water. He was surrounded by cats.

"He looked about as surprised to see me as I was to see him. He stood up, scattering cats everywhere, and wrapped an old purple blanket around himself. He had a short black cape around his shoulders. He set something on his head. I couldn't tell what at first, but it was a crown—"

"The king who loved cats!" Lucy interrupted.

"What?"

"Your story idea about the king who loved cats and the queen who loved birds."

"How do you know about that idea?"

"I read it in your book of story ideas—*The Book*

*of Story Beginnings*. And my father used to tell it to me before I'd go to bed—when I was little, I mean. I think Aunt Lavonne told it to him when he was a little boy."

"You *read* my book of story beginnings?" Oscar said in amazement.

"I found it in the smokehouse."

"The smokehouse! How did it get there?"

"Well, it was in the boat at first. In your raincoat pocket."

"I put it there when I was in the boat. I didn't want it to get wet," said Oscar.

"Yes." Lucy was thinking that there was something about Oscar's story that wasn't right. She was sure of it. But she was too interested to think about it for long. "Go on," she said. "Tell me about the King."

Oscar continued. "When the King saw me, he shouted, 'Who goes there?' and 'Approach!'" Oscar sounded like a lion as he rolled the *r* in the word *approach*.

Whatever was wrong with Oscar's story had something to do with the king who loved cats, Lucy decided. "Then what?" she asked.

"I *approached*," said Oscar. "There wasn't much else I could do. I had to go around the edge of the pond, picking my way through all the cats. I got close enough to see that the black cape around the King's shoulders wasn't a cape at all. It was a *cat*. It had yellow eyes.

"Then the King said, 'That *hag* sent you, didn't she?'" Oscar made his voice snarl.

"'What hag?' I said, only I said it kind of angrily because just then a kitten leaped up and dug its claws into my arm.

"'Our *wife,* you fool!' he said. But I still didn't know what he meant," said Oscar. "I couldn't think why he said *our* wife, as if she was *my* wife, too."

"He was a *king,*" said Lucy. "Kings always say *we* instead of *I.*"

"I could tell my question annoyed him," Oscar continued. "'The *Queen,* imbecile,' he said. 'Don't tell me you've never heard of her. Queen of Birds, they call her now. Ha! And here we sit, King of Cats and nothing more. Look at them! Look at our subjects!' he said. 'Did you ever see such a kingdom as ours?'

"There were all sorts of cats: tabbies, calico cats, black cats, white cats, Persian cats—you never saw anything like it in your life! That was his kingdom!" said Oscar.

"Then the King said, 'The Queen's got all the birds locked up in the palace. She's thrown us out of our own home!'

"'Why did she?' I asked.

"'That blasted canary!' said the King. 'Noisy little

cuss of a bird, singing the same thing over and over all day long. We wouldn't have minded if she'd kept the thing in a cage, where it belonged. But she was always one for letting it fly around the place. She liked the sunlight on its wings, she said. She even decorated a special room for it, all pink and yellow. And maybe even that would have been all right if she'd been careful about keeping the door closed. But no, she had to leave it open. And Tom here does what comes natural to a cat. He goes in to investigate.

" 'Next thing we know, feathers, squawking, shrieking, and sobs, and she says to get that beast away from her sight or she'll drown him,' said the King. 'She orders us out of the palace! Makes us a laughingstock for all! But did she care that they laughed?'

" 'Who are *they*?' I asked.

" 'They! Our subjects!' he said.

"And I said, 'You mean the cats?'

"And he said, 'Not cats, you chucklehead. People! Before we changed them into cats.'

" 'You changed people into cats?' I said.

" 'Well, what else were we supposed to do?' he said. 'They were laughing at us! A King can't be laughed at by his own people. So the next thing *she* does, she gives orders for every bird on the island to be given safe haven within the walls of our home.' "

"The queen who loved birds," said Lucy.

"Yes. And I suppose that given everything that had happened, it was silly of me to start finding things ridiculous and unbelievable just then," said Oscar. "But the King's story sounded so idiotic. What king would get so mad at someone that he would change his own subjects into cats? So I said, 'All these cats—you mean that they're really people? I don't believe you.'

" 'She sent you here to *taunt* us! To *laugh* at us!' said the King. 'To *spy* on us!'

"I told him that nobody had sent me. Only right then that kitten leaped up on my arm again, and I guess I didn't sound as polite as I ought to have, because the King shouted, 'Why, you insolent wretch!' And he reached behind him and tore off a branch from a bush. He raised it over his head and pointed it straight at me. He shook it and said:

'Spit! Spat! Enough of this brat!
Take this and that! You're a cat!'

"I didn't know what he meant. But the next thing I knew, I was falling down in the water. Then I was drowning, struggling to swim. My head popped up to the surface of the pond, and everything looked different," said Oscar. "And that was that!" he concluded.

"What do you mean, *that was that*?" said Lucy.

"I mean, that's how I became a cat. I *was* a cat—until tonight, that is."

"You've been a cat all this time?" Lucy said in disbelief.

"It didn't seem that long. You don't think too much about time when you're a cat."

"But that doesn't make any sense. You've been gone since 1914!"

Oscar was quiet for a moment. His hands were pressed against his eyes. Then he said, "I think I might have tried to get back at first. I tried to think about my family, my home. But it was hard. I kept thinking like a cat. I—I forgot everything."

Once again, Lucy had the nagging thought that there was something not quite right about Oscar's story. She tried to push the thought aside. "How did you get away from the island?" she asked.

"On a ship," said Oscar.

"A ship!"

"There were lots of ships that came to the island."

"Who sailed them? I thought you said everyone had been turned into cats."

Oscar shook his head. "Not everyone. There was a town near the Queen's palace. There were people there. That's where the ships came, full of birdseed and other food for the Queen's birds. We cats used to sit outside the palace and watch them deliver the food. It was maddening to hear all those birds."

"So you escaped on one of those ships?" said Lucy.

"That's right. I got curious and sneaked onboard a ship that was teeming with rats. I stowed away in the cargo hold and gorged myself for a few weeks. Then, one night, I stole out on deck. I saw land off the stern. The rats were getting pretty scant by then, so I took my chances and jumped. I swam forever—thought I was going to drown—but here I am. Your aunt Helen fed me sometimes. That was kind of her."

"Oscar!" Finally, Lucy had it. She knew what was wrong with Oscar's story.

"What is it?"

"When did you go back to the rowboat? When did you go back to get *The Book of Story Beginnings*?"

"I didn't."

"But how can that be? When did you write your story beginnings?" Lucy had assumed that Oscar had written the story about the boy who woke up to find the sea around his farmhouse *after* it happened to him. But now that didn't make sense, because Oscar hadn't had time to write the story beginning. And she had assumed that Oscar had written the story about the king who loved cats and the queen who loved birds *before* he found the sea outside The Brick. Otherwise, how could

Aunt Lavonne have told it to her father? But that made even less sense. How could Oscar have known about the King of Cats and the Queen of Birds *before* he met the King?

"I don't know," said Oscar. "I wrote the one about the king and queen a while ago, not long after I found *The Book of Story Beginnings* in the attic. I wrote another one about orphans for Lavonne. She was always wishing she was an orphan. I wrote the story about the boy in the boat on *that* night, of course. The night it all began."

"You mean you wrote about it before it happened?"

"Of course I did."

"But how can that be? That's too much of a coincidence."

"Who said anything about coincidence?" Oscar looked puzzled. Then a look of astonishment washed over his face. "You don't know, do you? You said you'd read it, so I never dreamed you didn't know."

"What is it?" said Lucy, terrified because she thought that at last she *did* know.

"Lucy, the things you write in that book come true. They turn into stories, and the stories come to life!"

# CHAPTER NINE
## A TERRIBLE MIDDLE

I wrote a story beginning in the book!" said Lucy. She was feeling sick.

"You did!" said Oscar. "Why would you do such a thing?"

"I—well, why did *you* do it?"

"I was a fool, that's what I was. I read the warning at the beginning of the book and I just plain ignored it," said Oscar.

"I didn't pay any attention at all to the warning. I was thinking about something else," said Lucy. She had been thinking about her parents' argument. Had it been only this morning?

"What exactly did you write?" asked Oscar.

"I just said that once there was a girl whose father was a magician. That's all."

"Yes?"

"Well, it was *my* father. And the book knew that! And when I came home last night he *was* a magician, and he changed himself into a bird, and then . . ."

"I chased him out the window, didn't I?" Oscar concluded. He let out a long, slow breath. "I didn't mean it," he added. Then he asked, "Why that story in particular?"

"What?"

"Why did you write about your father being a magician?"

"What does it matter?"

"I looked around the attic a bit. There were a lot of queer-looking books and papers and other things up there. Did all that come out of your story beginning?"

"No. Most of that stuff belonged to Aunt Lavonne."

"Lavonne! My sister?" Oscar raised his eyebrows.

"My father said she was convinced something magical had happened to you," Lucy explained. "So she spent her entire life learning about magic."

"What do you mean, learning about magic?"

"Well, she studied alchemy, spells, incantations, that sort of thing."

"That's ridiculous!"

"What's so ridiculous about it? You just told me a story that nobody is going to believe!" said Lucy. By *nobody,* she meant her mother. "Besides, Aunt Lavonne was right. I don't know what you call what's happened, but I call it magic."

Oscar was quiet for a moment. Then he said, "I suppose you're right. It's just that it's hard to picture my sister that way. Just thinking of her as an old lady, that's one shock—"

Just then, the screen door behind them squeaked on its hinges. When Lucy looked around, she saw her mother standing in the doorway in her nightgown.

"Lucy? What are you doing? Who is this?" said her mother.

Oscar came to the rescue. He rose to his feet and extended his hand. "My name's Earl Norby, ma'am," he said. "I live near town. I saw Lucy out on the porch, and we got to talking."

Lucy's mother ignored the offered hand. "Lucy, it's after midnight!"

"Mom—"

"And you, young man! I've half a mind to call your parents. I *would* call them if I wasn't afraid of waking them up! Do they know you're out at this hour?"

"I reckon so, ma'am. We go to bed kind of late at our house."

"Earl," said Lucy's mother, "I'm going to assume that if you got yourself here safely, you can get yourself home safely, even if it *is* twelve thirty in the morning."

"Yes, ma'am." Oscar looked contrite. "I'll be fine. I hope you'll let me visit Lucy again, ma'am," he added.

"Visiting hours are from eight A.M. to eight P.M.," said Lucy's mother, smiling slightly. Lucy wondered if she had ever heard so many *ma'am*s in her life. "Good night, Earl."

"'Night, Lucy," said Oscar as her mother drew her in the door. When Lucy glanced back, he was heading across the front lawn, roughly in the direction of town, which lay less than half a mile down the hill. She wondered what Oscar would think when he saw the carpet of electric lights that Martin had become since 1914.

"What were you thinking, Lucy?" said her mother as they went upstairs. "It's not enough that your father has to stay up until the wee hours—heaven knows what he's doing up there in the attic—but now you turn into a night owl as well!"

She waited while Lucy put her nightgown back on and climbed into bed. "And boys! Whenever did you get interested in boys?"

In spite of all that had happened, in spite of the panic that kept rising in her, Lucy felt embarrassed. "Mom! This has nothing to do with boys!"

"We'll talk in the morning," said her mother, closing the door.

Lucy lay in the dark, wide awake and exhausted at the same time. Her mind could not stop thinking. She had found Oscar, and he was just as she had imagined from reading his journals. She could talk to him. Lucy had never been any good at talking to people. But she could talk to Oscar as if he were her older brother.

But I've lost my father, Lucy thought. Where is he?

A sudden noise—a sharp spatter like the rattle of hailstones—startled her into alertness. She waited, holding her breath until she heard it again. There! She recognized the sound this time, even though she had never heard it before. She had read about it in a book. Someone was throwing pebbles at her window.

Oscar's hand, poised to toss more gravel, dropped when he saw Lucy's face press against the window screen. "I thought this must be your room. Are you all right, Lucy?"

Though she had never felt less all right in her life, she nodded.

"Listen, Lucy. There's got to be something we can do. We can talk tomorrow."

"All right." Lucy tried not to think about never seeing her father again.

"Go to bed and get some sleep," Oscar advised.

And strangely, as if he had thrown magic sleeping powder up at the screen instead of pebbles, Lucy felt suddenly as if she could sleep after all. "What will you do? Where will you sleep?" she asked.

"Oh, I'll be all right. I'll find some place to lay up. Besides, I'm not that tired." He waved, and Lucy watched him disappear around the house, into the backyard. Then she got back into bed.

Lucy was dreaming that Aunt Helen was showing her father how to cook. "Just check the recipe, Shel," she was saying. "It says to add eggs." Lucy's father started paging through a book that Lucy could see wasn't a cookbook; it was *The Book of Story Beginnings.*

"How long does it say to cook the eggs?" said Aunt Helen.

"Until the bell rings," said her father.

Then Lucy woke up. It was morning. She could hear the telephone ringing in her parents' room.

On any other day, it would have been one of those funny dreams she laughed about at breakfast with her father. Today the dream fled out of her mind as she listened to her mother pick up the phone.

"Hello," said her mother. "Oh, Helen . . . Yes, of course we're up. Well, I'm up, anyway. I don't know where Shel is. He always stays up so late. I'm not sure he even went to bed last night."

Lucy rolled out of bed and tiptoed into the hall to listen.

"The café? No, we haven't been yet." Lucy's mother turned around. "Oh, here's Lucy. Can you wait a minute, Helen?" She put her hand over the mouthpiece of the phone.

"Lucy—you haven't seen your father this morning, have you?"

"I just got up," Lucy stammered.

"What's that, Helen?" said her mother, listening to the phone again. She turned to Lucy. "Did your father say he was going anywhere this morning?"

Lucy shook her head.

"Sorry, Helen, he seems to have gone missing," said her mother, laughing. "But *I'd* like to go for at least a cup of coffee. You don't mind if we make it a short trip? I've got to work today. . . . Yes, I'll see if Lucy wants to come. . . . Yes, of course. Come on up. Goodbye."

"Aunt Helen wants to take us to breakfast at the café in town," said Lucy's mother, putting the phone down. "Can you hurry up and get dressed?"

"Mom, about last night," Lucy began.

"That boy? I must admit I was surprised. How long

were you out there? You can't stay up that late; you should know that."

"I do know that." Lucy followed her mother out into the hall.

"It certainly is a new world out here," said her mother, pausing at the top of the stairs. "I can't believe Earl's parents let him run around after midnight! What do his parents do? Have they got a farm?"

"I don't know," said Lucy, wondering how she could ever tell her mother the truth. *Last night Dad changed himself into a bird and flew away, Mom. And Earl is actually our cat. Only his name's not Earl. It's Oscar.*

Her mother was already hurrying down the stairs. "Please get dressed, Lucy," she called over her shoulder. "Aunt Helen will be here any minute."

But Lucy didn't get dressed. She waited at the top of the stairs until she heard the sound of Aunt Helen's car pulling into the driveway. "Lucy! Are you ready?" called her mother.

"Not exactly!" Lucy called back.

Her mother appeared at the bottom of the stairs. "You're not ready at all."

"Can I stay here?"

Her mother hesitated. When they had lived in the city, her parents had never considered Lucy old enough to stay home by herself.

"Dad must be around somewhere," said Lucy. It was such a lie that she felt ashamed. But she didn't want to go to the café. She *couldn't* go to the café.

"Well, I guess it's all right," said her mother. "I won't be gone long."

Lucy found Oscar right away, curled up on the floor of the smokehouse. He sat up and blinked as she threw open the door. He stood up and stretched, twisting his back this way and that. "Not such a great place to sleep as I remembered. I didn't mind it when I was a cat," he said, rubbing the back of his head. "Did your father come back?"

"No. And I've got to find him," said Lucy. "Last night you said we could talk today. You said there had to be something we could do."

"Well, sure," said Oscar.

"I hope you have something in mind." Lucy was surprised at how angry her own voice sounded.

"I—I don't exactly," Oscar stammered.

Lucy could feel her anger transforming into tears.

"But I'll try to think of something," Oscar added hastily. "Lucy, I'm really sorry. But I'm not exactly sure when I last had anything to drink. The pump that used to be out back of the house is gone."

Lucy felt almost grateful to him for giving her a

reason to turn away. She hated crying in front of people. "Come on," she said.

In the kitchen, she poured him a glass of water. "Do you want some breakfast?"

"Yes, please."

Lucy put bread in the toaster and poured two bowls of corn flakes and milk. Oscar studied the cereal box and ran his finger down the plastic milk jug. He and Lucy both seemed to notice that his hands were dirty at the same time. "There's some soap at the sink," she told him.

"We had a sink when I lived here," said Oscar as he washed his hands. "In case you were wondering." He washed his face, too. "We also had an outhouse, but I didn't see one outside."

"Uh-huh." Lucy was moving leftovers around in the refrigerator, looking for the orange juice.

"I expect you've got a water closet in the house. . . ." Oscar suggested delicately.

"A water closet?" said Lucy, puzzled, and then she said, "Oh!" and showed him the downstairs bathroom.

Oscar ate hungrily, stopping only once to tell Lucy politely that her mother's strawberry jam was every bit as good as his mother's. Lucy didn't tell him that it came from the supermarket.

When he was done eating, he wiped his mouth with

his napkin. "That was wonderful," he said, sighing with pleasure.

As if he'd never had cereal and toast before, thought Lucy. Then she remembered what he *had* been eating. Cat food—and mice!

"Where's *The Book of Story Beginnings*?" asked Oscar.

"It's up in my room. Why?"

"I don't know. I just wanted to look at it, I guess. Maybe it will give us some ideas about how to get your father back."

"I don't see how," Lucy complained. But a second later, she *did* see how. An idea had jumped into her mind. "Oscar, we could write something in the book!"

"What do you mean, write something in the book?"

"We could write that my father comes back home."

"It's a book of story *beginnings*," said Oscar. "That sounds like an end to the story beginning you already wrote."

"It could be the beginning of a new story," Lucy argued. "Once upon a time, a man changed himself into a bird and flew out the window. The next day he came home from his journey. . . ."

"You can't just go and write anything you like in that book," said Oscar. "It's dangerous. You've got to be careful."

Lucy opened her mouth to protest, to say that of course she knew they had to be careful. But Oscar held up his hand to stop her. "Just listen for a moment. The story beginnings we've written so far have already had disastrous effects." He leaned back in his chair. "I'll tell you what I think has happened," he said. "I think we're in the middle of a story. A terrible middle. And I'm afraid anything else we write in that book will only make it worse."

"How could it be worse?" said Lucy. "My father's gone. And you—well, you've come back in the future and . . ." Her voice fell off because what she had been about to say—that Oscar's family was dead—sounded so terrible and final.

"I'm not sure there's much we can do about me," said Oscar. "I couldn't sleep last night thinking about it. This kind of thing happens all the time in stories. Take 'Beauty and the Beast,' for example. That poor fellow stays a beast for hundreds of years. When the enchantment is lifted, he hasn't changed a bit. He's the same age as he was before. What happens to his family? We never find out."

As he continued, Oscar's voice became more resolute: "What I mean to say is, maybe my family isn't important to *this* story—I mean the one you started when you wrote your story beginning. As awful as it sounds, that's how it feels to me. I can't get back what's gone. But I feel as though there must be some way we can help your father. If he's disappeared—well, maybe he'll come back. But if he doesn't, maybe there's some way we can find him. If we really are in the middle of a story, maybe there's some way we can give it a good ending."

It struck Lucy that Oscar sounded like a hero. She admired him and felt sorry for him all at the same time. For some reason, the combination of emotions made her feel embarrassed, and she changed the topic. "Where did the book come from?" she asked.

"I found it in the attic." Oscar looked unhappy. "It was in Ma's trunk. I never told her I took it."

"Where did *she* get the book? It looks really old."

"I think she must have brought it with her when she ran away with my father."

"She ran away with your father?"

"Ma was only seventeen, and my grandfather forbade her to see my pa. She told him she knew what she wanted, and what she wanted was to marry Pa, and believe you me, when Ma decides she wants something, nothing stands in her way. I think she might have taken the book from my grandfather's library. Ma talked about him having a library."

"So the book was your grandfather's," said Lucy. "Do you think he knew it was magic?"

"I'm not sure. Ma didn't want anything to do with him."

"There was another story beginning in the book," said Lucy. "It was in a foreign language."

"Norwegian," said Oscar. "That's another thing that made me think the book might belong to my grandfather. He came from Norway, like Ma."

"Can you read that story beginning?" asked Lucy.

Oscar nodded. "I know a little Norwegian from Ma. Why?"

"Maybe it'll tell us something important—how to use the book. How *not* to mess everything up when we do. Wait here and I'll get it."

Lucy hurried upstairs and found the book. But as her hand closed around it, she heard a noise—a car pulling into the driveway. She looked out the window. It was her mother and Aunt Helen.

*Oscar!* thought Lucy. She ran down the hall and down the stairs, through the parlor, through the dining room, and into the kitchen just as her mother and Aunt Helen pushed open the kitchen door.

"Earl?" said her mother. "What are you doing here?"

# CHAPTER TEN
## A BETTER BEGINNING

Oscar stood up from the table. "Good morning, ma'am," he said.

"Earl stopped by while you were out," Lucy explained.

"It's good to see you in the light of day, Earl," said her mother with a little smile. "This is Lucy's aunt Helen. Helen, do you know Earl? I'm sorry, Earl, I've forgotten your last name."

"It's Norby, ma'am."

"Earl Norby!" Aunt Helen exclaimed. "You're not related to *old* Earl Norby, are you?"

Lucy saw Oscar give a start.

"Who's old Earl Norby?" asked her mother.

"Why, he's the town's oldest citizen! The church had a big party last August on his birthday. Wonderful man—lives over at the nursing home in Onawa now, but he comes up to visit his daughter every so often. Come to think of it, Denise mentioned just last week that he was coming today. Her son Ted and his family are here from Des Moines. You must be one of Ted's children, Earl—" Aunt Helen's voice broke off. She sounded puzzled.

"I don't suppose I'm related, ma'am," said Oscar, looking uncomfortable.

"Where do you live, Earl?" Aunt Helen's eyes traveled up from Oscar's bare feet to his pants, which buttoned just below his knee, and then up to his dirty white shirt with its sleeves turned up at the elbows.

He looks like he stepped out of an old photograph, thought Lucy. She remembered the photograph she had seen upstairs. Did Aunt Helen recognize Oscar?

"Earl lives near town," said her mother.

"Would it be all right if I showed Earl around?" Lucy asked, anxious to get Oscar away before Aunt Helen started asking more questions.

"Go ahead," said her mother.

"Earl looks so familiar. But I don't see how he *could* be a Norby," Lucy heard Aunt Helen say in a low voice as she and Oscar left the kitchen.

"Why did you say you were Earl Norby?" Lucy whispered as they climbed the stairs.

"I don't know. Earl was my best friend. Lucy, you don't think — well, it must be true — that old man your aunt mentioned — he must be *my* Earl Norby. Gosh, it would be good to see him."

Then they reached the top of the stairs and Oscar saw his room. He stood in the doorway for a moment. "It's changed some. That's my desk all right, though. And my bookcase," he said at last. His eyes rested momentarily on the photograph Lucy had noticed before — the one of Oscar and his mother and Lavonne and Morris. Lucy wondered if he would pick it up.

He looked away instead. "I see some of my books are still here," he said, kneeling down and running his hand along the titles. "I've never heard of some of these," he remarked, hesitating at a battered-looking paperback copy of *The Hobbit*.

He looked up. "Let's see *The Book of Story Beginnings*."

As Lucy sat down beside him, Oscar took the book and opened it. He studied the paragraph in Norwegian, whispering the syllables. "That word there means *books*," he said. "I think it says, 'Once there was a man who loved books. He loved books so much that they became real for him—more real than his own life. Books became his life.'"

"Maybe that's important—the part about books being real."

"Hmm."

"What I mean is, this book makes whatever you write in it become real."

"Right," Oscar murmured. Lucy could tell he wasn't really listening.

"Well, what do *you* think is important?" she said, frustrated.

"I was thinking about stories," said Oscar. "It's just like the book says, isn't it? A story has a beginning, a middle, and an end."

"Right. And we're in the middle of a story. We already know that!"

"It's more than that. What we are is *characters* in the middle of a story. We've got to start thinking like characters," Oscar explained. "We've got to get ourselves to the end of the story. The middle is figuring out how to get there."

"I can't think of a way to end this story," said Lucy. "I just want to find my father and bring him home!

Only we haven't got the slightest idea where he's gone!"

"Except that he flew across the sea," said Oscar. "That's *something.*"

"Right," Lucy said sarcastically. "Maybe he flew to the same island you did. Maybe the Queen of Birds has him locked up in her palace! How are we supposed to know?"

"Jump into the story," said Oscar. "There's got to be a way to find him—otherwise it wouldn't be a story."

"All I know is that stupid book has got him lost and—oh!" Lucy stopped short as an idea came to her. "Oscar, listen!" She had to wait for words to catch up with her idea. "What you said—that a story has a beginning, a middle, and an end. What if we could change my beginning—or add to it just a little bit? What if we could have my father turn himself into a bird, fly out the window—just like it happened—and then have him fly to a particular place—a place where we could find him?"

"Not a new beginning, exactly—just a better one," said Oscar.

"Better for us! We'll never find my father if we don't know where he is."

"Do you think it would work?"

"It's worth a try," said Lucy, who was already hunting for a pencil in a drawer of the desk. She found one and held it up triumphantly.

"Where would you put him?" said Oscar.

His question set them both to thinking. Lucy wanted her father to end up close to home. "He could fly over the sea for a bit, then come back and roost in the barn," she suggested.

"What kind of bird is he?" asked Oscar.

"I don't know—a crow, I think."

"I don't think crows roost in barns."

"So he doesn't have to roost. He just likes to swoop down to the barn every day like all the other crows to eat corn near the feedlot. I've seen the crows down there— lots of them!"

Oscar continued to look skeptical. "It doesn't sound like a very interesting story."

"Who cares if it's interesting?"

"A story has to be interesting," Oscar said with conviction. "You have to care. Otherwise it's not a story."

"Maybe he's gone wild or something like that. We have to tame him."

"How would you tame a crow?"

"With love! Affection! Food! I don't know!" Lucy was getting annoyed.

"Your father will get mixed in with all the other crows," said Oscar. "How will you pick him out?"

"I think I'd know my own father!" said Lucy, though she wasn't sure that was true.

"What if he gets killed by a farm cat?" said Oscar. "'Be mindful of stories that you begin'! That's what the poem says."

"Any story I begin could lead to something dangerous," Lucy countered. "And you have to agree that the feedlot is a pretty safe place, considering."

"I don't think it's a good idea," said Oscar. "You don't know what will happen."

"I've got to do *something,*" said Lucy. She opened the book to the page where her story beginning was written and read aloud: "'Once upon a time, there was a girl whose father was a magician.'

"Now I want to say that the girl's father invented a potion that could change—no, transform—one thing into another," she said.

"You'd better explain what you mean by 'transform one thing into another.'"

Lucy thought for a moment. "How about 'invented a potion that could transform one thing into another—a mouse into a salamander, the land into sea . . .'"

"'A cat into a boy,'" Oscar finished. "I guess that's all right. Write that down and go on. What's next?"

Despite his initial hesitation, Oscar seemed to be entering into the spirit of the thing. Lucy felt encouraged. "'A cat into a boy,'" she murmured as the pencil raced across the page. "'One night the girl's father used the potion to change himself into a bird. To the girl's dismay, he flew out the window and'—rats!" She stopped midsentence. "I forgot to say that he'd already changed the land into the sea."

"Just say 'out the window and over a magical sea he'd created with the potion.' That ought to take care of it," said Oscar.

"Good idea." Lucy added Oscar's suggestion, then paused. So far she hadn't written anything that hadn't already happened. The paragraph glared at her, waiting for the next sentence. "Here goes," she said, and wrote: *Her father flew over the white-capped waves until he was tired and hungry. Being a crow, he wanted corn. And the best place to find corn was the barn near his house. His wings carried him swiftly home and he flew down to the feedlot.*

"Hey!" she yelped.

"What is it?"

"My writing! It's disappearing."

Sure enough, the last sentences she had written, starting with *Her father flew over the white-capped waves until he was tired and hungry,* were rapidly disappearing. Letter by letter, word by word, an invisible eraser was rubbing its way across the page. Oscar and Lucy stared as the end of the last sentence, *flew down to the feedlot,* vanished completely. Lucy's story beginning now ended with the sentence *To the girl's dismay, he flew out the window and over a magical sea he'd created with the potion.*

Lucy took the pencil and rewrote the sentences as best as she could remember them. They watched as the invisible eraser chased the point of the pencil across the page. Lucy didn't even have time to cross the *t* on *feedlot* before the word disappeared.

"Let me see the book," said Oscar. He flipped back to the start and read aloud:

> "Know this, too, before you write:
> Though day must always lead to night,
> Not all beginnings make good tales;
> Some succeed, while others fail.
>
> Let this book its judgment lend
> On whether and how your beginning ends.

"That's it, Lucy!" he exclaimed. "The book must have judged your story beginning and decided it wasn't going to make a good tale. How do you like that? It's kind of funny, in a way!"

"I don't think it's funny! What are we supposed to do now?"

"Come up with a more interesting beginning. Something that makes you want to hear more," said Oscar. "You came up with one yourself earlier. Having your father fly to the island—having him get caught by the Queen of Birds. That's the sort of thing we need. Not that idea exactly, but something like it—"

"Why not that idea?" Lucy interrupted. "You said yourself it would be an interesting story."

"A bit too interesting for me, thank you! Don't forget how long I was on that island. It sounds like you want to consign your father to the same fate."

"Who said anything about consigning him to the same fate? All I said was he could get caught by the queen. I never said he had to stay there. We could go rescue him."

"And how would we do that?"

"Well—I have a plan," said Lucy. But she didn't have a plan.

"Yes?" said Oscar, waiting.

"Well, we've got a boat." A plan began to construct itself in Lucy's mind. "And we've got *The Book of*

*Story Beginnings*. We could write that my father gets captured by the queen—"

"That's crazy!"

"What's crazy?" said a voice from the hall, and they both jumped. Neither of them had heard Lucy's mother come up the stairs.

"Nothing." Lucy wondered how much her mother had heard. "We're just looking at books."

"Are you as much of a reader as Lucy, Earl?" said her mother, sounding pleased.

"Yes, ma'am," said Oscar. "I love books. I want to be a writer someday."

"That's a wonderful goal. Don't lose sight of it," said Lucy's mother. "I wanted to be a writer myself once. . . ." Her voice faded for a moment. Then she said briskly, "Lucy—I'm going to have to shut myself up in my office today or I'll never get through the stack of work on my desk. I know you'll help yourself to lunch. Earl, you're welcome to eat here if you like."

"Thank you, ma'am."

"Your mother's nice," said Oscar when Lucy's mother was gone. "What's the stack of work on her desk?"

"She's an editor."

"For a newspaper?" Oscar sounded surprised.

"No." Lucy shook her head. "She edits articles for

books and journals. People send her things, she edits them, then sends them back. Science stuff mostly—aerospace, genetics, biotech, that sort of thing." She rattled off a few of the subject areas she had heard her mother mention.

Oscar was looking at Lucy with a blank expression, and she realized that he couldn't possibly have heard of the things she'd just described. In fact, he looked tired suddenly—and sad. His eyes flickered over the photographs on the bookcase. He's thinking of his family, thought Lucy. He knows he doesn't belong here. "What about my plan?" she said, filling the silence, trying to draw him back to the present. "What do you think?"

"Sure, Lucy," said Oscar.

But she could tell he hadn't really heard her. "Are you all right?" she asked.

Oscar looked at her then. "I'm fine. Just tired is all." He smiled a little. "I think I must still be on cat time," he said. "I used to take a nap every morning about this time."

It didn't take long to get Oscar settled on the floor of the smokehouse with a blanket and a pillow. "Don't worry! We'll think of something," he told Lucy.

But Lucy was already thinking of something, and

when she returned to the house, she stood in the front hall, thinking about it even more. She listened for a moment to the whispery sound of her mother typing at her computer. Then she climbed upstairs to Oscar's room, where she sat down and read what she had written in *The Book of Story Beginnings:*

*Once upon a time, there was a girl whose father was a magician. The girl's father invented a potion that could transform one thing into another—a mouse into a salamander, the land into sea, a cat into a boy. One night the girl's father used the potion to change himself into a bird. To the girl's dismay, he flew out the window and over a magical sea he'd created with the potion.*

Lucy's hand closed around the pencil, and she could almost feel herself writing. "Just a few more sentences," she murmured, imagining Oscar's voice rising in protest. The pencil joined the paper, and she began to write.

*The bird flew across the sea to a strange island ruled by a king who loved cats and a queen who loved birds. The queen took the girl's father and kept him prisoner. When the girl learned what had happened, she knew she must free her father. She and her . . .*

Lucy hesitated, not sure what to call Oscar. *She and her great-uncle set off in a boat to rescue him,* she wrote. Best to be exact, she decided. She didn't want there to be any confusion.

Then a wave of panic swept over her. How were she and Oscar going to find their way to the island? Writing hastily, as if to make up for careless planning, Lucy added one more sentence: *They knew they could get to the island by following the path made by the moon on the water.*

Lucy waited breathlessly. She closed the book, then opened it again. She closed it and opened it again and again, just to make sure. The new beginning—the *better* beginning, she reminded herself—had not vanished this time.

# CHAPTER ELEVEN

## THE TRANSFORMING POTION

A noise—the steady tread of feet on the stairs—made Lucy snap shut *The Book of Story Beginnings*. She slid it into the bookcase just as her mother looked in from the hallway.

"Did Earl go home?" said her mother.

"Yes." Technically speaking, it was true—Oscar *was* home. "He was tired," Lucy added.

"I should think so!" said her mother. She turned and opened the door to the attic closet. Lucy listened to her mother's feet on the attic stairs, then jumped up to follow. Why was her mother going to the attic?

When Lucy reached the top of the stairs, she looked across the attic floor. It was littered with paper and broken glass. The window was still open from the night before. Her mother was gazing out, and Lucy moved to her side, hit by a sudden flash of hope and fear that she would see an ocean outside. But there were only the tops of the oak trees below the slope of the hill, and far beyond, the distant fields of glittering green corn.

It will happen tonight, she promised herself. Tonight the sea would appear, and she and Oscar would find the island by following the path made by the moon on the water.

Then she began to worry. For all she knew, it could be tonight, tomorrow night, or some night a year from now — or never.

It *will* be tonight, she admonished herself. She couldn't let herself believe anything else.

Lucy's mother leaned over to peer into the mouse cage on the table. The mouse — the *familiar,* thought Lucy — was curled up asleep in the sawdust at the bottom of the cage.

Lucy's mother straightened, surveying the chaos on the table and floor. "This place is a mess," she said. "Was it like this when you were up here last night, Lucy?"

"Walter got into the attic. He jumped on the work-table and knocked some things down." Lucy blushed at telling only half the truth.

Her mother stooped down and picked up a sheaf of papers from the floor. She shook them, and a black feather drifted and twirled in the air. She watched it absently for a moment, then looked down at the pages in her hand. Lucy strained to see the rows of Aunt Lavonne's lacy handwriting. She saw that her father had written in red pen in the margins of the paper.

Her mother read aloud: "'Notes on a Theory of Transformation. The sleeper dreams of an egg and knows an egg. He dreams the egg is hatched and . . .'" She frowned and set the pages down on the table. She picked up another pile of papers, read silently, then glanced down. For the first time, Lucy noticed a round gold medallion with a pentagon-shaped hole in its center. Her mother scooped up the medallion by its silver chain, then let it clatter back onto the table.

"Lucy—last night—did your father seem upset about anything?" she asked. Her mother's face looked troubled, and Lucy wondered if she was remembering the argument she had had yesterday with her father.

Lucy picked up the medallion. She put it around her neck and held it in front of her, studying the intricate design around its center so that she didn't have to look at her mother. "Dad seemed okay," she said. Another half-truth—maybe even a complete lie this time.

Her mother began shuffling the papers, tapping them methodically on the table, first on one side, then on the other until they were straight. She laid them down carefully.

"Mom . . ."

"Lucy . . ." They had spoken at exactly the same time.

"You first." Her mother smiled, her dark eyes like two wet stones.

"No, you," said Lucy.

"I was just thinking it would be fun to do something different for dinner tonight," said her mother. "We can all go to the burger place in town when your father gets home."

"Sure," said Lucy, feeling relieved and disappointed at the same time. For a moment, she'd had the wild idea that her mother had guessed the truth after all.

"We can do more as a family here. I've been so busy—it's silly of me. There's so much more time in the country. Time to be a family." Her mother smiled. "Let's surprise your father and clean this up, shall we?"

While she laid out papers and equipment on the table in rows as neat as city blocks, Lucy's mother chattered blithely. Mostly she repeated things Aunt Helen must have told her—about the town of Martin, about school, about the church youth group. Lucy swept the floor, wishing her mother would stop talking so she could tell her what had happened.

And then her broom hit something that went rolling and clinking across the floor.

"What's this?" Her mother stooped and picked up the bottle of transforming potion. She pulled out the glass stopper and sniffed. "Well, it's definitely not perfume," she said, wrinkling her nose.

"Can I see it?" Lucy was afraid her mother would spill the potion.

Lucy peered through the bottle's narrow neck. Was there any potion left? It was hard to tell. She replaced the stopper and closed her fist around the bottle. She would need it when she found her father.

Later, when her mother was closed up in her office again, Lucy lay on her bed in her room. She was thinking about *The Lion, the Witch, and the Wardrobe,* a book she had read so often it was indistinguishable from her own memories. She knew Narnia, the kingdom in the book, almost better than the characters did.

She was actually thinking about time. She was thinking about how no matter how long you stayed in the other world of Narnia, you always returned to your own world at the exact moment you left it. It was a very convenient arrangement, thought Lucy. Unfortunately, *The Book of Story Beginnings* had not made things so nice and neat. Oscar had been away for decades, yet it hadn't seemed like such a long time to him. Lucy wondered whether time ran more slowly on the island of cats and birds.

Was that a good thing? She tried to puzzle it out. Suppose it took Oscar and her a day to get to the island, a day to rescue her father, and a day to get back. Those three days of island time might very well translate into three weeks, or three months, or three years and more back in Martin, Iowa. There was no way of telling.

A new concern now dwarfed all of Lucy's other worries. Even if she and Oscar were successful in rescuing her father, even if they returned home safely, there was nothing to say that they would find everything as they had left it. They might come home to find that Lucy's mother was an old woman. She might have moved away. Or worse, like Oscar's mother, she might be dead.

Lucy allowed her imagination to punish her. She imagined herself in a rowboat on a cold, gray sea. Oscar and her father were in the boat, too. She was pulling hard on the oars, while they were straining to see through a thick fog. "It's land, all right!" said Oscar. Then he and her father began to speak in low, frightened voices. Lucy glanced over her shoulder to see what was worrying them. Through the fog, she glimpsed The Brick on the shore. As she stared, its shingles started to fall off. The porch began to sag, then crashed down on one side. One by one, the windows shattered, as if invisible stones were crashing through the glass.

"Row faster, Lucy!" screamed Oscar. But she couldn't row fast enough and neither Oscar nor her father would help her. When she looked again, one side of the house had caved in.

"Are you all right, Lucy?"

"What?" Lucy opened her eyes.

Her mother was leaning over the bed. "Did you fall asleep?"

"Just thinking."

"What were you thinking?"

"Nothing really." Another lie. "What time is it?"

"It's almost suppertime. Your father's not home yet, though. I thought you and I should walk down to the burger place—just us girls. Does that sound okay?"

"Sounds fine." Lucy tried to match her mother's cheerful tone.

The burger place was a little white house at the edge of Martin. It had a window that slid open so that you could give your order to the teenagers who worked inside. Aunt Helen had taken her once, and Lucy had embarrassed herself by asking what kind of *soda* they had. In Iowa you were supposed to call it *pop*.

Most people drove to the burger place, so Lucy and her mother drew attention walking down the highway. Two teenagers sitting on the hood of a station wagon stared at them as they came near.

"Take my wallet and order what you want, Lucy. I just want a soda," said her mother, sinking down on the bench of a picnic table. She seemed to have used up all her cheerfulness on the walk down.

Lucy carefully ordered two *drinks* and a hamburger and fries. She would have to lie again and pretend she was hungry or her mother would worry. She had just brought everything back to the table when she saw Uncle Byron's pickup coming down the road. He pulled up beside the picnic area and got out.

"Hello, Jean, Lucy," he called.

As he walked toward them, a police car pulled up behind Uncle Byron's truck. A tall, spare man with thinning hair climbed out. "Excuse me there, fella—I got to tell you that you're illegally parked," he said, his sunglasses glinting in the sun.

"Well, I guess you'll just have to slap me with a fine—or set me up at the county jail," Uncle Byron drawled. Then he grinned. "How're you doing, Ray?" He stood up to shake hands. "Jean, Lucy—I'd like you to meet the toughest law enforcement officer in Iowa, Sheriff Ray Jensen. Jean's my brother Shel's wife, Ray. I told you how they were moving here from back east."

"Sure! Living up at The Brick, aren't you?" Sheriff Jensen shook hands with Lucy's mother. "I used to hang out with this rascal here and your husband when we were kids. I hope you're finding Iowa to your liking."

"Yes, very much."

"I've been meaning to stop in and say hello. How's Shel?" said Sheriff Jensen.

"Oh, just fine," said Lucy's mother.

"Too busy to come out to supper, eh?" said Uncle Byron.

"What? Oh, yes . . ." Lucy's mother sipped at the drink Lucy had given her. "Actually, Byron, I haven't seen Shel all day. Have you seen him?"

"I can't say I have. He didn't go up to Sioux City, did he? I heard him say just the other day that he wanted to go."

"He went to Sioux City yesterday," said Lucy's mother. "And wherever he went today, he didn't take the car."

No, thought Lucy. He had definitely *not* taken the car.

"Sounds like we got ourselves a missing person," said Uncle Byron, winking at Lucy. "Aren't you supposed to handle things like that, Ray?"

"Now Byron, I'm too busy writing parking tickets for folks like you." Though Sheriff Jensen played along with Uncle Byron's joke, he was watching Lucy's mother. Her mouth was tight and closed, and her eyes looked watery. "How long has Shel been gone?" Sheriff Jensen asked, his voice more serious.

"Since last night—probably only this morning," said Lucy's mother. "I'm sure he just forgot to tell me where he was going."

"Shel hasn't changed a bit, Ray," said Uncle Byron. "He's just as absent-minded as he was as a kid. He's probably off daydreaming somewhere. Right, Lucy?"

"Right," Lucy stammered, feeling her face grow hot. She hoped nobody had noticed.

Lucy's mother never watched television, not unless she was sick. All the same, when they came home from the burger place, she went straight up to her bedroom and turned on Aunt Lavonne's tiny black-and-white set. When Lucy looked in on her a half hour later, she was asleep, curled up next to the phone as if she hoped it would ring. The thought that her father wasn't going to call—the thought that her mother didn't know—

made Lucy feel so alone that she could hardly bear it. For a moment, she thought of waking her mother, telling her everything, telling her what she planned to do. But her mother would never believe her.

Instead, she began preparing for what she was already calling the *voyage*. In the kitchen, she rummaged for provisions. She found apples and bananas. She stockpiled soft drinks and store-bought cookies, putting everything into plastic grocery bags. She made four peanut butter and jelly sandwiches, then thought better of it and started to make four more.

"Lucy?"

She dropped the knife and whirled around. Oscar was standing at the screen door.

"Where have you been?" she asked.

"I went to see Earl."

Lucy held the door open for him. "You did what?"

"I slept for a while this afternoon. Then I walked into town and asked some boys I saw if they knew where Earl Norby was staying. Your aunt Helen said he was visiting somebody named Denise." Oscar looked down at his nightshirt and knickers, at his bare feet. "I guess my clothes must look out of place. Those boys sure looked me up and down. But they told me where Earl was, and I found the house all right. I thought I'd just knock on the door. But there he was, sitting alone out on the front porch." Oscar shook his head. "I'm such a fool! I didn't recognize him right away."

"What did you say to him?" asked Lucy.

"I didn't have to say a word. Earl took one look at me and said, 'Oscar? Oscar Martin?' And I said, 'Earl?' And the two of us just stared at each other." Oscar grinned. "I think Earl thought he'd died or something, so as quick as I could—as best I could—I told him what happened to me."

"Did he believe you?"

"Earl's sharp, Lucy. And he's my best friend. Of course he believed me! And oh, Lucy—it was so good to see him. There was so much to catch up on—I guess nobody ever had quite so much to catch up on as I do." Oscar grinned. "Did you know they have airplanes that can get you to Europe in the same day? They're called *jets*. Earl flew in one all the way to Paris, France!"

Oscar looked as if he expected Lucy to fall out of her chair in surprise. She tried not to laugh. It was a surprise to find that she *could* laugh.

"And Earl has a machine inside his chest, Lucy— it keeps his heart going."

"A pacemaker?"

"That's right. Say, is that a sandwich you're making? Would you mind awfully if I had one? I'm pretty hungry."

Lucy pushed the sandwich across the table, wondering whether Oscar would notice the other sandwiches, or ask why there were so many.

"Mostly we talked about the old days," continued Oscar. "That's what Earl calls them. For me, they don't seem old—they seem—well, they seem like yesterday. Earl said the same thing: 'It seems like yesterday,' he kept saying. But I could tell that *yesterday* for him isn't the same as it is for me." Oscar shook his head. "He told me about my family—what happened after I left. I had to find out, Lucy—coming back and finding them gone—it's just . . ." Oscar looked down at the table. "It's just hard, that's all."

She and Oscar weren't so very different now, thought Lucy. Depending on what happened, it might very well be her sitting across the table years from now, trying to find out what had happened to her mother. "Oscar—I need to tell you something," she said, her voice small. "I have a plan for finding my father. It involves using *The Book of Story Beginnings,*" she began. But that was only half true. She didn't just have a plan. She had already put a plan into action. "What I mean to say is—while you were sleeping, I wrote something in *The Book of Story Beginnings,*" she said.

"What exactly did you write?" Oscar's voice was guarded.

*The Book of Story Beginnings* was on the counter. Lucy handed it to him and watched as Oscar read her story beginning. When he was done, he looked up. "'She and her *great-uncle* set off to find him in a boat'?" he read aloud. "Is that supposed to be me?"

"Well, yes . . ."

"Not a very elegant way of putting it."

"You're not mad at me, are you?" It was a silly question. Lucy could tell that Oscar was angry.

"Do you realize what you've done?" he said.

"I had to do something. I have to find my father."

"Just tell me then. What do we do now?"

Oscar had said *we*. Lucy clung to that hopefully. "I thought we could use the boat. Pull it around to the front of the house. I can use my father's transforming potion to make the sea appear. Then we follow the moonlit path, just like you did. . . ." She didn't tell Oscar that she had only just thought of using the transforming potion.

"You make it sound so easy! Like going off to a Sunday school picnic!"

"Please, Oscar. Please help me. With any luck, we can get to the island, rescue my father, and get back here in a few days—maybe a week. I know we can do it." She didn't dare tell Oscar that a week might turn into years.

She took his silence as encouragement. "My mother's asleep," she said. "I've packed food and things to drink. We could leave now—"

"What you want to do is too dangerous!"

"I have to try to find him!"

"How will we get back? Have you thought of that?"

She hadn't. "I—I have to find him," was all she could say.

Oscar didn't say anything for a minute. Then he threw up his hands. "Let's go," he said.

Everything was harder than Lucy could have imagined. First they had to tilt the rowboat on its side and drag it out of the smokehouse. They heaved and hauled it through the backyard and pulled it around the house. Every time the boat scraped on the gravel driveway, Lucy was terrified her mother would wake up. Finally they dragged it across the front lawn to the end of the walk.

"This is what my father did," Lucy told Oscar. She tilted the bottle of potion up and let a drop fall onto a pencil she had brought along. Then, with a trembling hand, she lifted the pencil in the air. "Sea!" she said firmly. Only her throw was so bad that the pencil didn't even make it across the road in front of The Brick.

Nothing happened.

Then Oscar tried, throwing a stick so far that they almost lost sight of it as it arced through the darkness. Yet the same thing happened again, which was to say *nothing,* and Lucy stood there numbly, wondering what to do next. "I was so stupid to think this would really work," she said.

"And just what did you think would work?" said a voice behind them. It was Lucy's mother. Her arms were folded across her chest.

"Mom—"

"Lucy—in case you haven't noticed, it's dark and it's late and as far as I know, those two things have always meant that your father and I like to know where you are and what you're doing. You can explain to me later why you seem to have forgotten that fact, and why there's a rowboat in our front yard. Earl—I believe I sent you home at a late hour last night, as well. Good night!" She clamped her hand down on Lucy's shoulder and steered her toward the house.

# Chapter Twelve
## Aunt Lavonne's Notes

Seeing Lucy and her mother cross the lawn, Oscar decided that the strangest thing of all was having other people living in his house. He watched them go in the front door, then saw the lights in the front parlor turn on. How bright the electric lights looked in the darkness!

In a way, it helped that everything was so strange. The entire day had felt like a stroll past the sideshows at a circus. All the fantastic sights made it hard to think about anything else. And there were so many things that he didn't want to think about.

But now it was night, and the night was almost too familiar for comfort. The same stars he had seen all his life were greeting the moon as it rose above The Brick. And even with its newfangled electric lights blazing, Oscar couldn't help thinking that The Brick was *his* house, *his* home. He couldn't help thinking of Ma and Pa and Lavonne and Morris inside it. He closed his eyes; it was as if nothing had changed at all. He might look now, he thought, and find that everything was all right.

It wasn't. Oscar wheeled about, nearly falling over the rowboat at his feet. It was only then that he realized he was still holding the bottle of potion in his hand. Lucy and her crazy plan, he thought. He sat down in the boat, facing away from The Brick. There were two bags at his feet. They were made of a crinkly sort of paper that Lucy had called *plastic*. He felt inside one and pulled out a sandwich wrapped in yet more plastic. He was hungry.

He was about to take a bite when he had an idea. He opened the bottle of potion and let a drop fall on the sandwich. "Apple turnover," he said, picturing in his mind one of Ma's freshly baked pastries, steaming hot from the oven.

"Ouch!" Oscar fell backward, dropping a hot turnover in the bottom of the boat. He stared at the mess of crumbs and sticky brown apple filling. "Well, I'll be!" he said. "How did that happen?"

He took another sandwich from the bag and tried

using the potion again, setting the sandwich down this time before he said *apple turnover.* To his disappointment, however, nothing happened. He tried two more times without success. "Hang it all!" he said. "Why did it work just that one time and not the others?"

He ate the sandwich and a bit of ruined turnover. Then, turning to look at the house, he saw that the lights were off now. Lucy and her mother must have gone to bed. He contemplated waking Lucy up, throwing gravel at her window again so he could tell her what had happened.

But it was a mistake to even look at the house. Oscar was once again overcome by the feeling that nothing had changed. He yearned to go inside The Brick. What if he were to go up to his own room? Or what if he were to knock on Ma and Pa's bedroom door? What if he were to call out, *I'm home . . . ?*

"Stop it!" Oscar told himself. He put the bottle of potion in his pocket. He would tell Lucy about the apple turnover tomorrow. Tomorrow it would be light again, and the world would be strange again, and he wouldn't have to think about home. He really ought to try and get some sleep.

One of the problems with having been a cat for so long was that Oscar felt wide awake when he shouldn't.

For the longest time, he lay staring into the darkness of the smokehouse.

He thought about *The Book of Story Beginnings*. If only he had never found it! He'd been so sneaky— taking it without telling Ma. Had she known that it was magic? Was that why it was locked away in the attic? He would never know. He could never tell Ma how sorry he was.

*It's all my fault,* he thought. Even Lucy's father being gone was his fault. He hadn't meant to chase him out the window. But he never would have chased him out the window if he hadn't been a cat. And he wouldn't have been a cat if he hadn't written in *The Book of Story Beginnings*.

He wanted to help Lucy. It seemed like a cruel sort of twist for that magic potion of hers not to work all of a sudden. On the other hand, thought Oscar, it was the sort of thing that happened in stories—a twist in the plot. Every so often, it helped to remind himself that this *was* a story.

The potion changed Lucy's father into a bird, thought Oscar. It changed me back into myself, and it changed that sandwich into an apple turnover. But what about the other times we used the potion? Why didn't it work then?

He yawned. It was a relief to feel tired at last, and

as he closed his eyes, Oscar remembered something Pa had once told him. The best way to solve a problem was to sleep on it. The mind had a funny way of coming up with answers when you were sleeping, Pa had said. It was one of the great blessings of rest.

When Oscar awoke, he didn't know where he was. He had been dreaming about the attic. In his dream, a cat had been running up and down a long table, scattering papers in the air. Oscar had reached his hand into a cloud of papers swirling about his head and grabbed one. He was just starting to read it when he woke up.

He blinked. He wasn't in the attic. He was in the smokehouse, and he could see sunlight around the edges of the doors.

*Notes on a Theory of Transformation.* That was what the paper in the dream had said. But Oscar knew he had seen those same words on a real piece of paper. He had read them on that first night, when he had lapped up the spilled potion and found himself in the attic. He hadn't thought much of it at the time. He had put the paper back down on the table. But it's probably still there, thought Oscar. And if Lucy's father made the transforming potion, maybe he wrote down instructions for using it.

Oscar stood up and stretched. His bones hurt from

sleeping on the pine boards of the smokehouse floor. His mouth was dry and his tongue felt rough. He pushed open the door and saw that the sun was high up, glaring at him. It had to be late morning. Lucy was sure to be up. He could ask for a drink, maybe even breakfast.

But she wasn't home. The house was empty, and Oscar saw that the automobile was gone from the driveway. So he helped himself to breakfast, finding a loaf of bread in the cupboard and the jar of strawberry jam in the kitchen's big white icebox. He drank cup after cup of cold water from the kitchen sink. It all felt like trespassing, even stealing, and he hurried to clean up afterward.

Then he went upstairs, ignoring an impulse to look around the house, to poke his head into the various rooms. It had been eerie enough sitting in his own room yesterday with Lucy; he had felt like some kind of ghost. He went straight up to the attic, climbed through the trapdoor hole, and looked around.

Someone had cleaned things up since the other night. The broken glass was gone, and the papers that had been strewn all over were stacked in neat piles on the table.

The first sheaf of papers he picked up wasn't what

he was looking for, though it was interesting enough. *A Theory of Transportation*, someone had written at the top of the first page. There was a sketch on the page—a round circle with a pentagon in the middle. There were scratchy designs around the pentagon.

Oscar tried to read the notes that accompanied the sketch. There was a long discussion of space and time that didn't make any sense to him. But a few sentences at the end caught his interest:

> To use the traveling talisman, the would-be traveler must put his finger through the hole in the middle and speak aloud the desired destination. Be it the sands of Egypt, the ancient lands of the East, or even the far-off moon, he will find himself there. But beware he who would thus conquer space and time. Let him think before he acts, lest he stop some wheels in their turning and start others in motion.

Oscar wondered if the round thing in the picture was supposed to be the traveling talisman. It must be some sort of magical object, he decided. Put your finger through the hole in the middle, say where you wanted to go, and there you were. It sounded like a handy sort of thing to have.

Handy, and rather silly. For the first time, it occurred to Oscar that Lavonne might have written the notes he was reading. Lucy had said that most of the things in the attic were Lavonne's, and that she had been interested in magic. He pictured his sister waving a magic wand. It was the sort of thing he might have laughed at once upon a time.

He didn't laugh now. Instead, he paged through the rest of the papers in his hand. He set them down and picked up another sheaf. And another, and another, until at last he found what he was looking for at the top of a paper filled with rows of black ink and small notes in red around the edges. " 'Notes on a Theory of Transformation,' " he read aloud.

Before Oscar could read further, however, he heard noises downstairs—the kitchen door squeaking open, footsteps on the floor, and faraway voices. He tiptoed over to the window and looked down. The automobile was back. He hadn't even heard it come up the drive.

Now the voices were getting louder. Lucy and her mother were coming up the front stairs. Oscar crept over to the trapdoor to listen.

"I have a headache, Lucy. I'm going to lie down," said her mother. "Will you be all right?"

"I'll be okay."

"I'm sure your father will call this afternoon."

"I know."

From the sound of her voice, Oscar could tell that Lucy was standing in the hallway near the attic closet. He heard a door close. He hesitated a moment, then spoke as loud as he dared: "Lucy!"

The door to the attic closet opened and Lucy's face looked up at him. "What are you doing up there?" she whispered.

"I've got something to show you. . . ."

"Shh!" Lucy threw a worried glance over her shoulder.

"Come on up!"

"All right. But be quiet!"

"Where were you?" he asked her when they were both in the attic. Lucy was wearing a dress, not the denim trousers she had been wearing last night.

"At church," she said. "And afterward we went to Aunt Helen and Uncle Byron's for dinner. It was awful."

"Why?"

"Everyone's finally figured out that my father is really gone. My mother thinks he's left home—run out on us or something like that because they had a big argument the other day. Everyone's really worried. And Sheriff Jensen was there. That made it worse."

"Who's Sheriff Jensen?"

"Some friend of Uncle Byron's. Aunt Helen invited him because he knows my dad. So it was supposed to be fun—only my dad wasn't there, and it all turned into one big interrogation."

"Interrogation!"

"Well, maybe that's not the right word," said Lucy. "But he *is* a policeman, and when everybody got all worried about my father, he started asking questions. Like, who was the last person to see my father? That was *me*. And when did I last see him? And did he seem all right when I last saw him? Anyway, my mother started to cry, and Sheriff Jensen actually said he'd get some people out looking for my dad."

"Maybe you should tell what really happened," said Oscar.

"I can't. She'd never believe me."

Then Oscar remembered the sheaf of papers in his hand. "I think I've found something," he said. He laid the papers on the table, smoothed the top one with his hand, and read aloud:

"Notes on a Theory of Transformation
The sleeper dreams of an egg and knows an egg.
He dreams the egg is hatched and a bird rises
from the shell. Awake, he sees an egg and knows

*a star, and the star will shine. But how shall we wake the sleeper from his dreaming? How shall we enter his chamber and wake him to power? We can show him the door, but how shall we give him the key?"*

Oscar scowled. "This isn't any good. I thought it would tell us how the potion works. You see, I got it to work last night after all."

"You did?"

Oscar told her about the apple turnover. "But I couldn't get it to work after that," he said.

Lucy studied the paper more closely. "This is Aunt Lavonne's handwriting," she said.

"I don't see why she bothered writing such nonsense." Oscar felt almost annoyed with Lavonne, as if she weren't an unfamiliar old lady but still his younger sister.

"She probably didn't write it. She told my father about some old book on alchemy. I bet the book was written in Latin or Greek, and this is her translation of something it said."

"But what does it mean?" said Oscar. "'The sleeper dreams of an egg . . .'"

"It could mean anything," said Lucy. "The sleeper isn't necessarily a sleeper. The egg doesn't have to be an egg. They're probably symbols for something else. My father said the alchemists used symbols for everything."

"What do you suppose this means?" said Oscar, pointing to a note in red ink in the margin of the paper:

Sleeper = Imagination
Door = Word
Key = Potion

"That's my father's handwriting." Lucy screwed her eyes shut, and Oscar could tell she was thinking. "He said something about imagination," she said after a moment. "When he was telling me about the transforming potion, he said that the potion was a *catalyst* for the interaction between imagination and language."

"What's a catalyst?" Oscar wondered.

"Something in chemistry, I think."

"You haven't got a dictionary, have you?"

They found one on the bookshelves at the end of the attic. "It says a catalyst is an agent that induces catalysis," said Oscar.

"I hate it when they do that! What's it say under *catalysis*?"

"Something about chemistry, just as you said. Then it says more: 'an action or reaction between two or more persons or forces precipitated by a separate agent and especially by one that is essentially unaltered by the reaction.'"

"What does 'precipitated by a separate agent' mean?" said Lucy.

"*Precipitating* can mean making something happen more quickly than you'd expect," said Oscar. "I know because I got it wrong once in a spelling bee and had to look it up afterward."

"Maybe the imagination is one force and words are the other," said Lucy. "The potion is the separate agent that precipitates their reaction!"

"That's it, Lucy!" Oscar closed the dictionary. "When you tried to make the sea appear, were you really imagining it?"

"I don't think I was."

"I wasn't either when I tried to make the ocean," said Oscar. "But when I turned that sandwich into an apple turnover, I was really picturing it in my mind."

"It's not enough just to say what you want! You have to imagine it!" said Lucy.

Oscar took the bottle of potion from his pocket. It gleamed like a dark jewel in the light from the window. "We ought to test it," he said.

"You're right." Lucy looked down at the table. "Try this," she said.

Oscar hesitated.

"It's a paper clip," said Lucy.

"I know. We had those back then. I was just wondering what to change it into."

Lucy thought for a moment. "What about a butterfly?" she said.

"All right." Trying not to let his hand shake, Oscar tipped a drop of potion onto the paper clip. "Butterfly!" he said firmly, concentrating his thoughts. And suddenly a black-and-yellow swallowtail fluttered up in front of him.

"I was imagining a monarch!" said Lucy, her voice filled with wonder.

"I was the one holding the bottle," said Oscar. The swallowtail danced in the air like a puppet, just as he had pictured it in his mind. Then it skipped along the ceiling and out the open window. Its wings shimmered in the sunlight as it floated across the grass and out of sight.

# Chapter Thirteen
## The Broken Moon

That night Lucy's mother seemed to take forever going to bed. Lucy, who had pretended to be tired soon after supper, had to sit in her room and wait. The phone rang at nine, and then again at ten thirty. It was Aunt Helen each time, and each time, Lucy's mother said the same things: "No, we haven't heard a thing," and, "Yes, I'm sure he'll call tomorrow. . . . I'll let you know right away," and, "I'm sure everything will be just fine."

Only it wasn't going to be fine, Lucy knew. Oscar was waiting for her outside. They were going to leave tonight. In the morning, they would be gone, and her mother might never know what had happened to her.

When at last she was sure that her mother was asleep, Lucy stole down the stairs and out the front door. As she crossed the lawn toward the rowboat, Oscar stepped out from the trees. "Have you got the potion?" he said.

"Here." Handing it to him, Lucy nearly dropped the bottle. She was so nervous that she felt cold. Her teeth were chattering. She looked back at The Brick and saw a disappointing moon rising above the house. It was nowhere near full, nor was it a familiar, satisfying crescent. It looked broken—the wrong kind of moon for an adventure. Lucy's hand felt inside her sweatshirt until she found the touch of cold metal. She was wearing the medallion she had found in the attic. *For luck,* she had told herself as she put it on earlier. *For luck,* she reminded herself now.

"Are you ready?" asked Oscar.

Lucy nodded. They had already agreed that Oscar would handle the transformation, given that he had a better mental picture of the way the sea ought to look. "The sea!" he said. Two words, and there it was, rolling in from the horizon like a black shadow, colder and darker than Lucy had imagined it, bringing with it a chill, salty wind.

"Let's go," said Oscar.

Lucy sat in the stern as Oscar pulled the boat away from shore. She watched him lean toward her, the blades of the oars slicing through the air until they caught the water behind him. Then the oars came forward in a swift, strong sweep as he stretched back toward the bow. Again and again and again the boat sprang forward, and Oscar never stopped gazing at the shore behind Lucy. She wondered whether he was thinking of another time—of Lavonne, racing back to the house to wake everyone.

Oscar stopped rowing. He rubbed his knuckles. "Where's your moon path?" he said.

"What?"

"I thought you said we were to follow the path made by the moon on the water."

Lucy looked back at the moon. It was so high in the sky above The Brick that it left only a flickering patch on the water about halfway between the rowboat and the shore.

"Common sense says we ought to row out to sea," Oscar suggested.

"I'll row," Lucy offered.

"Give it a try," said Oscar.

Lucy had watched Oscar while he rowed, so she knew in her mind what she was supposed to do. But she had trouble forcing her arms to obey her thoughts. If she got the least bit tired (which she did almost immediately), one or the other oar would twist in her hands, slicing through the water like a knife. Or an oar would catch the top of a wave and splash Oscar. The stern zigzagged back and forth against the horizon.

"You're doing fine," said Oscar. "It takes a while to get a feel for rowing."

"But we're not getting any farther out from shore. I think we're getting closer!"

"Suppose I row for a bit," said Oscar. "At least far enough out so we don't have to see The Brick perched at the water's edge like that. I don't know about you, but it makes me nervous."

Lucy had to agree. There was something disturbing about being so close to the border of two worlds. When they had stood on shore, it was the sea that had looked mysterious and strange. Now it was The Brick that looked unreal. It seemed impossible to Lucy that her mother was still sleeping inside the house.

A half hour later, Oscar stopped his rowing. "We can't see land anymore," he said. "There won't be a moon path for a while," he added. "Not until the moon begins to set, anyway. We might as well just rest. Otherwise we're likely to row back to shore again."

Try as she might, however, Lucy couldn't rest. For a long time she watched the moon, now useless and small above them. She watched the water that stretched to the horizon in all directions. Somewhere there was a shoreline, she thought, with The Brick overlooking the water. Her mother was there. And somewhere, her father was on an island. But where? She felt as though someone had thrown a blindfold over her and whirled her around and around.

She pictured her mother checking on her, not finding her in bed, calling for her. Would she think she had run away? How long would she look for her before she gave up? A hundred years from now, would someone be trying to solve the mystery of Lucy Martin's disappearance?

She looked at Oscar. He was stretched out in the bow—stretched out as much as he could be in such a tiny space. His legs were draped over the seat, his arms resting on the sides of the boat. The oars were pulled in. She had thought he was asleep, but now she could see his eyes looking at her in the moonlight.

"What's it like?" she said. "Finding yourself in the future?" She felt cruel for asking the question, like a scientist sliding Oscar's feelings under a microscope.

Oscar pulled himself up and leaned over the side, rippling the cold water with his hand. "It makes me think of a time when I was little, when Pa took me on a train to Chicago," he said. "And I fell asleep. When I woke up, Pa was gone. He'd gone up to the next car to talk to a cattle farmer he knew, but I didn't know that. I didn't even know passengers could go from car to car. I just thought Pa had left the train and forgotten me. I remember looking out the window, thinking that if I could just find something I recognized—a farmhouse or a tree or a road—I could get off the train and go home and find Pa. But nothing was familiar. And I was so little that I didn't really understand why. I didn't know we were miles away from Martin. I thought the reason I couldn't recognize anything was that the train was going so fast." Oscar drew his hand out of the water and rubbed it dry on his shirt. "That's what it's like," he told Lucy. "Just like that fast train—nothing's familiar and I can't get off."

Not just everything being unfamiliar, thought Lucy. But finding your mother gone—dead! She didn't dare ask Oscar how he felt about *that*.

"Tell me about your mother," said Oscar.

"What about her?" said Lucy, startled because she thought he had read her mind.

"She wanted to be a writer once," said Oscar. "What does she like to write about?"

"I—I don't know," said Lucy. "She doesn't exactly have time."

"Sounds like my ma," said Oscar. "Never having enough time for music."

"She played the violin," said Lucy. "I read about it in your composition books."

"My what?"

"Your journals."

"You read my journals?" Oscar sounded shocked.

"Well, I found them and—"

"Those were meant to be private," said Oscar.

"Well, they didn't say private! Aunt Lavonne read them. My dad read them," said Lucy.

Oscar sighed. "I suppose everyone read them. Even Ma and Pa."

"But there wasn't anything terrible in them," Lucy said quickly. "I liked reading about your family. They seemed so happy. Your parents got along so well. Not like mine."

"My parents?" Oscar sounded surprised.

"Well, yes!" said Lucy. "My parents are always arguing. They never agree about anything."

"I don't know why you think my parents do!" said Oscar. "They're completely different. Pa's always working. And Ma—she likes to play music all the time. She says she *has* to. She plays her violin whenever she can, so things kind of go to seed around the house. She can't stand housework. She tries for Pa's sake, but he's so persnickety. He's always getting mad at Ma—they're always fighting. . . ." Oscar stopped short. "Or they *were* always fighting," he added softly.

"It didn't sound that way from what you wrote."

"Well, they did."

"But they *loved* each other," said Lucy.

"Sure." Oscar shrugged.

"That's *important*," said Lucy. She thought of her own parents—how they were always fighting. Yet now that her father was gone, her mother seemed so— *lost* seemed to be the right word.

She watched Oscar again, wondering what he was thinking. Then she said, "You wrote about one fight they had. Your pa moved out of the house."

"Oh!" Oscar's voice was full of pain. "I forgot I wrote about that."

"But they made up with each other!" Lucy said.

"I guess you could call it that," said Oscar. "What happened was Morris got the croup. Ma sent me to fetch Dr. Carter, and she sent Lavonne up to Uncle Ned's house. Pa rushed home, and everybody worried all night. Morris was better by dawn, and Pa stayed for breakfast and there was never any more talk about it. That's how most things went with them. I never heard anybody making up."

Maybe that's the way parents were, thought Lucy. They fought in front of you and made up in private. It was a strange thought—a lonely kind of thought that wasn't very comforting.

"One of us should get some sleep," said Oscar. "The other can stay up and watch for the moon path."

"I'll watch," Lucy volunteered. It was silly, but she felt as though the boat needed her to stay awake. She needed to steer it toward her father so she could bring him home.

"Lucy!"

Her bed was shaking. Not only that, her bed was hard and shaped all wrong. Why would anyone make such an uncomfortable bed?

"Lucy, wake up!"

Startled, she opened her eyes and sat up.

"It's the moon path!" Oscar grabbed the oars, swung the boat around, and began rowing.

Though the moon was still a good ways above the horizon, the path it made on the water was faint. The sky was turning light gray. It took Lucy a second to figure out what was happening. As the moon was setting, the sun was rising. It wouldn't be long before daylight entirely erased the moon path from the water. "I fell asleep!" she wailed.

"It's no use," said Oscar, dropping the oars as the moon's path flickered away to nothing. All around them, the sea was brightening.

"We could keep rowing," said Lucy. "Just keep going away from the sun."

"Aren't we supposed to follow the moon path? Isn't that what you wrote?"

"Yes." Lucy thought about what she had written: *They knew they could get to the island by following the path made by the moon on the water.* Those had been her exact words. Would it have been wiser simply to write that they *got* to the island by following the moon path? She wondered if she could scratch out a few words. Then she remembered that she had forgotten to bring *The Book of Story Beginnings.*

"I say we use the potion," said Oscar. "I could imagine the island into existence—right over there." He gestured toward the west.

"All right," said Lucy. "But it does seem like we're using an awful lot of potion. I don't want to waste it. I'll need it when I find my father."

"It won't be a waste if we can make the island appear." Oscar rummaged through one of the grocery bags and found the bottle of potion. He also pulled out an apple. He let a drop of potion fall on it, then hurled it through the air. "Island!" he shouted.

They heard a small plunk, and Lucy thought she could see the apple floating in the water.

"What happened?" said Oscar. "I was imagining the island. Believe me, I know exactly what it looks like!"

Lucy thought for a moment. "I wonder if you

already imagined it," she said. "When you made the sea earlier, you imagined the same sea that you saw back in 1914. The island was in that sea, so it must exist in this sea as well. Maybe you can't imagine something that already exists."

"I guess we'll have to wait for your moon path after all." Oscar sighed.

It was the longest day ever. The sun was at high noon before they figured out that they were going to get dreadfully sunburned if they didn't do something about it. After much debate, Lucy agreed to use the potion to change one of the grocery bags into an enormous beach umbrella (Oscar called it a parasol) that was large enough to shade them both. Eventually a gust of wind whipped it out of the boat. The parasol collapsed and sank before they could retrieve it.

As night fell, they took turns rowing, moving confidently along the path of light the rising moon shot across the water. After several hours, however, the path faded because the moon had risen too high.

"We'll have to take another rest. Wait for it to set a bit," said Oscar.

Lucy let the oars drop. The muscles in her arms and back were aching. Her hands were blistered and raw.

"The moon looks smaller than it did last night. It must be waning," said Oscar.

Waning! thought Lucy. What if they were out here tomorrow night, and the night after, and the night after that? What would they do when the moon disappeared altogether? "I'm sorry," she said. "I should never have suggested we do this." She cupped her hands in front of her mouth, sheltering her palms from the cold air. "I should never have written what I did in *The Book of Story Beginnings*."

"Now you sound like me—sorry for what you can't undo," said Oscar, shifting his position so he could stretch out in the stern. But a second later, he sat up, a look of astonishment on his face.

Lucy turned to see what he was gaping at.

It was a ship—a quaint, old-fashioned ship with a striped sail. It made Lucy think of model ships in old movies.

"You shout!" Oscar commanded. "Let me row!"

"Hey! Over here!" Lucy shouted as Oscar took over the oars. He rowed as if a steam engine were powering his arms. And still the ship sailed on, the distance between it and the rowboat steadily increasing.

"It's no good. We've got to signal it somehow," said Oscar, gasping for breath. "What about a flare?"

"A flare!"

"Yes—we could use the potion to imagine a flare."

Thinking of flares made Lucy think of the *Titanic*.

Was that before or after Oscar? "Do you know what a flare looks like?" she asked. "Have you got any idea how to shoot one off?"

"I think I could figure it out," said Oscar. "But if you like, we could use a lantern."

"Why not a big flashlight?"

"Go ahead! Hurry!" Oscar stood up, rocking the boat dangerously, waving his arms at the ship.

Lucy imagined the largest flashlight she could, modeling it on one she had seen at music camp last summer. "Flashlight!" she said, remembering at the last second to say, "with batteries."

She fumbled with the switch. Then Oscar held the flashlight up above his head. He waved the beam of light slowly back and forth.

"They don't see it," said Lucy. "Try switching it on and off."

Oscar handed the flashlight to her. "Over here! Over here!" he shouted as Lucy flashed the light at the ship.

"They can't see it. We're too far away!" cried Lucy.

"No! No, look! The ship's turning around! They've seen us!"

# CHAPTER FOURTEEN

## CAPTAIN MACK

A s the ship turned broadside to the rowboat, Lucy saw shadowy figures standing near the stern. One of the figures raised a hand and beckoned. "Come alongside 'n' state your business!"

Oscar propelled the rowboat toward the ship's hull, which rose up before them like the wall of a fortress.

"Put some muscle into it! We ain't got all night!" a voice called. To Lucy's surprise, she saw that it belonged to a woman. She could see the woman's broad face peering down. Other, smaller faces grinned down as well, looking ghoulish in the darkness.

"They're *children*!" whispered Oscar.

"It's the law of the sea to help a sailor in need," said the woman. "But so help me if you ain't in need and you've slowed us down for nothin'. . . .

"Fetch a rope, Mavis!" she said, and one of the smaller faces disappeared. A minute later, a rope snaked its way down. "Hoist yourselves up!" ordered the woman.

"You first," whispered Oscar. He grabbed the rope and held it taut for Lucy.

"Don't forget to tie up your boat," the woman called as Lucy tumbled over the rail onto the deck. A grinning girl helped her to her feet.

By the time Oscar flopped onto the deck, even more children—Lucy counted eight in all—had gathered around to stare. The oldest was a sturdy-looking boy with a wispy beard sprouting on his chin. The youngest was a little boy who kept yawning and rubbing his eyes. He sat down on the bottom rung of a ladder that led up to a small deck at the ship's stern.

"Now'd be the time for statin' your business!" The woman thrust her thumbs behind a pair of blue suspenders. These held up a pair of brown pants that looked like they had been made out of an old potato sack. The pants were tucked into a pair of battered brown boots.

"We're lost!" Oscar and Lucy spoke in unison.

"You're lost!" scoffed the woman. "I guess you are! Out in the middle of nowhere without a sail. What happened to you? Were you put off your ship?"

"What?"

"How'd you get here? Can't tell me you rowed that old tub all the way out here. What'd you do? Get caught as stowaways?"

"No!" said Lucy and Oscar together.

"Where're you headed?"

Not knowing what else to say, they told her the truth. That they were looking for an island inhabited by cats, and ruled by a king who couldn't get along with the queen, who kept all the birds on the island in cages. The description tumbled out of them haphazardly because they were so anxious. Lucy wondered whether the woman might be a pirate. If so, she looked like she had invented the phrase *Make them walk the plank!* Her thick gray hair looked like it had been hacked off at the shoulders, probably with the knife that was tucked into her right boot. Her chin was crumpled up toward her nose, pulling her mouth down in what looked like a perpetual sneer.

But as they described their destination, there was a twitch in the sneer. "Cat'n'berd Island," she said in a twangy drawl.

"You know it?" said Oscar.

"Headin' there myself. Got a load of birdseed be-low deck to deliver." Just as the woman said this, there was a thud from behind her. The little boy who had been yawning was lying on the deck looking dazed.

"Charlie's so tired he fell right over, Auntie," said the girl who had helped Lucy up earlier.

"Don't just stand there gawkin', Millie. Take your brother to bed," said the woman. "And don't forget to call me *Captain*."

"Yes, Auntie—Captain." The girl picked up Charlie and disappeared into a doorway next to the ladder. There was a little house beneath the stern deck. The ship's cabin, thought Lucy.

"As for you," continued the woman, turning toward them again. "What business has the likes of you got on Cat'n'berd Island?"

"We need to see the Queen," Oscar said boldly.

"Well, ain't that somethin'!" The woman grinned. "Jarvis!" she said to the boy with the wispy beard. "He says they need to see the Queen!"

Jarvis and the other children snickered.

"Now look here—you're either daft as sea slugs or you're lyin' through your teeth," said the woman. "No one sees the Queen less'n they're somebody the Queen wants to see. And less'n you got feathers sproutin' on your head, she don't want to see you!" This comment brought on a new round of giggles from the children.

Oscar glanced at Lucy and rolled his eyes. "The Queen *will* see us," he told the woman. "I can promise you that. And if you take us to the island, we'll pay you."

"How much?" asked the woman, as quickly as a cash register drawer sliding open.

"How much do you want?"

The woman's eyes narrowed. "Fair's fair," she said after a moment's calculation. "Say twenty silver coins."

"We haven't got any coins," said Oscar. "We haven't got any money."

Lucy had two dollars and some odd cents in the pocket of her jeans, but she didn't see the point in bringing that up right now. "We've got a rowboat," she offered.

The woman smirked as if she had been offered a toy boat. She said, "I also seen you got a lamp."

"You want the lamp?" Oscar sounded relieved.

"Gimme the boat 'n' the lamp, and I'll see you get to Cat'n'berd Island."

"All right with you, Lucy?" said Oscar.

"All right." Lucy hoped the batteries in the flashlight would hold out.

"Deal, then!" said the woman, smiling broadly. "Hate to sound hard, but fair's fair. I got a family to feed. Haulin' folks back and forth between islands never made nobody rich. Jarvis! Let's get goin' again. Stupid to waste this good wind."

"Yes, Auntie—Captain," said Jarvis.

"And you two—Hugh, Mavis—climb over and secure that rowboat. Both ends now, and we'll haul her out of the water. Mind the lamp. Hand it up careful or I'll have your ears."

As Hugh and Mavis scrambled over the side, the woman gave an agreeable nod to Oscar and Lucy. "Captain Amelia Mack at your service. Jarvis is first mate, but don't tell *him* that. It'll go to his head. The rest of my crew . . ." The captain took notice suddenly of the remaining children on deck—two small boys and a girl who were staring at them with big eyes. "The rest of my crew needs to get back to bed! See that they're tucked in straightaway," she told Millie, who had just emerged from the ship's cabin.

"Yes, Auntie. . . . Can I come back when they're all in?"

"Don't let me see your face till mornin'," Captain Mack said firmly.

"My sister Sadie's lot," she said as Millie herded the children through the door. "Eight of 'em she had.

•: 176 :•

Always dyin' of curiosity she was, to know whether the next one'd be a girl or a boy, whether it'd be pretty or plain, whether it'd have curly hair or straight. And there she is carryin' the next one in line last winter when her husband ups and dies of the flu. Silly man, about as useful as a sail full of holes. Yes, I know," she said, looking at Oscar and Lucy as if they had spoken. "It ain't right to speak ill of the dead, but it was the plain truth. There he goes, leavin' the family bereft and all, and then Sadie goes and has the baby and wouldn't you know *she* dies, leavin' behind a houseful of kids and a baby besides and only me, their aunt, to take care of everyone.

"I'm no saint, if that's what you're thinkin', takin' 'em all on board," said Captain Mack. "Had seven of 'em already as crew, and it wasn't much trouble to take on Charlie, though he's too young to be much use for anythin' but givin' everybody practice shoutin', 'Man Overboard!' But I couldn't have the baby, naturally. Had to farm her out. Money out of my own pocket, too, payin' for a full-time nurse, but nobody ever said I ain't good to my own kin. And fair's fair—I guess I owe Sadie somethin' for the work I've got out of the rest of 'em. They're a good crew, though I won't swell their heads by tellin' 'em so," the captain concluded.

Just then, Hugh crawled over the side of the ship

with the flashlight. The captain watched with interest as Lucy showed her how to switch it on and off. "Never seen one like it," she said. "Should come in handy." She checked to make sure that Hugh and Mavis had secured the boat properly and sent them off to bed.

"You two will have to sleep on deck," she told Oscar and Lucy. "Somewhere out of the way."

"Jarvis!" she called as she climbed up the ladder to the stern deck. "You need to steer by the stars. If you expect to get there by the seat of your pants, you might just as well go naked!"

"Lucy—you know what this ship is, don't you?" Oscar whispered. "It's the *ship of orphans.* It's that story beginning I wrote! I guess this means that one more story has gotten mixed up with all the rest."

For breakfast, Millie brought them hard biscuits and coffee. Lucy, who had never been allowed to try coffee before, sipped it curiously, trying to force herself to like the bitter taste. Oscar drank his eagerly, all the while pelting Millie with questions about the ship. He seemed to know a lot about ships, though it did sound to Lucy as though most of his knowledge came straight out of *Treasure Island.*

"The ship's called the *Rosalie,* after my dead granny," said Millie. "She was Auntie's mother. Auntie wants me to be captain of the *Rosalie* someday. That's because I'm her favorite. I'm named after both her and Granny—Amelia Rosalie. You can call me Amelia Rosalie, if you like," she said, smiling at Oscar and leaning toward him. "I got a secret," she added. "I don't want to be captain at all."

"No?"

"No—not one bit," said Millie. "I hate ships. There's mice and rats down below. I hate mice and rats. And nothin' but work, work, work, all day long," she complained. "What I want is to be a lady. Do you really know the Queen?"

"Well, I guess you could say we do—in a way," said Oscar, and Lucy could guess what he was thinking. After all, he had invented the Queen in his story beginning. For that matter, he had invented Millie as well. She must be the girl he had described in his story about the ship of orphans, the girl who dreamed of lords and ladies, of kings and queens.

"I guess you must know everything there is to know about life at court," said Millie. "I know how to dance. I can waltz. You got to count *one-two-three, one-two-three,* just like this." She jumped up and did a few steps for Oscar's benefit. "I know how to hold a fork, and use a napkin the right way. And I know how to curtsey. I've practiced."

But just as she dipped down, Captain Mack strode over, looking peeved. "None of your airs now, Missy," she said. "Go and give Jarvis a break at the tiller."

"Givin' you her nonsense about wantin' to be a lady, I'll wager," said Captain Mack when Millie was gone. "It's all I can do to knock it out of her—train her to run the ship proper."

"It's a beautiful ship," said Oscar.

"Bought the *Rosalie* six years ago," said the captain, warming to what was clearly a favorite topic. "And a good, solid ship she is. Not so fast as the three-mast ships that can make the trip to Cat'n'berd Island in two days. But more sail power's costly, so I do the best I can. In a good wind like this, we should make it to Cat'n'berd Island by dawn tomorrow."

The *Rosalie* had left its home port, a place called Pig's Head Island (because it was shaped like a pig's head, Lucy was told when she asked) only three days before. "Give us a day at Cat'n'berd Island to unload and collect our money, and we can be home in a week, weather permittin'," said Captain Mack. "This time of year, I can take nine, maybe even ten loads of seed. Got to be quick, though, or all the business gets taken by the three-mast ships."

"The birdseed's for the Queen's birds, isn't it?" Lucy said.

"Well, sure!" Captain Mack looked surprised that Lucy would need to ask.

But Lucy was thinking of her father. "And do you deliver it directly to the Queen?"

"Not likely! I drop off my cargo at port, take my money, and go. What use have I for her silly goin's on?"

"Is she silly?" Lucy was watching Oscar amble toward the stern. Millie's face brightened when she saw him coming.

"All this bird business!" said the captain. "Mind you, I'm not complainin' or anythin'—birds are my livelihood, after all. The quarrel between those two has been plenty good for some of us. But it ain't been good for everyone, that much I'll say. And there's many who would agree with me—if cats that used to be people could express their opinion. No, indeed! That island's a sorry place what with her in charge."

"In charge! What about the King? Isn't he in charge?"

"Oh, he's a fool!"

"Doesn't he change everyone into cats?"

"Ha! You can't call *that* bein' in charge. That's just spite." Captain Mack squinted at the sky for a moment, checking the sun's position. She waved her hand at Millie, who was showing Oscar how the tiller worked. "A hair to the north, girl!" she called. "Check the compass or we'll end up sailin' off the edge of the world."

"Yes, Auntie!"

"Why doesn't he change the Queen into a cat?" Lucy asked. "Has she got magical powers?"

"Not a speck of 'em."

"Well then, why couldn't he change her into a cat?"

"Well, I suppose he *could*," said Captain Mack. "But that's not the same as sayin' he *would*. Got him wrapped around her finger, that one has. Even if they ain't on speakin' terms."

"Will they ever make up?"

"Not likely! She likes birds. He likes cats," said the captain. "What folks say is, the Queen doesn't just like birds. She *loves* 'em. They say her palace is one of the seven wonders of the world. Some rooms all red and green and gold—filled up with parrots. Others all rainbow-like, filled up with little finches. Swans and seagulls and such—all displayed as if they was in a museum. Must be somethin' to see.

"But wouldn't you know, millions of birds ain't enough for her!" added Captain Mack. "Just last week, I heard a captain of a ship out of Bramble Island sayin' he'd found a big black bird. Sold it to the Queen for thirty silver coins." The captain snorted. "Thirty silvers for an old crow!"

"Are there lots of crows around here?" Lucy asked eagerly.

"Nah! I ain't seen one for ten years!"

Lucy gripped the rail of the ship.

After the midday meal of hard biscuits, dried beef, and sour oranges, Captain Mack disappeared into the cabin at the stern. Millie told Oscar and Lucy that her aunt usually slept during the afternoon so she could be alert for the night watch.

Oscar and Lucy took shelter from the sun in a strip of shadow cast by the main sail. Lucy told him everything she had heard, including the encouraging news about the crow. "Do you think it could have been my father?" she wondered aloud.

"Sure." Oscar was watching Mavis and Hugh and the other small children jump rope. In the absence of their captain, the members of the crew appeared to do more playing than sailing.

"I've got an idea," Lucy continued. "We can use the potion to make a bird. Then we can use the bird to get into the palace—pretend we want to sell it to the Queen."

"Sure."

"You didn't even hear what I said."

"I did! It's a good idea, Lucy." Oscar looked at her,

then back at the children. "I was just thinking about how queer all this is."

"What?"

"Well, everything. This ship, Captain Mack, the crew. They're all just part of a story I began. That's all. But see how complete everything is. The sail there—it's got a tear near the corner. How did the tear get there? I reckon if you ask Captain Mack she'll tell you. And the crew—each and every one of them's a completely different person with a past and a future. There's Millie—she never stops talking about how bored she is. She wants to go with us when we go to see the Queen. Don't look at her, for heaven's sake! She'll be over here in a second. She's been making eyes at me all day, worse than Earl's sister Charlotte."

Millie was sitting on an overturned barrel peeling potatoes. Every so often her eyes flickered in their direction. Sometimes they did more than flicker and opened wide like two pansies as she smiled coyly at Oscar.

Meanwhile, the jump rope thwapped against the deck, whisking beneath Mavis's quick feet as she jumped, her brown braids flapping. She was chanting a rhyme Lucy had never heard before:

> *"The moon is a cookie,*
> *with sugar on its cheeks.*

*We like to eat it every night*
*for weeks and weeks and weeks.*
*We nibble and we nibble,*
*until it's all but gone.*
*And then we beg for more again,*
*so we can sing this song.*
*How many cookies can we eat?*
*One, two, three . . ."*

Mavis counted up to thirty before she missed. She stamped her foot and accused Hugh of pulling up on the rope to trip her. They began to argue, and Jarvis, who was dozing in the sun, told them in a bored voice to shut up so a person could get some sleep.

"I never imagined any of this!" said Oscar, his voice quiet with wonder.

Captain Mack came up on deck as the sun began to set. Millie followed behind, lugging a steaming black kettle. Hugh came too, carrying a basket of bread. "Stew's on!" called the captain.

Everyone ate ravenously, using bread to soak up fish and potato stew from wooden bowls. Then Hugh climbed up proudly to take Jarvis's place at the tiller so Jarvis could have his supper. "Tell a story, Auntie," Hugh called down.

"Yes! Yes! A story!" Even Jarvis joined in the cries.

Captain Mack told a story about how long, long ago, the moon got so thirsty it tried to drink up the sea. The earth poured salt into the ocean to stop her. Everyone laughed as Captain Mack demonstrated how the moon spat out the salty water.

"Do you know any stories?" Millie asked Oscar, giving him a dimpled smile.

Lucy glanced at the captain. Every time Millie smiled at Oscar, or giggled at him, or moved a little closer, the captain looked annoyed.

Oscar told "Rapunzel." Lucy wondered whether the children had ever heard it before, because they listened so intently. When it was over, they wanted it again.

"No," said the captain in a firm voice. The agreeable look she had worn at the beginning of Oscar's story had vanished. "It's gettin' late, and we'll all need some sleep before mornin'."

"Oh! Let's sing songs first," begged Hugh and Mavis.

The children clamored so loudly that Captain Mack waved her hand. "Go on then," she said.

So Oscar sang "Billy Boy" for them, his voice clear and strong.

Lucy could tell the captain liked the song. She was tapping her foot and humming along by the third verse.

But by the last verse, she looked suspicious. Her eyes kept traveling from Millie's face to Oscar's.

"Again! Again!" Millie cried, and the other children chimed in as well.

So Oscar sang the song again, and this time everyone joined in—everyone except the captain. Lucy glanced at Oscar. He seemed unaware that Millie was gazing raptly at him, or that the captain was glowering at him.

*"Oh, where have you been, Billy Boy, Billy Boy?*
*Oh, where have you been, charming Billy?*
*I have been to seek a wife,*
*She's the joy of my life,*
*Sheeee's a young thing and cannot leave her mother.*

*"Did she bid you to come in, Billy Boy, Billy Boy?*
*Did she bid you to come in, charming Billy?*
*Yes, she bade me to come in,*
*There's a dimple in her chin,*
*Sheeee's a young thing and cannot leave her mother."*

"That's enough there now!" said the captain after the second verse. "Why's this Billy Boy messin' about with girls too young to leave their mothers?"

"It's just a song," said Oscar.

"Everyone to bed now," said the captain. "You too, Millie. Your bedtime's no different than the rest."

Though Millie looked as if she would die of shame, she joined the line of shuffling children without protest.

"Interestin' song," said the captain to Oscar when they were gone. "But no decent young man ought to play up to a young girl like that. Deceitful's what it is. Same goes for your story! What's that lad up to, goin' behind the old woman's back, crawlin' up that tower like a spider to steal away the girl?"

"It's just a story," said Oscar.

"We'll see land by dawn tomorrow." The captain turned abruptly and hoisted herself up the ladder to the stern deck. "Go to bed now, Hugh!" they heard her say.

"Did you ever hear the like?" said Oscar as he and Lucy laid themselves down on some burlap bags near the bow of the ship.

"I think . . ." Lucy was thinking that Captain Mack was a bit like a mother hen protecting her young. But before she could say so, a yawn overtook her.

"What were you going to say?" asked Oscar.

"Nothing," Lucy murmured sleepily. A mother hen, she thought, smiling to herself. And here she had been afraid Captain Mack was the sort who would make them walk the plank.

Perhaps that was why what happened the next morning came as such a shock.

# Chapter Fifteen

## Extreme Thirst

Lucy awoke to find Oscar shaking her and Jarvis standing over the both of them. "There's land," said Jarvis.

Lucy stood up, unsteady on her feet, and looked out over the bow. Straight ahead was a line of rocky cliffs rising above a dense forest and a narrow strip of white sand.

"That's the island," said Oscar.

"Hold up here, Jarvis! Jack—help your brother with the anchor." It was the captain. "You'll get out here," she said. "Jarvis'll row you to shore."

"Where's the Queen's palace?" Lucy asked.

"Queen's Harbor's at the other end of the island." The captain's voice was gruff, and her face bore the same scowl that had greeted Lucy and Oscar when they had first boarded the ship.

"But we want the harbor—we'll go the rest of the way with you," Oscar said.

"Fair is fair," said Captain Mack in a steady voice. "I said I'd take you to the island, and so I have. This is the island and this is where you'll get out."

"But this is the wrong end of the island," said Oscar.

"We made a bargain. I said I'd take you to the island, and I've kept to that bargain."

"You said you were in a hurry. It's a waste of time for you to leave us here," said Oscar.

Captain Mack leaned forward until her face was close to Oscar's. "Waste of time is right, *Billy Boy*—or whatever your name is. But I seen the way Millie was lookin' at you last night. Nothin' gets by me. You can bet I made her tell me your plans."

"What plans?" said Oscar.

"You're lucky I don't make you swim to shore!" said the captain. She turned and stomped off, slapping the rowboat as she passed it. "Jarvis—Jack! Let's get this tub lowered." She disappeared into the cabin at the stern.

"Oscar—what is she talking about?" asked Lucy.

"I don't know."

It didn't take long for the rowboat to bump down the side of the ship. As Jarvis was climbing down into it, Captain Mack reappeared.

"If it's money you want, we can pay you," said Oscar.

"What I want is for you to get off my ship."

"What have we done?"

"Why?"

"Tryin' to lure away a girl too young to know her own mind—that's what!" Captain Mack sneered at Oscar. "Ready to follow you to the moon she is— more likely hell before you're done! Don't think I ain't seen you carryin' on with my Millie—puttin' ideas in her head."

"It was Millie who was talking and carrying on!" said Oscar.

"And to think it was I who let you on board! Get off my ship before I push you off!"

Lucy half expected the captain to brandish her knife at any moment. Or perhaps she would produce a plank after all and send them to the sharks. Surely there would be sharks in an adventure story. "Come on!" she said, tugging Oscar by the arm. She threw one leg over the side of the ship, then the other. "Come on!" she called as she slid down the rope.

From above, she heard Millie's voice, swollen with sobs. "No, Auntie! No!" A second later, Oscar dropped into the boat.

"No, Auntie!" Millie cried again. "It ain't his fault!"

Jarvis pushed the boat away from the ship and began to row.

"What did you say to Millie?" Lucy asked Oscar.

"Nothing!"

"You must have said something."

"Mavis found Millie's things all packed," said Jarvis with a grin. "And Mavis can't keep her mouth shut five minutes. It was Mavis that told Auntie."

"Told what?" said Oscar.

"Millie was all set to run off with you when we got to port."

"Run off with us!" said Oscar.

Jarvis smirked. "Millie told Mavis all about it. Said you could introduce her to the Queen. Millie's always fancied being a lady. Auntie don't take kindly to that. She wants to make Millie captain one day."

"Oscar, what did you say to Millie?" asked Lucy.

"I told you! She did all the talking. She didn't like being on the ship. She wanted to run away. She wanted this. She wanted that. She went on and on . . ."

"That's our Millie. Can't shut her up," said Jarvis.

"I just said if she didn't like it, she should do what she wanted," said Oscar.

"Great! Just great!" Lucy said. "You told Millie to do what she wanted, and what she wanted was to run away with us!"

"How was I to know?"

"Do you mind wadin' in to shore?" Jarvis interrupted. "Auntie'll skin me alive if I don't get back to the ship right away."

"But you can't just leave us here!" Oscar protested.

"Got to." Jarvis waited as they climbed over the side. The water was up over their knees. "Just follow the shore around, and you'll come to Queen's Harbor," he called as they splashed through the surf. "Wait!" he called again. He held up a cloth bundle and tossed it to Oscar. "Mavis says Millie wants you to have this!"

When they reached the shore, they discovered that the bundle was food. "More biscuits and oranges and dried beef," said Lucy. "That's good."

"It's hard to feel very grateful." Oscar looked apprehensively at the dark and tangled forest beyond the beach.

"Which way should we go?" said Lucy. The beach curved away in two directions.

"Let's follow the ship," said Oscar.

But the wind was strong, and the ship moved more quickly than they did. Soon it disappeared from sight behind one of the many outcrops of rock that jutted into the sea.

Whenever they rounded one of these outcrops, Lucy grew hopeful, thinking she might see the Queen's palace. But after being disappointed countless times, she began to find walking tedious. The fact that they were trudging through sand only made it worse. With every step, her feet sank down just far enough to make the next step come out wrong. "I hate walking on sand," she complained. "And I'm thirsty."

"There's a stream up ahead." Oscar pointed at a bright ribbon of silver lying across the sand. "Only . . ."

"Only what?" called Lucy as she bounded toward the stream.

"Only I think I recognize this place," said Oscar as he caught up with her.

"It's too sandy to drink here, isn't it? But if we follow it up into the jungle, don't you think we could . . ." Lucy stopped, having just realized what it was that Oscar had said. She followed his gaze along a line of rocks that jutted up from the beach, then curved inland to grow into a high cliff that towered above the jungle. "What do you think?" she asked.

"I think I don't like it here in the least. I think we ought to be on our way."

"But surely it can't hurt to get a drink of water."

"I think this is where I landed in the rowboat," said Oscar. "The King might be nearby. Come on!"

Lucy continued to plod after him. At last, however, when they had skirted yet another outcrop only to find another stretch of empty beach, she sank onto the sand. "I suppose we picked the wrong way to come around the island," she said as Oscar sprawled next to her. "Who knows if we'll ever get to the Queen's palace? We'll die of thirst before we do."

"Maybe we could use magic to make ourselves a drink of water," Oscar suggested.

Lucy was watching him reach into his pocket for the bottle of potion when she noticed something out of the corner of her eye. She turned her head in time to see three kittens—one black, one white, and one calico—come rolling out of the jungle onto the sand. She stared, mesmerized, thinking they looked like they belonged in front of a fireplace chasing a ball of yarn. The three kittens were joined by a big cat—their mother, Lucy thought—and another cat—their father, she decided—and then a crowd of aunts and uncles and cousins all popping out onto the sand.

"Oscar . . ." she said.

"Run, Lucy!" Oscar jumped up and jerked Lucy to her feet.

"Stop!" called a man's voice as they stumbled across the sand.

"No!" Oscar pulled at Lucy.

"Stop! Please!" called the man again, in such a desperate voice that Lucy yanked her hand loose from Oscar's and turned around.

It was the King. There could be no doubt about that, thought Lucy, though he looked even less regal than Oscar's description. His battered crown was propped askew on dirty, tangled brown hair streaked with gray. A sleek black cat was rubbing against the King's bare ankles and feet. The three kittens were crawling up the hem of his tattered purple robe.

"Please don't run away." The King sounded even more pathetic than he looked. "We haven't had any company for a year."

Lucy looked down at the hundreds of cats lolling and strolling about in the sand.

"Our loyal subjects. Alas—not the sort of company with which one can converse," said the King.

"One *could* if one hadn't changed them into *cats*!" Oscar muttered.

The King's gaze narrowed on Oscar. "Have we perhaps had the pleasure of making your acquaintance in the past, sir?" he said.

"I don't think so." Oscar's voice was steady.

"Quite right—unlikely that we have met." The King shook his head. "So difficult for us to entertain these many years. Our wife, you see . . ." He paused to pick the kittens off his robe. "You would not guess it to look at us, but we are married to the most beautiful woman in the world." More kittens were climbing up the King's robe; the faster he picked them off, the more they swarmed.

"I thought you said he called the Queen a hag!" Lucy whispered to Oscar, perhaps more loudly than she should have, for the King looked up with a frown.

"We had a quarrel with the Queen some years ago," said the King. "Since then, she has seen fit to call *our* home *her* home."

"Don't get him started talking about the Queen," Oscar murmured.

"He seems harmless enough. Nothing like you described," whispered Lucy.

The King's frown curved into a tight smile. "Your companion does you a discourtesy, dear lady, in not presenting you to us," he said, and it took Lucy a moment to realize that he was expecting Oscar to introduce her. It took her another moment to realize that Oscar wasn't about to do any such thing.

"I'm Lucy!" She made a stab at a curtsey, bending her knees and bobbing her head.

The King looked pleased. "We welcome you, Lady Lucy, and would be delighted if you would consent to visit us at court—that is to say, if you are able to overlook the shortcomings of the rough setting which circumstances compel us to call our court." He gestured toward a gap in the trees. "You must be fatigued—or thirsty perhaps."

"No!" said Oscar. "Thank you, but we must be on our way—"

"Yes!" Lucy interrupted. "I mean, yes, please. We're actually extremely thirsty."

"Well, then—it would be cruel to allow you to suffer any longer. We may not be able to offer much, Lady Lucy, but we can give you water, if you will grant us your leave to guide you." The King held out his hand to help Lucy navigate through the cats. He pushed aside a cluster of vines so she could follow him into the shadow of the trees.

Lucy knew Oscar was behind her because one of the cats shrieked.

"Watch your feet!" the King called. "Cats have tails!"

As she hurried after the King, Lucy could hear leaves rustling in the underbrush. Every so often, a cat would zip across the path in front of her or dash up the trunk of a tree. Lucy jumped every time, but the King and Oscar seemed unperturbed. They're used to it, she thought.

The sunlight flickered green through the leaves of the trees. Heavy vines drooped and crisscrossed above Lucy's head, so low that she had to duck at times. Once a cloud of tiny biting insects swarmed about her. She swatted at them until the King turned, waved his hand, and said something that made them fly off. A charm, thought Lucy, turning to look at Oscar. He gave her a pleading look.

"I just want to get a drink," she whispered.

Meanwhile the King chattered away. Unfortunately, it didn't matter what he was talking about—the merits of long-haired cats as opposed to short-haired, the typical number of kittens in a litter, and whether cats preferred mice to fish—somehow he always brought the Queen into the conversation. As a lecture on the qualities of a good mouser devolved into a rant against the Queen, Lucy could sense Oscar's fear coiling up like a spring.

By the time they stepped out of the forest, the King

was telling Lucy about his quarrel with the Queen. "So Tom eats her canary and she says to get that beast away from her sight or she'll have him drowned. The next thing we know, we're tossed out of our home and she gives orders for every bird on the island to be given safe haven within the walls of the palace! And now we are left with *this*!" The King swept his arm wide.

They were in an immense clearing filled with round wooden buildings—houses that might have been neat and pretty once upon a time, but were now falling apart from disrepair. The houses were so close together that neighbors could step from one doorstep onto the doorstep across the way or shake hands without ever leaving their doorsteps at all. Only there weren't any neighbors. There were only cats—hundreds of them— passing in and out of the open, derelict doorways.

"On the bright side of things, Lady Lucy, the crystalline waters of the well in this village are unrivaled in the kingdom," said the King.

"He's not so bad," Lucy murmured to Oscar.

"Just try not to say anything to upset him."

The King led them to a round stone well with the tattered remains of a thatched roof above it. There was a crank with a rope for pulling up the water.

"There was a time when we should not have had to draw our own water," the King lamented as he turned the crank. "And now we draw water not only for ourself but for our subjects as well." A wooden bucket filled to the brim with bright, beautiful water rose out of the dark well. Lucy forgot everything but her thirst as she leaned forward. She held out her hands to bring the bucket to her lips.

"No! No! This won't do!" snapped the King. He let go of the crank and it whipped around like an airplane propeller. Lucy grabbed at empty air. The bucket slapped the water below.

"It won't do at all!" the King muttered as he stomped over to the edge of the clearing. He leaned over to pick something up from the ground. Then he broke off a tree branch, long and thin like a violin bow. He bent it and ran it through his fingers, as if he were testing its strength.

Lucy ignored Oscar's frantic whispers. She watched as the King returned to the well. "Won't do at all!" he said, and raised the tree branch up in the air.

"Run, Lucy!" whispered Oscar, pulling on her arm. But before she could move, the King began:

"For ladies fair, we can't have *that*
  To drink from a bucket, one must be a cat!
  The lady at the well

requires this spell:
Drip and droplet,
You're a—"

"No!" Oscar shouted, so forcefully that the King looked up in astonishment.

"Not if I can help it!" Oscar raised his arm above Lucy's head. When she looked up, she saw the potion bottle in his hand. A drop of blue liquid fell out and landed on her nose.

"Bird!" said Oscar.

# CHAPTER SIXTEEN

## A RARE BIRD

*Danger! Danger! Danger!* Not as much a word repeating itself as a sensation, like the blood pumping rapidly through her heart, or the beat of her wings grabbing like hands at the air, as if she were scrabbling up a rock wall. The feeling of danger lessened the higher she rose, and that was good.

She pulled herself up and floated in a circle, her wings twisting, the tips of her feathers shifting slightly as they balanced her weight on a warm updraft of air. Her eyes scanned the crowd of cats below almost mechanically. Her vision was so acute that she could practically see their hungry eyes and sharp, eager teeth.

Yet she wasn't afraid now. Her strong wings pulled her in a straight line toward a high cliff that rose like a fist out of the forest. Its steep face rushed toward her as she approached, and she pulled herself even higher, exhilarated at the prospect of safety that the cliff offered. Then her bright red feet grasped the rough gray stone of a protruding ledge, her wings fluttered efficiently, and everything was still and peaceful.

But only for a moment, for she was thirsty. The word *water* did not come to mind, but the knowledge of water did. Her wings flapped, and she flew upward again, her eyes scanning the cliff until she saw a glint of bright silver—a puddle on one of the rock ledges. She dropped down with precision. The ledge was much larger than the last, and she took several steps toward the water. She bent her head and drank.

Her head came up with a quick jerk that surprised her. She wasn't used to it moving so quickly. She turned from the puddle and found, somewhat to her annoyance, that she couldn't take a step without her head jutting forward. She heard a soft cooing noise that was soothing to her nerves. She bobbed about and listened to it until she realized that it was coming from her own throat. Feeling that there was something not quite right about that, she ruffled her feathers and sat down like a stone to think. In fact, the word *think* popped into her head, shocking her with its power. *I can think! These are words!* said her thoughts, and she listened as hard as she could for more words to come because she knew that words were somehow very important.

Fighting back the desire to make the soothing noise in her throat, she studied a dusting of sand and gravel on the stony surface in front of her. Then her beak came down and snapped up a speck of gravel. She swallowed it, and it was almost a minute before more words came into her mind. When they did, they hit her like a slap. *I don't eat gravel!* she thought. For one second, she thought she would be sick.

She clung to the feeling of revulsion because it helped her think. Using scraps of thought and emotion as guideposts, she began to work backward in her memory. She remembered all the cats, of course. But that memory brought out nothing more than a strong impulse to fly, so she veered away from it.

The word *Lucy* was important, she was sure, for many different voices seemed to be babbling it inside her head. Trying to pick out one voice from another was difficult, however—like trying to hear a whisper in the middle of a crowd.

*Lucy—sweetie!* said one voice, for one second louder than all the others, and she briefly recognized her mother's voice. So *Lucy* was her *name*. She squeezed her eyes shut (an act that went completely against instinct) so that she could listen harder. Another voice said *Lucy*. It belonged to a boy with a long face and light brown hair. Then another voice said, *It works, Lucy!* It was her father, holding a little blue bottle in his hand.

She found that if she sat perfectly still, it was easier to listen to the voices. It was easier to keep her thoughts in line. She remembered her flight from terror to the safety of her rocky perch. She remembered the long-faced boy—*Oscar* was his name—holding a little blue bottle over her head and saying *Bird!* The blue bottle made her think of her father again, and in the excitement, she fluttered her wings and forgot everything she had just recalled. Gradually, however, she managed to piece together enough of what had happened to understand that she was *Lucy*. She wasn't a *bird*, but a *girl* who was searching for her father.

Unfortunately, she kept forgetting important things almost as soon as she remembered them. Still, she found she could always start over by repeating the name *Lucy* in her mind. She must have reconstructed the story dozens of times, progressively padding it with more and more memories. One of these memories was her own voice saying to Oscar, *Who knows if we'll ever get to the Queen's palace?*

*If I'd only been able to fly. There's one advantage to*

*being a bird,* her mind thought. Just then, her head darted forward and her beak snatched up another bit of gravel. The movement sent her mind spinning, and she promptly forgot everything again. She had to sit perfectly still until her mind reasserted itself. *Why don't you fly to the Queen's palace?* it said.

In a moment, her wings were flapping and she was airborne, turning to follow the curve of the cliff. Another advantage of being a bird was a strong sense of direction. She knew she must not retrace the route she had already taken on foot. She must keep the cliff on her left and the glittering sea on her right. Then she would be going toward the Queen's palace.

She dove down, swooping across the tops of trees until the seashore lay below her like a road. She watched her shadow flicker on the wet sand. The thrill of the cool sea air rushing past was almost enough to make her lose her sense of purpose. *Lucy! Lucy! Lucy!* she told herself.

The beach ended abruptly, cut off by a cliff that jutted into the water. Lucy flew straight up and over the cliff, only to see something on the other side that made her stop short and land on a point of rock. Below her, the shoreline tucked inward, forming a natural harbor bordered by cliffs. Nestled at the back of the harbor was a city. Row upon row of round houses gripped a hillside so steep it seemed ready to slide into the sea. The houses were built so close together that their gleaming slate roofs looked like scales on a fish. Towering above them was a magnificent building.

What sort of building was it? Lucy had to work hard to remember the word *palace,* and then had to work even harder to figure out why it was that she cared about a palace in the first place.

She dropped down from the cliff and headed across the water toward the city. As she drew near, she saw that the houses near the shore were in a ramshackle state, with windows knocked out, doors knocked in, and chimneys knocked down. The streets were filled with pieces of slate that had come off the roofs. The houses closer to the palace were in better repair, and she saw several men talking outside one of them. She landed on a nearby rooftop to rest, and one of the men pointed at her.

A second later, Lucy was flying away. Something of greater interest had caught her eye. A ship was bobbing in the water next to a long wooden dock. She circled downward and perched on the ship's tall mast, nearly toppling over before she caught herself.

There was something familiar about the ship. But she immediately forgot to wonder what it was. Her attention was drawn to the ship's deck, where a crowd of children was hard at work. Two of them were heaving large canvas bags out of an open hatch. Two more dragged the bags across the deck to the top of a narrow gangplank leading down to the dock. Two more—a boy and a big girl who looked older than the rest—were lugging the bags down to the dock.

"Can't we take a rest, Auntie?" said the big girl, dropping a bag on the dock.

"Careful now, Millie, or you'll spill the cargo!" scolded a short, stocky woman. "Go and get the next bag while Jarvis and I stack these. Jack'll help you."

*How do I know these people? And what is in those bags?* Lucy wondered as she watched the girl trudge sullenly up the gangplank. A younger boy was already waiting for her to grab one end of the next bag. The girl seized it and dragged it down the gangplank. The boy stumbled behind, struggling to keep hold of his end. Lucy could see the canvas bag stretching as it caught on something sharp at the foot of the gangplank. "What's the *matter* with you, Jack!" snapped the girl as the boy lost his grip on the bag. The girl tugged, and there was a ripping noise. The bag burst open, spilling out a golden mass of a sandlike something. Some of it fell into the water, but most of it spread out onto the dock.

"Confound it!" said the stocky woman. "Ain't we had enough trouble this trip?" She strode toward the scene of the disaster, but Lucy got there first, causing the girl to leap to her feet with a squeal.

"I couldn't help it, Auntie!" whined the boy named Jack. "Millie pulled so."

"Shush!" the woman hissed. "All of you—quiet now and careful."

Lucy could feel her head bobbing back and forth like a metronome as she gobbled up the contents of the torn bag. It wasn't sand after all! It was edible, and it was good, and the more she gobbled, the less she thought about caution. In fact, she forgot everything but a need to grab every last bit of birdseed.

"Give me your apron, Millie," said the woman's voice, as soft as a creaking board. Lucy heard the words but couldn't understand them.

"But Auntie—"

"Hush up and hand it over! Quick now!" Still soft, but urgent. Lucy felt a small stir of alarm.

Now the voice was gentle and soothing. "There now, pretty bird. Pretty, pretty bird."

And then the world was gone, and Lucy was enveloped in a cloud of something scratchy and white and horrible. She shrieked and fought, tearing with her claws and biting with her beak. She felt herself bouncing through the air. Voices were swearing and shrieking, someone was laughing, and then Lucy was thumped down and something else was thumped down around her. The horrible, scratchy whiteness pulled at her. It fell off her body and slid away across a wooden surface. Lucy skittered to one side, crashing into a wooden wall. A shadow fell over her. Looking up, she saw eyes peering at her through wooden slats. There were wooden slats all around her.

*Cage!* said her thoughts.

"What kind of bird is it, Auntie?" said a child's voice.

*Not a bird!* Lucy's thoughts insisted.

"Ain't never seen one like it. Looks rare." Lucy could see the bright blue eyes of the woman—*Auntie* she was called—studying her. She *knew* who the woman was, if only she could think clearly.

"Look how lovely it is!" said the big girl, the one called Millie. "Soft and gray like a lady's silk dress. And it's got rainbows around its neck."

"Its eyes ain't so pretty," said the boy named Jack. "Look at 'em, all red and beady."

"Red as rubies," said Auntie. "And like as not more valuable. I'll wager this little prize here's worth more 'n twenty sacks of birdseed."

"Oh, Auntie!" said Millie. "You mean we'll take the bird to the *palace,* don't you!"

"Banish that look from your eyes, Missy. I'll be the one to present this beauty to the Queen."

*Palace. Queen,* thought Lucy. Why were those words important?

"Course, I'll need something a little more elegant than this here crate. Jarvis—get yourself up to town. Find something to carry this critter in."

"Oh, Auntie! Jarvis don't know elegant from his own cars," said Millie. "He'll bring back an old barrel and want to stuff the bird in it. Let me go. I know what's elegant."

There was a long pause while Auntie considered this statement. "All right, go along then," she said. "But don't stray beyond arm's reach of Jarvis. And Jarvis, keep your eye on your sister. Don't look at me like that, Missy! Understand now if you so much as think of runnin' off I'll spank you like you was five years old, no matter how much a lady you think you are."

"Leave that bird alone now," Lucy heard Auntie say when Jarvis and Millie were gone. But the youngest boy dropped by every so often to let a shower of birdseed drop through the slats of the crate. Lucy pecked away cheerfully, forgetting that she was in prison. Soon, however, the whisper of *Lucy!* was in her brain again and she forced herself to sit still and think. Once she had managed to recall everything she had already recalled and forgotten, she remembered why the ship and its crew were so familiar to her. The woman called *Auntie* was named *Captain Mack*. Lucy even worked out—with a feeling of triumph—why it was that Captain Mack wanted to take her to the *Queen* at the *palace*.

Unfortunately, just as she figured it all out, Millie came galloping up the gangplank with Jarvis behind her. Frightened, Lucy flew into the side of the crate, and in that moment, she forgot everything all over again. *Sit still!* Her thoughts were urgent. *Watch! Listen!*

"Here it is, Auntie!" she heard Jarvis call. There was a thud next to her crate. Lucy tilted her head, peering through the slats at a globe-shaped something made of curved bits of brass.

"Exactly what do you call that?" said Captain Mack.

"It's a lamp, Auntie! Ain't it lovely?" exclaimed Millie, clasping her hands together. "You hang it from a hook, put a candle inside, and it throws shadows all around—leaves and fruit and flowers. Just see how fine it is. I bet it belonged to a rich family."

"A lamp! What in blazes are we supposed to do with a lamp?"

"If you squint your eyes, it looks just like a cage, Auntie," said Millie. "This part opens so you can put a candle in. The bird will fit in just as well."

"How much did you pay for it?"

"Only five silvers."

"Five silvers! Every bit of money spent!"

"You wanted somethin' more elegant than that crate and that's just what this is," said Millie. "If it'd been left up to Jarvis, you'd have had to take the bird in a ratty old basket that cost only three coppers. It stank of fish, and you'd have been turned away at the palace gates. Then see how happy you'd be to have your five silvers in your pocket, Auntie."

"Watch your tongue, Missy!"

"Oh Auntie—Captain—I know just the right things to say to royalty. I know I do! Please take me with you to see the Queen!"

"Stop your blatherin'!"

"You want to make the right impression," Millie argued. "There's more to sellin' a bird than just sayin' 'Here you go' and 'Where's my money?' Royalty have their own way of doin' things. You got to be tricky— think like they do—or you won't get half what you should for the bird."

"And just how did you get to be such an expert on the ways of royalty?" said the captain.

"I know all sorts of things about royalty, Auntie."

"She does act like a spoiled princess most of the time," said Jarvis. "If you don't take her along, we'll never have no peace."

"Yes, oh yes! Please take me," Millie clamored.

"I promise I'll never complain about peelin' potatoes, or swabbin' the deck, or haulin' bags of birdseed, or anythin'."

"Hard to pass up an offer like that," said the captain, rolling her eyes.

"Then you'll take me! You'll take me!" Millie danced around the captain.

"I'll think about it," gasped her aunt, stepping backward as Millie leaped upon her like a wild wave. "Watch yourself, girl, or you'll tip us over the starboard side!"

*I ought to worry,* thought Lucy when she grasped the fact that she was to be sold like a slave. But she couldn't worry, for she felt herself overcome by a blissful contentment. Having glutted herself on birdseed, she felt wonderfully at peace, so much so that she hardly noticed Jarvis's big, bony hands lifting her gently into her new cage. He set her down on a flat, wax-spattered metal bar that braced the inside of the lamp. It must have held a candle once upon a time, but it would do for a perch now. Lucy gripped it tightly with her feet and began to coo. A soft feeling settled over her, like the faded silk scarf that Millie draped over the lamp, and soon she was asleep.

# Chapter Seventeen
## The Ways of Royalty

When Lucy awoke, everything was so dark that her first thought was *night*. She sat very still, fluffing up her feathers and pulling her head into her chest until she remembered who she was.

Then, suddenly, the darkness disappeared with a whoosh. Lucy started at the sight of an enormous grinning face. "Good mornin', Birdie!" said the face. *Millie,* Lucy remembered.

Millie draped the silk scarf she had pulled from Lucy's cage about her shoulders and turned around. Only then did Lucy see that her cage was inside a small room. She watched, puzzled, as Millie stared at herself

in a scrap of glass hung on a wall. She couldn't understand why there were two faces, one on Millie herself,
and one in the piece of glass. She watched the two Mil-
lies comb their corkscrew ringlets. She watched them
pinch and slap their cheeks and bare their teeth like
twin horses. Then the glass Millie disappeared and the
other Millie was lifting Lucy's cage. *Sit still!* Lucy told
herself as her cage swung through the air and Millie
began to sing:

> *"Lords and ladies dancin' at the ball,*
> *Silks and satins and jewels upon 'em all,*
> *See the ladies curtsey, see the gentlemen bow,*
> *Lords and ladies dancin' at the ball."*

A door opened; Lucy had a glimpse of dark walls
everywhere. Then another door opened and she was in
the sun. She recognized the smell of the harbor and
fluttered her wings.

"There you are at last, Millie! Danged if this ain't
the best day we've seen for sailin' in weeks!" said a
voice just as Lucy's cage came down with a bang that
nearly knocked her off her perch. "Get the breakfast
like a good girl and we'll haul that bird up to the
Queen," said the voice, and Lucy remembered that it

belonged to Captain Mack. "We can visit the baby on the way back and still have time to set sail today."

"Oh, Auntie, no!" said Millie. "We can't possibly go to the palace so early. Why, if we did, we wouldn't even get to see the Queen."

The word *Queen* was rattling around in Lucy's mind. Why was that word important?

"Royalty never receive anyone before noon at the very earliest," Millie continued. "They take their time in the mornin'. I expect the Queen sleeps till noon. Then she'll have her breakfast in bed. And she'll have to be dressed and have her hair curled. That's the sort of thing her ladies-in-waitin' help her with."

"That's what Millie wants," said a new voice. "To be a lady-in-waitin'."

"Oh, be quiet, Mavis," Millie snapped.

"I ain't waitin' till afternoon to sail," said the captain. "But I suppose we could drop in to see the baby aforehand, on our way to the palace, 'stead of on our way from."

"It ain't proper to visit much before three."

Captain Mack gave a snort. "I guess if Her Majesty ain't up when we get there, she'll miss her chance to buy our friend here, in which case we can have bird pie for supper."

*Bird pie?* thought Lucy. Fortunately, Mavis poured a handful of birdseed into her cage just then.

After breakfast, Millie disappeared below deck. "Makin' herself into a lady," Mavis observed.

Lucy's confusion over the word *lady* wasn't exactly put to rest when Millie reappeared some time later. Millie's red hair was piled on top of her head. The silk scarf was tied around her waist, and she wore a necklace that sparkled in the sunlight, making Lucy thirsty because she thought the glass beads were drops of water.

"How do I look?" said Millie.

"Like a complete fool. Now get the bird and let's go!" said the captain.

*I'm the bird!* thought Lucy as Millie grabbed her cage. And then it was all a matter of keeping her thoughts together as the cage bobbed down the gangplank, across the dock, and up into the streets of town. Lucy had an excellent view of dirty cobblestones and Captain Mack's feet marching along ahead of Millie's. *Dark,* thought Lucy as they turned down a narrow, shadowy street. Her cage swung to a stop as Millie set it down on the ground. Lucy watched Captain Mack step up to a battered wooden door and knock on it.

"Who is it?" called a tired, cross voice, barely audible over the cries of a baby. The next moment, the door flew open, revealing a gaunt-faced woman balancing a remarkably fat, pillowy baby on her sharp, bony hip. The baby's curly hair was red like Millie's. The baby's face was red as well because it was shrieking.

"There you are!" said the woman over the din. "I seen your ship in the harbor and wondered when you'd be up to take this brat off my hands. Here! Take her!" And with that, she shoved the howling baby at Captain Mack.

The captain dipped under the weight of the child. "Now just one minute, Jane!" she said. "You promised to take care of Phoebe. Yes, you did! And I been payin' you handsomely for it!"

"It ain't worth it," said Jane. "It ain't worth ten silvers a week. It ain't even worth ten golds a week. My man and I ain't had a wink of sleep with that child in the house. Up all night wantin' to be fed, wants even more durin' the day. Just look at her! She's fat as a pig and heavy as lead. My back is near broke."

"Now, Jane." Captain Mack tried unsuccessfully to bounce the baby on her hip. "I'll grant you Phoebe's a nice, big, healthy child. And maybe she can be a bit fractious."

"Fractious!" screeched Jane. "She's got a wail that makes a body want to pitch her out the window. And I can't promise that I won't pitch her out the window.

My man swears he will if I don't. Take her today. We're done with her!"

Captain Mack gave Phoebe to Millie. "Now really, Jane," she began again. Then she paused, looking surprised, as Phoebe swallowed a sob and smiled at her big sister.

"No, and no again, Captain," said Jane. "I've had her things packed ever since I saw your ship come in. She's just had her diaper changed, and I put in a bit of bread and cheese for her to eat if she gets hungry on the way back to your ship, which she's sure to do, mark my words." And with that, Jane closed the door. It opened once, just long enough for Jane to drop a large basket at the captain's feet. Then *slam,* and Lucy jumped.

"Well, that's that," said the captain.

*What's that?* Lucy's thoughts were trying to catch up.

"We can take Phoebe back to the ship and leave her with Mavis while we go to the palace," said Millie, shifting Phoebe to her other hip.

"Waste of time," said the captain. "Let's get the bird business taken care of."

*Palace. Bird business.* Lucy had forgotten everything again.

"Come on now, Phoebe!" said the captain, trying to take the baby. But Phoebe howled and clung to

Millie. The captain threw up her hands and said, "That's the way of it. You'll just have to hold her while I transact our business, Millie." She picked up Lucy's cage and the basket of Phoebe's things.

"We can't take her to see the Queen, Auntie. It'll spoil everything!" Millie protested. "Stop it, Phoebe!" she added as the baby grabbed at her bead necklace.

"Nonsense!" Captain Mack began walking, stepping along so briskly that Lucy's cage swung back and forth like a bell. "If Phoebe starts to fussin', you can wait outside the palace while I talk to the Queen."

A bored-looking guard met them at the palace gates. "We've got business with Her Majesty," said Captain Mack. She held up Lucy's cage, and he waved them into the courtyard.

Almost immediately, they were surrounded by an army of shrieking peacocks whose tail feathers were spread out like shields. Lucy threw her body against the walls of her cage, trying to get away.

"Oh, Auntie! Ain't they beautiful?" Millie exclaimed. "What are they, do you reckon?"

"I don't reckon. I know. They're peacocks. Used to see 'em all about the island. Common as rats."

"They're prettier than our bird," said Millie.

"Prettier, maybe. But not near as quiet and well behaved."

All around her, Lucy could hear a great noise. As they crossed the courtyard toward the palace's entrance, she recognized it: the cackling, cawing, screeching, squawking, chirping, chortling, tweeting, trumpeting, whistling, and hooting of thousands upon thousands of birds.

"Look at the doorway, Auntie!" said Millie as they waded through a flock of geese.

*Doorway.* What was that? Then Lucy saw the grand stone entrance to the palace. It was carved to resemble an enormous cat arching its back.

"The King had it made that way, I expect," said Captain Mack as they passed beneath the cat's curved belly, walking between pillars carved to look like legs.

Just inside the doorway, Lucy saw enormous tree trunks everywhere. It took her a moment to understand that the tree trunks were towers of cages that were stacked, one on top of another, in massive pillars that rose to a ceiling high above. The pillars flickered with color in the light from the tall windows on either side of the entrance hall. Soon Lucy saw that the flickering colors were birds fighting and squabbling with each other. Their feathers floated like colored snow in the shafts of light that fell between the cages.

"Hullo!" Captain Mack shouted over the squawking. "They'll never hear us over this racket," she said. "Come on, Millie!"

"But we can't just march into the Queen's presence unannounced!" Millie wailed.

*Queen!* thought Lucy. *Queen, palace, Father.*

"If we're lucky enough to find the Queen in this jungle, we'll apologize nice and proper," said Captain Mack. "Hullo!" she shouted again as she plunged forward.

They must have taken one wrong turn after another, for they passed through room after room, each one filled with birds. In one room decorated in pale peach and pink, hundreds of yellow canaries darted about in a golden cage the size of a carriage house. For a moment Lucy thought she was looking at the sun. Another room was painted a soft blue, with abalone and pearl flowers decorating the walls. Graceful swans glided to and fro in a glassy pool surrounded by fragrant lilies. Another room was starkly white, whiter than the cooing doves that filled it. Another was sinister and dark, haunted by hooting owls, and Lucy shuddered. Still another room was bright and flamboyant, filled with tropical flowers and parrots that mocked each other. There were rooms with blue birds, rooms with red birds, and still other rooms that seemed catch-all closets for birds, and it was in one of these that Lucy recalled again that she herself was a bird. Her father was a bird, too, a *crow,* and he was here in the palace. Had she already seen him? Lucy couldn't remember.

As they moved into another room with cages stacked to the ceiling, a different type of movement caught Lucy's eye. A girl atop a high ladder was tossing handfuls of something from her apron into the shrieking cages. "There's your lady-in-waitin', Millie—takin' care of a lot of birds," muttered the captain. "You there! We want to see the Queen!" she called.

The girl gave a start and dropped a shower of the something on Captain Mack and Millie. *Birdseed!* thought Lucy as it sifted through her cage.

"The Queen's in the throne room." The girl nodded toward a large door in a nearby wall.

"We're here to conduct some important business with her," said Captain Mack, shaking seeds from her clothing.

"Go on in." The girl gave a careless shrug.

"But Auntie—we need to be announced," whimpered Millie, trotting behind the captain.

"Ha! Them that could have announced us has been changed into cats, that's plain enough. Beyond that guard at the gate, and a few more like that girl back there, there ain't a servant to be found on this island."

"Ooh, Auntie! Look at the ceiling!" squealed Millie as they entered the throne room.

Lucy turned the word *ceiling* over in her mind for a moment, remembering at last to look up. She saw a domed ceiling that was divided into nine triangular stained-glass windows. In each window there was a cat made of golden glass, leaping in the air, swiping its paw playfully at a flying red bird.

"Sit still, you!" cried a voice, startlingly near. Lucy couldn't see where it came from, for the throne room, like every other room, was filled with bird cages. "Sit still, please!" said the voice. "I'll never manage to paint you if you dart about so. Get back here, Delilah!"

Just then, a clucking white hen came hurtling down a narrow passageway between the cages, heading straight toward Captain Mack and Millie. Lucy tried to dash away but crashed into the side of her cage.

"Stop, Delilah!" the voice ordered, and a woman wearing a paint-spattered smock appeared in the passageway between the cages. "You there!" said the woman. "Keep her from getting out of the room!"

Millie planted herself in the doorway, keeping tight hold of Phoebe, and Captain Mack shifted positions between two other potential escape routes while the woman dashed this way and that after the hen. At last she pulled off her smock and threw it over the frantic bird. "Got her!" she shouted triumphantly. "There, there, Delilah," she added, gathering the smock up firmly but tenderly. "There's no reason to be so very upset. I only want to paint your portrait, and I've lots more grain if you'll only be patient."

"Oh, Auntie! It's the Queen!" said Millie.

*Queen!* thought Lucy. *Queen, palace, Father.* She watched as the Queen bent her head over the smock. She stared, fascinated, at the tiara holding back the Queen's golden hair. Her sharp eyes noticed that some of the rubies and emeralds in the tiara were missing. The embroidered flowers and hummingbirds on the Queen's dress looked worn and faded. Lucy could see dangling threads where some of the stitches had pulled out. Then the Queen looked up, and Lucy saw pink cheeks and lips, sky blue eyes, and a paint-smudged nose.

"Your Majesty," said Captain Mack, bowing. "We're here to conduct a bit of business."

Just then something—many things—exploded from the vicinity of Millie. Lucy, not realizing that Phoebe had broken Millie's necklace, thought of seeds bursting from a pod. Phoebe stared at the limp string in her hand, then erupted in wails.

"A baby!" cried the Queen. "A real baby! Oh, look at the poor thing. May I hold her?"

She put her smock down and the hen rushed away, clucking madly.

"Now then," the Queen said, lifting Phoebe from Millie's arms. "There's no need to cry. . . ." she began, and then her speech became unintelligible to Lucy, who found herself unable to interpret baby talk. Apparently Phoebe could, however, because she stopped crying, smiled at the Queen, and pointed her finger at Lucy's cage. "Bird!" she said.

*Bird!* Lucy felt proud for understanding something without having to think very hard.

"Yes, it is a bird! Aren't you a clever girl!" said the Queen. "What's your name, you sweet thing?"

"It's Phoebe, Your Majesty," said Millie, wincing as Phoebe grabbed for the Queen's tiara.

"Do you like pretty things, Phoebe?" said the Queen, untangling the crown and handing it to her. "Phoebe! Such a plain little bird name for such an enchanting creature," she remarked to Millie. "If she were mine, I should call her *Robin* or *Meadowlark*. Something happy and light."

Captain Mack cleared her throat. "Your Majesty — about our business . . ."

"Business?" The Queen was scrunching her eyes

shut, then opening them in mock surprise. Phoebe chortled.

"We got a bird here to show you, Your Majesty."

"A bird?" murmured the Queen, smiling at Phoebe.

"Quite an exotic bird, Your Majesty. I don't think I've ever seen one to compare for looks and temperament. Never seen one like it in these parts, that's for sure."

"Good heavens! A pigeon!" said the Queen. "I haven't seen one since I was a girl."

*Pigeon.* Lucy was racking her memory, trying to remember what a *pigeon* was.

"We was thinkin' that Your Majesty might like to acquire this fine pigeon for your collection," said Captain Mack.

"You're giving me a pigeon?"

"Not exactly givin', Your Majesty. We was hopin' to transact a business deal."

"Oh, you want to sell me your pigeon."

Just then Phoebe dropped the tiara. Millie snatched it before it hit the floor. Looking pale, she handed it to the Queen, who promptly returned it to Phoebe. Then the Queen began to walk through a passageway in the cages. Captain Mack and Millie followed behind, Millie leaping again for the tiara when Phoebe dropped it over the Queen's shoulder.

"See what I have here, Phoebe," said the Queen.

*See what?* Lucy wondered. The Queen was standing in an open area among the cages, pointing at what looked like a window with clouds in it. But the window was propped up at an angle in the middle of the air.

"I'm painting, Phoebe," said the Queen. "This is my canvas. I'm making a picture. These are my paints and brushes."

After carefully analyzing the table, which was littered with jars, rags, and brushes, Lucy realized that what she had thought was a window was a painter's canvas set up on an easel. She saw white paint splashed against a background of dark blue and purple.

"See the pretty hens?" The Queen gestured toward the canvas, and Lucy could see that the blobs of white paint did look rather like the three bossy hens that were strutting about on the floor, snapping up bits of cracked corn. "I just can't seem to get the tail feathers right," said the Queen, frowning.

Captain Mack cleared her throat again. "About our bird, Your Majesty . . ."

"Oh yes, your pigeon. I fear she would be lonely here."

"Beggin' your pardon, Your Majesty. But it's hard to see how she could be in this place. . . ."

"But there are no other pigeons. I really don't think that—"

"We found the bird wanderin' wild, Your Majesty," said Captain Mack. "It was a wonder cats hadn't pounced on her. If you ain't interested, we got no choice but to set her free again."

"But she'll be killed!" said the Queen.

"Beggin' your pardon, Your Majesty, but I ain't got room for a bird on board my ship!"

The Queen wavered a moment, long enough for Lucy to worry over the meanings of the words *cats* and *killed*. Then the Queen sighed and said, "Oh, very well." She lifted a brass bell from her table and rang it. "One more bird won't make a difference, I suppose. Though there's barely enough to feed the ones we've got already. I know I ought to let some go, but I can't bear to think of their fate. Those dreadful cats . . ." Her voice trailed off as a girl—the birdseed girl, thought Lucy—sauntered into the room.

"Cora, how much have we got in the treasury?" said the Queen.

"I'm sure I don't know, Your Majesty."

"Well—it doesn't matter. You are to get twenty silvers and—"

"Beggin' Your Majesty's pardon," said the captain. "Twenty silvers hardly seems a fair price for such a fine pigeon."

"Very well—thirty silvers. Cora, fetch thirty silvers from the treasury."

But Cora had already reached into her pocket and pulled out a handful of coins. "I just remembered, Your Majesty, that I took some money this morning to pay the grocer," she said.

"More likely you meant to steal it!" grumbled the Queen, and when Cora was gone, she added, "The girl is a thief, I'm certain. But what with help being so hard to find these days . . ."

"*I* like to work," said Millie.

"Been a real pleasure, Your Majesty," said Captain Mack. "Now, if you'll just tell us how to get out of here, we'll be on our way."

"But you can't leave!" said the Queen, clutching Phoebe.

"Got to, Your Majesty! Now then, I'll take the baby." Captain Mack had to force the Queen to let go of Phoebe.

"We'll find our own way out, Your Majesty," said the captain. "Come on, Millie!"

As they disappeared down a passageway through the cages, Lucy heard Phoebe's wails fading away and Millie's disappointed voice coming back. "Oh, Auntie . . ."

"I do so love babies." The Queen sighed, and Lucy saw one tear, then another, roll down her face. At last the Queen picked up a brush and began dabbing paint on the window tilted up in the air—on the *canvas,* Lucy reminded herself.

It was a long time before Lucy remembered the word *sold.* She began the laborious process of thinking about herself. She thought about where she was, and what she should do next. And it was then that she noticed the sound of crows cawing.

# Chapter Eighteen

## Fellow Sorcerers

Oscar squinted in the sunlight as he watched Lucy fly up and away.

Then his eyes fell and he saw the King. He was clutching the tree-branch wand, thrusting it forward with a trembling hand the way Oscar's algebra teacher used to thrust his pointer at fellows when he caught them whispering in class. "*You* are a sorcerer!" said the King.

Oscar shook off all thoughts of algebra class. "Put down that wand!" he told the King. He wondered if he sounded foolish. He remembered saying pretty much the same thing to Clyde Wilcox back when he was ten years old. "Put down that rock!" he had told Clyde, a bully the size of a Hereford steer, and Clyde had gone ahead and thrown the rock anyway.

"Are you a sorcerer?" The King's voice sounded puzzled now.

"Yes," said Oscar, hoping it was the right thing to say. Behind his back, his hand curled around the bottle of potion. His other hand fumbled with the stopper.

The King tapped his wand against the lip of the stone well. "You changed the Lady Lucy into a bird! Why?"

"You were about to change her into a cat!" Oscar slipped the bottle into his pocket.

"We were not! We would not!" The King sounded offended. "We were in the act of changing this stone into a goblet so that the Lady Lucy would have a more suitable vessel for drinking." He opened his fist to show Oscar a small gray rock.

"A goblet?"

"Naturally. We would not change a lady into a cat," said the King.

"But you do change people into cats—you can't deny that!" Oscar looked down at the cats crowding around the well.

The King looked haughty. "We will merely observe that, of occasion, necessity has called upon us to protect the authority of the royal house. After all, it is our duty and our right to command respect among our subjects."

"But what about Lucy?"

"What *about* the Lady Lucy?"

"What will happen to her?"

"That seems up to you, sir. Obviously, you must change her back."

"I would if I could!" said Oscar. "Only just now— well, she isn't exactly here!"

"Most unfortunate, sir," said the King. "Especially as it seems rather doubtful that the Lady Lucy will return. It seems more likely that she will be captured by Her Majesty. Such has been the fate of most of the birds on our island. Of course, there is also the possibility that she will be found by one of our subjects. They are fond of birds."

"Fond of birds!" Fear seized Oscar.

"Quite fond. Especially when they are hungry," said the King.

As much as Oscar wanted to hunt for Lucy, he could not think how or where to begin. And when the King commanded him to carry water from the well over to a long stone trough buried in the ground nearby, he did not protest. He wasn't sure it was safe to protest. What if the King decided to change him into a cat again?

Where would he be then? And what would happen to Lucy? It seemed to Oscar that his only hope lay in being friendly with the King, in fostering the notion that he and the King were fellow sorcerers.

He lugged bucket after bucket to the trough until he heard the sound of voices approaching. He saw six men striding into the clearing. They walked in pairs, carrying long wooden poles that sagged under the weight of three enormous baskets. The baskets were bulging and spilling over with silvery, smelly fish.

"Supper here, Your Majesty!" said one of the men.

Oscar watched as they dropped the fish into the water trough. The cats went wild, screeching and clawing and hissing as they climbed over each other to get at the fish.

The King took a smaller basket from one of the men. He glanced inside it. "That will be all," he said, and the men nodded and disappeared into the jungle.

"We will have supper before dark sets in," the King said, gesturing toward a ring of blackened stones. Inside the ring were the cold remains of a fire. Oscar watched as the King raised his makeshift wand in the air:

"Ash and char is what you are,
    Yet what you *were* is our desire.
    So rise up now and turn to fire!"

The words had the same effect as throwing kerosene and a lit match into the ring of stones. As the air puffed, then crackled with flame, the King viewed the fire with satisfaction. "Always the best bit of magic!" he confided. "Wouldn't you agree, sir?"

Oscar nodded. He wondered whether magic spells needed to rhyme, or whether the King simply did it for show. Was he so clever that he could make rhymes up on the spot? He watched the King raise his wand again, noticing that he had focused his gaze on a broken roof tile on the ground near the fire. His voice sounded bored:

"Two hunger here, boy and man,
They need a well-greased frying pan.

"We will have fried fish," said the King, leaning over to pick up the cast-iron frying pan that had taken the place of the roof tile. He propped the pan over a pile of glowing coals near the edge of the fire. As the fat that greased the bottom of the pan began to melt, the King pulled four plate-shaped fish out of the small basket left by the fish bearers. Oscar saw that each fish was nicely cleaned. "Flounder!" said the King, sounding pleased. He flopped a fish into the pan and it sizzled.

"When first we found ourselves in these circumstances, we took more time for creature comforts," said the King as he sat down on a flat rock near the fire. "A chair, a table . . ." He pointed to some rocks nearby. "But it seemed odd to us to eat alone in that fashion. Still, if you would prefer, make yourself more comfortable." The King eyed the pocket where Oscar had put the bottle of potion.

He thinks I'll perform a spell, thought Oscar. "This rock suits me fine," he said, sitting down.

The satisfying sound and smell of fish frying occupied the space between them for a moment, and then Oscar asked, "Why don't you use magic to make whatever food you like?"

"Magic food! Surely you jest!" said the King.

Oscar pretended to be interested in the fish, gently lifting it with a twig to check its progress. He wondered what was wrong with magic food, but of course he didn't dare ask. What if the King guessed that he wasn't a sorcerer? He had better watch out, just in case membership in the brotherhood of sorcerers really was his only defense against being turned into a cat.

"So you like fish, sir," said the King.

Oscar looked up from the picked-over remains of his supper, which lay on a leaf that the King had transformed into a tin plate. All being said and done, he thought, he should have been sick of fish after feasting on it raw for so many years. But he found to his surprise that he liked the taste of pan-fried fish as much as ever. "My pa and I used to go fishing," he told the King. "We used to cook over a fire, just like this."

Beyond the perimeter of light, Oscar could see the cats lurking. The fire was making them timid, he knew. Some looked sleepy and satisfied. These were the more aggressive cats who had prevailed in the battle for dinner. But other cats crouched closer, blinking at the light as they watched the humans licking their fingers. No doubt they were still hungry.

Oscar set down his plate, and Tom, the King's black cat—the only cat confident enough to come near the fire—began licking it clean. When several other cats pressed forward from the darkness, Tom arched his back and hissed until they slunk away.

There was never enough food for all of them, Oscar remembered. He thought of Lucy, wondering where she was, or worse, whether she was still alive.

"Your father is a fisherman, then," said the King.

"Oh, no. He's a farmer. We have a farm . . ." Oscar caught himself. It hurt to keep forgetting that Pa and Ma were gone, that they were *dead.* "We *had* a farm," he said. "Fishing was just something we did sometimes,

Pa and I. We'd go fishing in the Missouri—that's a river. You can catch all sorts of fish there, even catfish sometimes."

"*Cat* fish!" said the King with genuine interest. "We have never heard of it."

"Oh! It's the best thing you ever ate. Pa always says it's food fit for a king, so I guess you would like it. Ma doesn't care much for it."

"Her Majesty hates fish, too," said the King. "From the moment we were married, fish was forbidden at the royal table. Gives her a headache, she says. Wouldn't eat fowl either, of course, and what she would eat must be sautéed, or glazed, or fancied up with bits of fruit and such. Even with dinner she was an artist."

"An artist?"

"Nothing but painting and poetry all day long for her! We ask you, sir. Did you ever know anyone to look at a canary in a cage and see a poem—or a painting?"

"Well, I can't say. . . ."

"That's how Leona is." The King sounded half proud, half annoyed.

"Leona?"

"The Queen!"

Oscar had never thought of the Queen having a name. Did the King have a name, too?

"A crow never cawed, a turkey never gobbled, a hen never clucked but Leona must hear a poem in it," said the King. "But let a little cat open its mouth and Leona hears nothing more than a tiresome noise." The way the King's eyebrows drew together in a dark cloud reminded Oscar of the first time he had met him, when a chance remark had made the King fly into a rage. He wondered how the King and Queen could possibly despise each other so—all because of a silly quarrel about cats and birds. Then he reminded himself that he was responsible for their quarrel.

*Not a very pretty situation.* That was what he had written in *The Book of Story Beginnings.* The odd thing of it was, he could remember hearing Ada Hansen say the exact same thing to her sister Fanny only a couple of days after Pa had stormed out of the house to go live up at Uncle Ned's. The old gnarled pair of them had been standing outside Sunderlund's Store.

"Not a very pretty situation up there at the Martin house," Ada had said.

"My goodness, did you *ever*!" Fanny had replied.

Then the two of them had seen Oscar walking toward them, and their faces had smoothed out like cream in a saucer.

"Ada and Fanny Hansen are a pair of old cats!" That had been Pa's response when Oscar told him about it later. He had gone up to Uncle Ned's to try and persuade Pa to come home.

"I think you ought to come home, Pa."

"Did your Ma send you up here to tell me that?"

"No, sir."

"I didn't think so."

"But, Pa . . ."

Pa had put down the newspaper. "Son, if I am to believe your ma, she considers me an ignorant fool incapable of understanding anything more than the need to put food on our table. Your ma, on the other hand, is occupied with a far less worldly and far more important endeavor. I believe she calls it *expressing herself musically*. She seems to believe that people so vastly different from each other cannot live peacefully under one roof."

Oscar had known Ma didn't think any such thing. She had been in one of her dark and dismal moods (as she called them) ever since Pa left. And when she had seen Uncle Ned at church that morning, she had looked hopeful—until Uncle Ned shook his head over the pew.

"She doesn't think that, Pa!"

But Pa had just rattled his newspaper and disappeared behind it.

Shaking off his thoughts, Oscar realized that the King was still talking. His voice was angrier now. "As far as Her Majesty is concerned, those who love birds and those who love cats can never get along!"

"Maybe the Queen is just stubborn," said Oscar. He was thinking of Ma, who had been too stubborn to ask Pa to come home.

"Of course she's stubborn!" The King snorted.

Wary of upsetting him even more, Oscar lapsed into silence. In the distance, he could hear the unearthly sound of a cat fight. Closer, a machinelike noise rumbled, the sound of hundreds of cats purring. Hundreds of eyes blinked in the darkness, reflecting back the dwindling firelight. He watched Tom push his head against the King's knee, then leap to his lap. The black cat stretched upward to nudge the King's face with his nose.

The King looked down. "We are tired," he said wearily. He stood up and Tom leaped gracefully to the ground. "Come this way, sir!" the King commanded. He led Oscar to one of the cottages. "There's the bed, sir," he said, throwing open a wooden door.

In the dim light coming through the windows, Oscar saw what looked like a storage shelf built against the curved wall of the cottage. There was another shelf directly above it, leaving a space so small and cramped that Oscar found it hard to believe anyone ever could have slept there. On the other hand, he saw the remains of a mattress on the floor nearby, its cloth cover torn open and its feather stuffing strewn about like snow.

"Cats have ripped apart the bedding, but you'll find a way around that, no doubt. Nothing like a little magic, eh? We've managed to make our cottage next door quite livable," said the King. "Good night, then," he added abruptly, closing the door behind him.

Left in darkness, Oscar hesitated. The King was right. He could use the magic potion to make himself more comfortable. Goodness knows, he'd like a nice, soft bed. He was tired of sleeping in hard, cramped places. And he could make a lantern like the one Lucy had made—a flashlight. He could picture it in his mind.

He had just pulled the bottle of potion from his pocket when he thought of Lucy. Should he sneak out of the cottage to look for her? Oscar peered out one of the broken windows. It was so dark outside he couldn't even see to the edge of the clearing. How could he find her in the middle of the night?

It might be better to sleep for a few hours. He was exhausted. And it seemed to Oscar that he had better not use the potion after all. What if he used the last drop of it making himself a comfortable bed? He crossed the room and set the bottle on the lower storage shelf, at what he imagined might once have been the head of the bed. He lay down next to it so that it filled his vision.

Oscar didn't know he had fallen asleep, so he felt only joy when he heard his mother calling his name. Then he saw her. She was in the attic at home, her long yellow hair hanging down her back as she kneeled in front of an open brass trunk. "Where is *The Book of Story Beginnings*?" she cried, and Oscar's heart tightened up. Then she turned around, and suddenly it was Lucy's mother gazing at him instead, saying in a terrible voice, "Where is Lucy?"

Only then did Oscar know he had been asleep, because he woke up trembling. It took him a moment to get his bearings, to understand that the dark about him was the cottage, and that the even darker shape moving across the floor was a black cat. It was Tom.

Oscar sat up, bumping his head on the underside of the shelf above. "Ouch!" he cried. As he probed his throbbing head, he saw Tom creep closer. The cat's nose pushed at the bottle of potion standing near the edge of the storage-shelf bed. Tom pulled back on his haunches. His paw inched upward and tipped the bottle onto its side.

"Hey!" Oscar reached for the bottle, but Tom's paw came across his arm like a hand. His yellow eyes gleamed. Oscar righted the bottle and drew his hand away.

But Tom's paw came up and tipped the bottle on its side again. Very carefully, the paw pushed and rolled the bottle toward Oscar. Tom laid his paw on Oscar's hand and looked up expectantly.

# CHAPTER NINETEEN

## THE KING'S FAMILIAR

Oscar sat very still, watching the dark stripe of Tom's paw across his hand. He watched and he wondered, but it wasn't until his eyes met the black cat's clear gaze that Oscar pulled his hand away, opened the bottle of potion, and tilted it over Tom's head.

Though Oscar would have sworn he hadn't, he must have blinked as the drop fell. For all at once, exactly where Tom had been, there was a boy crouching—a boy not much older than Oscar himself, with a thin, bony face faintly drawn in moonlight and shadow. Oscar was close enough to see a spattering of freckles across the boy's nose. His wavy dark hair, greasy and unkempt and curling at the ends, fell almost to his shoulders. The boy's eyes, the color of tea, gazed at him with quiet, catlike authority.

Then, as quick as a match striking, the boy jumped up. He felt down the length of his arms, grasped his hair, and touched his nose, his ears, and his mouth. "Oh, sir! You've done it! You've gone and made me a boy again!" he said. "And I know what you're thinkin', sir. You're thinkin' I've disobeyed His Majesty. Oh—he'll be so mad at me. But I couldn't help it, sir." The boy tiptoed to the window to peer out. "His Majesty was asleep when I left him, sir. And he sleeps sound. That's why I took the chance. I don't mean to disobey. I only want to explain."

"What do you mean, you only want to explain? Who are you?"

"Oh, sir! It's all my fault, really. Please don't punish King Bertram!"

*Bertram,* thought Oscar. Was that the King's name? "How would I punish him?" he said.

"You're a sorcerer, sir!" said the boy.

"I'm not . . ." Oscar began, but he caught himself. He had better be careful.

"Please, sir! It looks like abuse of power, I know. But I can explain," said the boy.

"Abuse of power?"

"It ain't right. His Majesty shouldn't never have changed everyone into a cat the way he did—but he was driven to it. It's my fault, sir! Oh, please don't punish him!"

"All right! I promise not to punish him," said Oscar. "Not yet, anyway," he embellished for effect. "Just answer my questions, and everything will be fine. Tell me who you are."

"Why, I'm the King's familiar—Tom, sir!"

Oscar remembered that witches had familiars. Did sorcerers have them as well? "Did the King turn you into a cat?" he asked.

"No, sir!"

"But you're a boy, aren't you?"

"I was a boy once, sir. Just as you see. But now I'm the King's familiar. And it's my fault, sir! Mine!" Tom's panicked voice rose so high it cracked.

Feeling sorry for him, Oscar opened his mouth to set Tom straight—to explain that he had nothing to fear.

But Tom spoke first. "Oh, sir—may I tell you the whole story?" he pleaded. "From start to finish—then you'll see how I'm to blame, and not His Majesty."

"Go ahead, then. And really, Tom, you don't need to call me *sir*."

Tom nodded. "Yes, sir! I'll try, sir!"

"Tell me how you came to be a cat," said Oscar.

"That'd be when I was the cook's boy, sir," said Tom. "That was my job at the palace—washin' pots, carryin' wood for the fire, turnin' the spit for the roast—hard work, hot work, sir. And lucky I was to have it, for I'm an orphan—no father at all and my mother died practically before I was born. Never a day passed that I didn't feel grateful to the royal family for takin' me in. (The King was just a lad then. Prince Bertram he was, and it was his father and mother that was so kind to me.) Never a day passed I didn't say how grateful I was, too, until Cook'd beat me about the head she was so sick of hearin' it. But I *was* grateful, sir, and that's the truth of it."

Tom paused to fill his lungs before continuing. "Then one day, Cook says I'm to wash my filthy self and go see the Queen Mother—which is what we was supposed to call Prince Bertram's grandmother—and I says, 'Why?' Not to be insolent, sir, but just because I was that curious as to what the Queen Mother wanted with the likes of poor me. But Cook just gives me a wallop, so off I goes to get myself cleaned up as best I could, and I goes straightaway to see the Queen Mother. And she says, how would I like to serve His Royal Highness, Prince Bertram?

"So, of course, I says yes. And then the Queen

Mother tells me her plan, which is that I, Tom, will be Prince Bertram's loyal servant. It'll be my duty to watch him at all times, to protect him from harm, to make sure he's always happy and cared for. And how I'll be able to do this without anybody ever guessin' is because she—the Queen Mother, that is—will change me into a cat. She says I'm to be what's called a *familiar*. (As you well know, sir, all sorcerers has got to have familiars.) The Queen Mother herself had one, though I didn't know it till that day. Hers was a fluffy white cat, very pretty, goin' by the name of Cloud. And here old Cook was always complainin' about Cloud bein' so spoiled and useless!" Tom laughed gleefully.

"Was Cloud also a person?" Oscar asked.

"Yes, sir. Used to be a scullery maid named Tina. She was a present to the Queen Mother on her fourteenth birthday, just as I was to be a gift to Prince Bertram on his birthday. Sorcerers always get familiars when they're fourteen years old. It's the custom."

"It seems pretty unfair to me! Why do you have to be his familiar? Why can't he just have a cat?"

"But I am a cat," said Tom, looking confused.

"You're a boy!" said Oscar. "Why does the King need you to be his familiar? Why can't he just have one that's never been anything but a cat?"

"Well, I suppose he could. There's sorcerers that do,

of course. All sorts of animals is used as familiars—cats, birds, rats, mice. But the most powerful sorcerers has got ones like me—animals that once was people," said Tom. "We help concentrate their powers," he added proudly.

"Well, I can't believe you agreed to it!" said Oscar.

Tom looked perplexed by this response. "What the Queen Mother was askin' was the greatest of honors!" he said. "A familiar has many important responsibilities. It ain't just a matter of keepin' down the mice in the palace. I had to taste the Prince's food before he ate it to make sure it wasn't poisoned. And I saw to it that he was happy. Cats are a great comfort to people, you know. You just have to make your throat rumble, like this . . ." Tom tried unsuccessfully to purr. "Well, I can't seem to do it now. But I'd purr, you see, and rub against Prince Bertram's ankle, and he'd scratch my neck just here behind my ears. Oh, it is nice to be scratched there, sir! You can't imagine!"

Oscar didn't have to imagine. He *knew.* Tom's description was giving him odd, uncomfortable memories.

Tom went on. "I was very happy for the next few years. His Highness was growin' up into a fine young man. He was always learnin' things. There was his kingship studies, which he didn't much care for. Diplomacy, history, languages, mathematics, the correct use of

sword and shield. Then other things, not so serious—
dancin', conversation, literature, and court etiquette.
Prince Bertram liked them even less, I could tell.

"Then there was Prince Bertram's sorcery studies,
which was taught to him by the Queen Mother herself.
Very tricky thing, magic. I had to be sharp so I could
help the Prince. And there was laws of magic—rules
and regulations and such that has got to be learned inside and out. There wasn't room in my brain for 'em
all, but I did try to cram 'em in, sir, for I could see
Prince Bertram didn't have much interest.

"One of those regulations concerned abuse of
power, sir! Not usin' your magic against others. It's the
worst punishment for that, ain't it? I still remember
what the regulation said. I've thought of it often these
many years: *Abuse of power shall be punished by loss
of familiar and powers, said punishment to be administered as appropriate by the governin' body. . . .*" Tom
broke off tearfully. "That'd be you, wouldn't it, sir!
The governin' body—here to punish His Majesty."

Seeing Tom cry, Oscar felt embarrassed for him.
"Tom—I'm not here to punish King Bertram. I'm not
even a sorcerer—not really!" he confessed.

"You're not? But His Majesty said so. And you
worried him, sir. I could see you did."

"I may have worried him, but I'm not a sorcerer,"

Oscar said firmly. "Finish your story and I'll tell you mine. You were telling about the King's lessons," he prodded. "Abuse of power and all that. Tell me more."

Tom sniffled and wiped his eyes with his dirty sleeve. "A great many things happened after that, you see. All bad, and all at once. First, the Queen Mother took ill and died. Oh, it was very sad, sir. And the next thing was even more tragical, if you can believe it! Prince Bertram's father and mother was lost at sea! Died when the royal ship sank in a storm. On a voyage to Song Island they was, goin' to arrange Prince Bertram's marriage."

"His marriage to Queen Leona?"

"No, sir! That was the next bad thing. It was Princess Ida was supposed to marry Prince Bertram. She was considered a fine match, diplomacy-wise. But with his parents lost at sea, Prince Bertram—King Bertram by then—had to go himself to Song Island to complete the nuptial arrangements, and I went along.

"The trouble began almost as soon as we got there," said Tom. "It ain't my place to criticize, sir, but I think Princess Ida's folk was partly to blame for what came next. They kept her hidden away, you see. All part of the marriage custom is what they said. But what I say is, maybe the King might've fallen in love with the Princess if he hadn't had all that time to meet someone else first."

"Queen Leona?" said Oscar.

Tom nodded. "She was one of Princess Ida's ladies-in-waitin'. The loveliest woman you ever saw, sir. Even a cat like me couldn't have missed that much. The King fell under her spell right away. She made him weak from happiness. That's what confused me in my duties, sir. I ought to have remembered that the most important thing is diplomacy. Only—well, sir, happiness is easier for a cat to think about. That's why I made sure to bring the King and the Lady Leona together as much as I could. Cats are good at that sort of thing. The next thing you know, the King takes her home with him, leavin' a great stink behind at Song Island."

"So he eloped with her!" said Oscar.

"Yes, sir," said Tom. "And things was fine for a while. The King built a grand palace for the Queen. I don't think she cared much for it, though she made out like she did. Oh, she was somethin'—always goin' on about her paintin' and poetry while His Majesty was busy tryin' to be King. Between you and me, sir, I could see him was wishin' he'd studied more in his youth.

"So there he is, tryin' so very hard, when one day, someone makes a gift to the Queen. A canary—a plump, juicy little thing that sang from sunup to sun-down. The Queen was just crazy about that bird. Al-ways after His Majesty to make up some little poem about the creature. The King's good at makin' up rhymes—for his magic, you know—and at first, he goes along, but at last even he gets tired of it. Then she starts makin' up poetry herself. And she's got to paint the bird's portrait—not once, not twice, but over and over again. She loves that bird so much she's got to re-decorate her mornin' room. Paints it all pink and or-ange and yellow, to look like the sun, she says, and she shows the King how the bird looks so pretty flyin' about in there. Flittin' up and down and around and every whichaway until . . ." The agitation in Tom's voice had been steadily rising. Now he buried his face in his hands.

When he looked up, his expression was bleak. "I just couldn't take it no more, sir," he said. "There's only so much a cat can stand. There I was in that room, crouched near the King's heel, sir. There I sat, watchin' that canary dip and dive. I could feel my eyes glazin' over, and my jaw twitchin', and I just forgot myself and I *pounced.* I caught the little thing in mid-air and I *chomped it*! Chomped it right through the neck!" Tom licked his lips, as if recalling the taste of the bird. "The Queen screamed and carried on. Said I ought to be drowned, or hanged, and—"

"Yes, I know!" Oscar interrupted. "The King and Queen quarreled, and she kicked him out of the palace, and then everyone laughed at him, and he turned them all into cats."

"That's about the sum of it," said Tom. "You can see I'm to blame."

"I don't see how. You didn't make him change everyone into cats."

"But he's a good King, sir!" said Tom. "He never meant any harm."

"Never meant any harm? How many lives has he ruined? Yours, mine . . ."

"Yours, sir?" Tom cocked his head curiously.

"Yes, mine! He changed me into a cat years and years ago. I think anyone who steals a boy's life from him like that ought to pay for it," said Oscar. Even if he is just a character in a story, he said to himself.

Tom's eyes widened. "Why, I know who you are now! You're that boy he changed into a gray tabby some time back, ain't you! How is it that you are yourself again? You're sure you ain't a sorcerer?"

"Very sure," Oscar said firmly. And then, as he had promised, he told Tom his own story. He told him about escaping, about finding Lucy and getting changed back into himself by the potion. He left out the part about *The Book of Story Beginnings,* for he wondered how Tom would react to finding out that he was just a character in a story, or to finding out that Oscar was responsible for his existence.

He went on to explain about Lucy's father and how he had used the potion to change himself into a bird. Tom's eyes flashed. "Then it's the Lady Lucy's father that's the sorcerer!"

"I suppose so," said Oscar. "But it's not what you think!" he added when he saw the look on Tom's face. "I'm sure he doesn't want to punish the King."

Tom looked unconvinced.

"Lucy's father couldn't possibly punish anyone because he's a crow. And he's locked up at the Queen's palace," said Oscar. "I'm sure if he wanted to punish anyone, it would be me, for changing Lucy into a bird."

"Oh, sir! That *is* a terrible thing. And if you'll take my advice, you'd better find the Lady Lucy right away. There are thousands of cats on the island."

"Thanks for reminding me!"

"Like as not she'll be captured and taken to the Queen," said Tom. "There's folks all over the island on the lookout for birds. The Queen pays good money for 'em."

"Then the palace may be the best place to look for Lucy," Oscar said. "How far is it from here? How do I get there?"

"I'd say a half day's walkin'. If you like, I could take you."

"Oh, that's good of you, Tom!"

"Still some time left tonight," said Tom. "We ought to leave now, while the King sleeps."

"Do you think the King would try to stop us?"

"The King'd stop *me,* if he knew what I was about," said Tom. "And I expect he'd stop you—even if you was to go by yourself. His Majesty's starved for company. I could tell he liked talkin' with you, sir, even if he don't trust you. If he knew you was leavin'—and if he knew I was helpin' you—he'd be none too pleased, and that's puttin' it mildly."

"Let's go, then," Oscar whispered.

"Very good, sir." Tom crossed the room. "The door's been locked by magic, of course," he said, tugging on the knob. "But we ought to be able to take care of that. The King never learned nothin' but the most simple of spells. Which is to say that just about any old spell can undo one of his. What a locked door needs, sir, is a magic key."

To Oscar's surprise, Tom held not a key in his hand, but the bottle of potion.

"Where did you get that?" Oscar hadn't even noticed him taking it.

"Cats are quick and clever," said Tom.

"I'll take the potion," said Oscar after Tom had changed a pebble from the floor into a key.

Tom was putting the stopper back in the bottle. "I'll keep it safe for you," he said.

"No, Tom! Give it back." Oscar held out his hand.

Tom looked wounded. "Don't you trust me?"

"I'll need it when I find Lucy," said Oscar.

But when he reached for the potion, Tom skipped sideways. The wounded look vanished and Tom grinned. "I told you cats was quick and clever," he said as he dropped the potion into his pocket.

"Give it to me, Tom!" Oscar insisted.

But Tom was already turning the key, pushing the cottage door open. He peered about the clearing, sniffing at the air. And Oscar had no choice but to follow him.

They hadn't gone far into the forest when Oscar heard rustling noises. "What's that?" he asked.

"Cats. I told 'em to follow us."

"How did you tell them anything?" Oscar said in surprise.

"Oh, I told 'em all right. Never you mind how. The thing is, they think of me as their leader. Cats ain't exactly anxious to have a leader, but I must say I've managed pretty well."

"But why do you want them to follow us?"

"Don't you bother yourself about that," Tom said. "And now, if you don't mind, I think we should make haste. There's only an hour or so of dark left, and there's a cave I know where we can rest come daybreak. We'll all be tired then."

Stepping after Tom, Oscar wondered if he had misjudged the King's familiar. Tom had seemed so—*simple* was the word that came to mind. All *yes, sirs* and *no, sirs*. And yet Tom was leading an army of cats through the forest. Why would he want to take so many cats to a palace full of birds? What was he up to? Oscar was beginning to suspect that Tom wasn't half the simple fellow he had made him out to be.

# CHAPTER TWENTY

## DIPLOMACY

By morning, Oscar was quite sure that Tom was not a simple fellow at all. By evening, he was even more sure. And by the morning of the next day, he would have said that of all the words he could think of to describe Tom, the best one seemed to be *calculating*.

For one thing, Tom had a plan. Not a plan to rescue Lucy and her father—Oscar soon realized that Tom cared very little about that. No, as Oscar discovered, Tom's plan was more far-reaching. His intention in visiting the palace, as he had explained to Oscar, fell nothing short of ending the hostilities between the King and Queen.

Of course, Tom hadn't put it quite like that. "My aim is to patch things up between the pair of 'em," he had told Oscar. "Make the Queen see things from His Majesty's point of view. Sort of a matter of diplomacy, if you catch my meanin'." Tom seemed to put great faith in diplomacy. "Diplomacy can join the hands of snakes—that's what they say," he had remarked. "And snakes ain't got hands, of course, so you can see how useful a thing it is."

Upon first hearing Tom's plan, Oscar had been rather pleased. He felt a prickle of intellectual satisfaction at the prospect of his story beginning about the King and Queen coming to a happy end. What an intriguing twist for Tom to play such an important role in the plot.

Over the course of the next day and night, however, Oscar had begun to have some misgivings.

After leaving the King's village in the night, Tom had led Oscar and all the cats through the jungle to a large cave. They had stayed hidden there all day while Tom proceeded to implement his plan.

To begin with, he had used the bottle of potion. "We mustn't waste it," Oscar had protested. But Tom had pushed him away, and Oscar had found himself trapped suddenly near one side of the cave, surrounded by cats, while Tom had gone right ahead and changed a dozen cats into men and women. He called them his *captains*.

"Who knows whether the Queen'll listen to reason?" he had explained. "The captains'll help me if I have to force her hand. Besides, I may need help keepin' all the cats in line."

Before Oscar could ask what he meant by *force her hand*, Tom had begun to explain his plan to his captains. Oscar had tried to listen at first. But he had fallen fast asleep on the floor of the cave, waking only when one of Tom's captains shook his shoulder and said, "Come on! Up with you! The General says we've got to move."

The *General* was Tom, and from that moment on, Oscar had not been able to get close enough to say a single word to the King's familiar. Emerging from the cave, Oscar had found that it was once again dark outside, and he had found himself surrounded on all sides by cats who restricted his movements to a kind of forced march through the jungle. They had marched until dawn, when at last Oscar had stumbled out of the trees and into a town. Bleary-eyed and ravenously hungry, Oscar had marched up to the Queen's palace, where Tom and his captains and his army of cats had pushed their way through the outer gates.

Now they were in the throne room, and there stood

Tom, and there, facing him, stood the Queen. Tom's captains stood at attention all around the throne room; the cats sat clustered around them like soldiers. The birds were shrieking in their cages.

"Just who do you think you are?" said the Queen. "Remove these cats at once!"

Tom bowed, his greasy hair flopping forward. "Permit me to introduce myself, Your Majesty. I am Tom, humble servant of His Most Royal Majesty, King Bertram."

Somewhere in the room, a clucking noise began and ended abruptly. The Queen went pale.

"What brings me here is a mission of diplomacy," said Tom.

"Diplomacy!" said the Queen, her expression darkening.

There were more clucking noises. It sounded like a fox raiding a chicken house, thought Oscar. He had hoped to ask the Queen about Lucy and her father, but he could see that he wasn't going to get a chance any time soon. If Tom really wanted to patch things up between the King and Queen, as he had said, he wasn't starting off very well.

"His Majesty says he's willin' to let bygones be bygones," said Tom. "Only thing is, he'd like an apology."

"An apology! An apology for what?"

"Well," said Tom, "for throwin' him out of his own home, for one thing."

"I never threw him out!"

"You told him to get out or you'd see that his familiar was drowned, Your Majesty. Those was your exact words."

"And so it ought to have been drowned! That vicious beast ate my canary."

Tom scowled. "It ain't the King's fault that I ate— I mean, that his cat ate that canary. Cats eat birds. That's what they do."

"I see!" said the Queen. "And is that supposed to explain why the King has seen fit to change everyone in the kingdom into a cat? So they can eat my birds?"

"No."

"He wants me to apologize to him, does he? I never heard anything so preposterous in my life!"

"So you won't say you're sorry?"

"I won't say any such thing," said the Queen. "I'm not sorry and I haven't done anything wrong. I command you to leave!"

"I ain't leavin'," said Tom. "And if you look around the room, you'll see my captains standin' at attention. You can see my troops, ready to follow orders."

"What captains? What troops? What orders?" said the Queen.

"People is the captains. Cats is the troops, Your Majesty. And their orders is to attack your birds on my signal."

Oscar gave a start. Did Tom really mean what he said?

"You wouldn't dare attack my birds!" said the Queen.

"I would dare! On His Majesty's orders."

*Liar,* thought Oscar. The King hadn't given Tom any orders at all.

"Say you're sorry, or I'll give my signal," said Tom.

"Tom!" said Oscar. "What about Lucy? What about her father? They could be somewhere in this room!"

But Tom's attention was locked on the Queen. "Go on! Say you're sorry," he said.

"Never!" said the Queen.

Tom shook his head. "You give me no choice, Your Majesty."

Oscar grabbed Tom's arm. "Didn't you hear what I said? Lucy and her father may be here!"

Tom shook him off. "Diplomacy has got to be backed up by action," he said, raising his arm in the air. "Last chance, Your Majesty!"

"Get out of my palace!"

"No, Tom!" Oscar shouted. But Tom's arm came down, a signal that was accompanied by an uncanny yowl from his throat. The yowl was answered by others throughout the room. Oscar heard the sound of metal grating on metal, of hinges screeching and cage doors clanking open. He saw one of Tom's captains throw open a cage full of tiny wrens. Cats poured into the cage as the birds swarmed out. The Queen screamed.

In less than a minute, it was as if the throne room had been hit by a hurricane of fur and feathers. Oscar was surrounded on all sides by thick curtains of cats, their outstretched bodies slicing like swords through clouds of birds whirling by so fast they looked like streaks of colored chalk. All around his feet there was a horrible mess of cats chasing skittering birds across the floor, of birds defending themselves with their beaks and their talons.

Some of the birds were flying too high for the cats to reach. They flapped their wings, circling around and around the vast throne room until they grew tired. Then they swooped down low, looking for a place to rest. But there was no rest, for as soon as a bird landed—on a chair, on a table, on top of a cage—a dozen cats leaped up to pull it down into the fray.

Birds kept flying in Oscar's face. One even tried to land on his head, and he ducked down, covering himself until he realized that the bird might have been Lucy. He stood up, intersecting the arc of an attacking cat. Claws raked down his arm. "Lucy!" he shouted. "Lucy!"

It was no good. He would never find her now. Nevertheless, his eyes peered through the maelstrom of birds. And it was then that Oscar noticed the windows. It was then that he had an idea. The birds flying around the room didn't stand a chance unless they could escape. And the only way that could happen was if he opened a window.

He tried to run toward the windows, but it was really more like stumbling. Once he stepped on something soft that screamed. Once he stepped on something soft that didn't make a sound at all, and that was almost worse. Once he fell, coming face to face with a calico cat that had a robin hanging from its jaws.

When he reached the windows at last, he saw that they were made of large panes of glass that stretched toward the ceiling like cats' paws. The window sills were level with his head. To his dismay, Oscar found that the windows would not open.

All right then! He would break one of them.

Oscar looked around. There was an empty birdcage sitting on a marble table nearby. It was one of the smaller cages in the throne room, but it was large enough— about the size of the parlor stove back home. He slid the cage to the edge of the table without any trouble. Then, as he attempted to lift it into his arms, it smashed to the floor, barely missing the tail of an orange tabby.

It was too heavy! But it couldn't be; he wouldn't let it be too heavy. Oscar pulled the cage up in the air— up to his chest. He pushed it up over his shoulders and heaved it. The cage crashed against the glass and fell backward. Oscar leaped away just in time to avoid being crushed. Glass fell in a downpour as air rushed into the throne room.

But the birds didn't take any notice. The opening was large enough, but it was only one opening in an enormous room. He would have to break more windows.

He hurled the cage again and again and again, until at last he couldn't lift it anymore. And still the birds ignored the broken windows. They're too dumb to know what windows are, thought Oscar. They're too dumb, and Lucy will die, and it will be my fault!

Then he saw that a flock of sparrows had discovered the broken windows. They hopped along the window ledges, chattering excitedly before disappearing into the sky outdoors. A flock of starlings caught on next, then a crowd of grackles that paused to scold the cats below. Soon more and more birds were escaping, and at last, Oscar could see about him.

He surveyed the remains of the battle. The *carnage,* he thought. That was the only word to describe the scene. Everywhere he looked, there seemed to be a cat with a bird dripping out of its mouth. Or a cat patting and pawing at a twitching lump of feathers. Or a cat with a glazed, sated expression on its face. Everywhere he looked, there were feathers, swirling woefully in the air.

The room was filled with soft, dreadful noises. Oscar could hear cats gnawing on fresh bird, cats licking their chops, cats hissing at each other as they fought over their captured prizes. From far away, he could hear the sound of crying.

Lucy and her father must have gotten away, he thought. It was what he wanted to believe with all his heart.

# CHAPTER TWENTY-ONE

## A BIRD'S-EYE VIEW

A feeling of great security blanketed Lucy from all the many distractions in the throne room. That, and a feeling rather like smugness. As much as a bird could feel proud, she was proud of herself for having found a place of refuge. She had been the first to land there. Other birds—sparrows, finches, and a plucky cardinal— had soon followed, trying to escape the mayhem below, but they had all been nervous types, too fidgety to stay in one place for long, even a place as safe as the ledge above the main doorway of the throne room.

Fortunately Lucy was a bird who preferred ledges. She belonged on a ledge, or so she felt as she settled in. She was almost all pigeon now. From the moment the cats had entered the throne room, she had quite forgotten she was human.

Now, as she cooed very softly to herself, it occurred to her that it was growing more quiet. Of course, she didn't have a word like *quiet* at her disposal. She sensed only that there were fewer birds about. The ones that were dead she had forgotten, as if they had never existed. The ones that had flown out the windows she had forgotten as well. She did remember the windows breaking. She remembered the crash of glass and metal, and dreaded hearing it again.

Her eyes were drawn to a woman sitting in a heap near the windows. Broken glass glinted on the floor around her. The woman's head was buried in her hands, and Lucy could see her shoulders heaving as she made strange wheezing noises. *Crying,* thought Lucy, and the word surprised her.

Just then, a boy appeared from behind a group of empty birdcages. Lucy stirred uneasily. She recognized him; he was the window-breaking boy.

"Excuse me, ma'am," said the boy to the woman.

*Polite,* thought Lucy, and then the word flitted from her mind like a butterfly as she realized that she could understand what the boy was saying.

"Excuse me, ma'am." The boy's voice was louder this time, though still polite.

The woman looked up, and though her eyes were red and her cheeks were streaked with tears, Lucy instantly recognized her. The woman was called the *Queen*.

"Please, ma'am," said the boy. "I was wondering if you might have seen a pigeon."

"A pigeon!" The Queen's eyes traveled across the bodies and bones and feathers on the floor. "You want to know whether I've seen a pigeon?"

Lucy was quite sure that the word *pigeon* was important. Then she remembered why it was important. *I am a pigeon,* she thought, and the very impact of having a full sentence speak itself inside her mind was so overwhelming that she nearly fell off the ledge.

The Queen began weeping again, and Lucy began to mull over a vague suspicion she felt herself harboring: perhaps she wasn't really a pigeon. She was just about to seize upon the truth—she could tell by the way her heart was racing—when there was yet another distraction. A man strode through the doorway beneath her. Cats leaped out of his way like grasshoppers.

From her bird's-eye, top-down view, Lucy could see that the man was clutching a wooden staff. There were bits of leaves and twigs clinging to his tattered robe and his tangled hair. His head looked oddly bare to Lucy, and a question popped into her mind: *Where's his crown?* That was how she remembered that the man was called the *King*.

The King nearly tripped over the Queen. "Leona?" he said, stepping back.

The Queen looked up. "You!" she said, gulping back a sob.

"Leona—what has happened here? We came up through town—we saw birds flying out of the palace."

"What do you mean? You know very well what has happened, Bertram. It was your servant, carrying out your command, who caused this—this massacre." The Queen's voice trembled.

As the King surveyed the room, he noticed the window-breaking boy for the first time. "You!" he said in a voice that made Lucy jump. "You stole our familiar!"

"I did not!" said the boy.

"I suppose you are responsible for killing Her Majesty's birds!"

"No, I'm not!" said the boy.

The Queen stood up then. "I have no idea who this boy is—" she began.

"My name's Oscar," the boy interrupted.

"It was another boy—your own servant, Bertram—who killed my birds. He ordered your cats to attack them. It was a despicable thing to do!"

"Our servant?" said the King, looking puzzled.

"It was Tom," said the boy named Oscar.

"Tom?" said the King.

"Yes! He had me change him back into a boy, and then he led all the cats here to the palace."

"You changed him into a boy! So you did steal our familiar."

"I didn't!"

Just then, Lucy's eyes caught sight of movement across the room. Another boy was approaching the King and Queen, stepping over cats as he did so. A crowd of people followed him.

"There's Tom now," said Oscar.

The boy named Tom came forward and knelt before the King. "Your Majesty," he said, bowing his head.

"Murderer!" said the Queen.

"Tom! Did you kill the Queen's birds?" said the King.

"No, Your Majesty. The cats did that."

"Only because you ordered them to do it!" said Oscar.

"Who are all these people?" said the King.

"They're my captains, Your Majesty," said Tom. "They was cats before. And I changed 'em back into people so they could help me. That boy there had a bit of magic potion."

"This boy? This sorcerer?"

"I'm not a sorcerer!" Oscar exclaimed.

"So you say!" said the King. "And yet you have stolen our familiar! You knew we would be powerless once he had changed from animal to human."

"I didn't know any such thing!"

All the talk of sorcerers and change was bewildering to Lucy, and her mind closed itself off from the conversation. The word *potion* had caught her attention. She poked at it with her thoughts. She prodded it like a potential tidbit of food. She had a picture in her mind of a little blue bottle. Strangely enough, in this picture, the bottle was in Oscar's hand, and he was holding it over her head. Who was Oscar? Did she know him somehow?

"You are clearly a liar, sir!" said the King, shaking his finger at Oscar. "Not only do you have the audacity to steal our familiar, but you use him to conspire against us!"

The Queen broke in. "I don't understand this talk of people conspiring against you, Bertram, when it's clear that the only conspiracy is the one between you and your servant that led to the murderous attack on my birds."

"But Leona. You can't believe that we had any knowledge of that!"

"Of course you had knowledge!" cried the Queen.

"And stop saying *we*! There's only one of you, and that's quite enough!"

"Leona—please! You must believe us! You must believe *me,*" the King implored. "How could I know what this boy was planning? He came to my camp. He stole my familiar from under my nose. He stole my magical powers. And for reasons completely unfathomable to me, he has set my cats against your birds!"

"Please, listen!" said Oscar. "I didn't steal your familiar. And I didn't want the Queen's birds attacked. All I wanted to do was to find Lucy and her father."

Lucy's brain seemed to give a jump sideways. *I'm Lucy!* she thought, and suddenly a score of connections snapped together in her mind. She was Lucy, and her father was a bird, and of course she knew who Oscar was. He was helping her to look for her father.

"I don't know anyone named Lucy, and I don't know her father!" said the Queen. "All I know is that my birds are dead. I hope you're sorry, Bertram!"

"I am sorry, Leona. I'm as sorry as I can be," said the King.

"If you're sorry, then why don't you change all the cats back into people! It's the only way my birds will ever be safe!"

"Please, Leona—if I could, I would. But this sorcerer here has stolen my familiar. I can't perform magic without a familiar."

"There's always an excuse with you, Bertram. First your cat eats my canary and you won't do anything about that. Now it's all the cats—all of them your *pets,* and you don't care one bit about my birds!"

"Stop it! Stop arguing for one minute and listen!" Oscar's voice was so loud that Lucy took several sideways steps along the ledge. "You have to believe me, Your Majesty. I didn't have anything to do with attacking the Queen's birds. All I want is to find Lucy and her father. Don't you understand? They may have been killed!"

The word *killed* was one that Lucy understood immediately.

"Who is Lucy?" said the Queen.

"She's a pigeon, Your Majesty. And her father is a crow."

"How can a pigeon have a crow for a father?"

"No! He's not a crow—he's a man. He changed himself into a crow."

"I see," said the Queen. "And he changed Lucy into a pigeon."

"No, ma'am. I did that. I was afraid the King was going to change her into a cat."

"I was not going to change her into a cat," said the King.

"This is all very confusing. I hate magic!" said the Queen.

"Please!" said Oscar. "What about Lucy and her father? I've got to find them."

"Well," said the Queen, "come to think of it, there was a pigeon. Just came yesterday—a nice fat one with rainbow markings on her neck. She was in a rather odd-looking brass cage."

*I'm up here!* Lucy called. She called several times before she realized that no sounds were coming from her throat.

She tried cooing but saw that Oscar couldn't hear her. She ruffled her wings. She grabbed the air, lifting herself up off the ledge.

"Look!" cried a voice—Oscar's. Lucy dropped down, sliding toward him through the air.

"Let me get her!" cried another voice—Tom's.

"Get away! Get away!" shouted Oscar.

And then hands closed around Lucy, and she forgot everything except that she was terrified.

# CHAPTER TWENTY-TWO
## THE TRAVELING TALISMAN

For the next minute, Lucy was aware of nothing but a spectacular blur of sounds and colors and smells, all of them human and all of them horrible. She couldn't tell who was holding her. She couldn't understand the voices clamoring about her.

"Do something, Bertram! Change her into a girl!"

"I can't! I haven't got a familiar anymore!"

"Get the potion! Get it! Tom's got it!"

"Tom!"

"No, Your Majesty! No!"

"Give it to me! Give it to me, I say!" This barked order was accompanied by the sound of something whooshing through the air. Without knowing what it was, Lucy caught a flash of the King's wooden staff coming swiftly down. She heard a yelp of pain.

"Hold her tight!"

"Stop it, Lucy! Stop it!" The hands that were preventing her from escaping clutched even tighter. There was another hand above her—a paint-smudged hand that reeked of turpentine. It was holding something shiny and blue.

Then Lucy bit down hard on human flesh. "Ouch!" shouted a voice, and the hands let go. For one moment, she was flying upward. The next moment, her wings turned to lead and she plummeted to the ground. Her wing—no, her elbow—slammed into the stone floor. The rest of her followed like a sack of birdseed. And then came *pain,* and thoughts of pain, and thoughts of everything, and she knew who she was once again.

"Are you all right, Lucy?" said Oscar.

She had forgotten what it was like to be so heavy. Trying not to groan, she pushed herself up on her hands and knees. Something metal clanked against the floor. The medallion she had taken from the attic—the medallion she had worn for luck—was still around her neck.

"Your elbow is bleeding," said Oscar as he helped her up from the floor.

"It's all right," said Lucy. Gingerly, she touched her elbow. It wasn't all right at all. It hurt like fire.

"I thought you were dead," said Oscar. His voice was weak, and he was staring at her as if he couldn't believe she was really alive after all.

"I'm fine." Lucy felt embarrassed, actually; she wished Oscar would stop staring.

But he didn't. "Where did you get that?" he asked, and Lucy looked down, following his gaze.

"What? This?" she said, holding up the lucky medallion. "I took it from the attic? Why?"

Before Oscar could answer, Tom's voice broke forth. "But Your Majesty—you don't understand! The Lady Lucy's father is a sorcerer. I was tryin' to protect you from him."

"Oscar, what's he talking about?" said Lucy.

The King echoed her question. "What are you talking about, fool?"

"Don't you remember, sire?" said Tom. "When we was studyin' the laws of magic? That is, you was studyin' and I just listened. But I remember what the law said, just as if it was printed on the backs of my eyes: *Abuse of power shall be punished by loss of familiar and power, said punishment to be administered by the governin' body.* That'd be the Lady Lucy's father, Your Majesty. He's the governin' body—a sorcerer come to pass judgment on you."

Lucy murmured to Oscar, "What does he mean,

governing body? What's that got to do with my father?"

"Tom's the King's familiar, Lucy. Don't you remember that black cat that was always hanging around the King? It turns out he's really a boy. Somehow he got it in his head that your father has come here to punish the King for changing his subjects into cats."

"That's ridiculous!" said Lucy.

Oscar turned to Tom. "I told you already that Lucy's father never had any intention of punishing anybody," he told him. "But you didn't listen. What's more, you knew he might be in the palace. I think you wanted to kill him."

*Kill him!* Lucy stared at Oscar, then looked down at the birds scattered like dead leaves on the floor. "Oscar! Where is my father? He isn't here, is he?"

"What's this?" said the King.

"I've been trying to tell you," said Oscar. "Lucy's father is a crow. Tom came here to get rid of him."

"I didn't!" Tom protested. "I wanted to protect Your Majesty."

"By killing the Lady Lucy's father?" said the King.

"He was going to take away your powers," said Tom.

"That's no excuse for murder," said the King. "You are no longer our familiar. You are banished from our kingdom."

"Please, Your Majesty!" Tom pleaded.

"Get away before I throw you in the dungeons!" shouted the King. He swept his arm toward the door, and Tom, sobbing, went out.

"Where is my father?" cried Lucy.

Everyone was silent.

"He's dead, isn't he!"

"We don't know that, Lucy," said Oscar.

"How could he not be dead? Look at this place!" An unbearable pain in Lucy's mind—in her heart— was making her voice shrill.

"He could have flown out the window," said Oscar. "He must have flown out the window. It's a *story*, Lucy. It's got to end happily."

"Who says?"

"I thought you were dead, and here you are, safe after all."

"Suppose he did fly away! How will we ever find him?" said Lucy.

"I don't see why the poor girl thinks her father is here," said the Queen.

What could Lucy say? That she was sure her father was in the palace because she had written it in a book?

Oscar answered for her. "We heard someone sold a crow to you. We thought it must have been Lucy's father."

"But I haven't had any new crows," said the Queen. "Only that pigeon—that was you, dear," she said to Lucy. "And a robin not too long ago, and a wild goose, and a raven."

"A raven!" said Oscar. "They're black, aren't they? Don't they look like crows?"

"Well, I suppose one might say that a raven looks a little like a crow," said the Queen. "Much larger, though. Hard to mistake a raven for a crow, *I* think."

"Lucy! Could your father have turned himself into a raven?" said Oscar.

"He looked like a crow to me." Lucy had read a poem about a raven at school. *Quoth the Raven, "Nevermore."* It had never occurred to her that the raven in the poem would look like a crow.

"Where is the raven you bought, Your Majesty?" said Oscar. "Not in the throne room . . ."

"Heavens no!" said the Queen. "Ravens can't abide cages. I keep them on the small courtyard lawn, outside those windows there. I have to keep their wings clipped, of course."

Lucy and Oscar were already at the windows. "Lift me up! Lift me up!" said Lucy. Oscar made a step of his hands, and she pulled herself up to the window sill.

"Do you see him?"

"I can't tell. There's about a hundred ravens out there."

"Eighty-seven!" said the Queen. "Don't just stand there, Bertram! Do something!"

"What would you have me do?"

"I don't know—some sort of transforming spell," the Queen said impatiently. "After all, you do have a talent for changing one thing into another."

"I've already explained, Leona, that I no longer have a familiar. I have no power."

"The problem isn't changing Lucy's father back into himself, ma'am. We've got a potion for that. The problem is finding him in the first place," Oscar explained. "How do we get down to the courtyard?"

They followed the Queen through a small door at the far end of the throne room, down a steep flight of stairs, out an open doorway, and into a field of moving ink spots. There were ravens everywhere, circling about a large rectangle of weedy grass that was surrounded by high stone walls. Lucy watched as one raven—it *did* look like an enormous crow—leaped across the lawn toward them, its wings sweeping upward like exclamation points. "Dad?" she called.

But the raven veered away, bossing other ravens out of its path with its raucous cries. "This isn't going to work," said Lucy. "Even if he is here, we'll never get him to come to us."

All the same they tried. Lucy called for him over and over. She even tried singing "Billy Boy" in the hope that the familiar song would stir up memories. But none of the ravens showed any interest. They did nothing but mill about, peck at the ground, and chase each other.

"It's no use! He's been a raven for too long," said Lucy.

"Isn't there anything you can do?" Oscar asked the King.

He shook his head. "Even if Tom were to come back, I would be powerless. A sorcerer's familiar must have the form of an animal."

"Maybe we could test the birds one by one. We could put a drop of potion on each one to see if it turns into my father." Even as Lucy made this suggestion, she saw its shortcoming. What if they ran out of potion before they found her father?

"Lucy," Oscar said suddenly. "Could I see that necklace of yours?"

"This?" Lucy held up the medallion. "Why?"

Oscar took it from her. His finger traced the design around the pentagon-shaped hole in the medallion's center. "There was a picture of this in the attic," he said. "I think Lavonne drew it. But I didn't know you had the real thing."

"So what if I did?"

"Lavonne called it a traveling talisman."

"A what?"

"It's supposed to be magic. You put your finger through this hole and tell it where you want to go."

Lucy took the traveling talisman from Oscar and pointed at the hole. "You mean this?"

Oscar looked alarmed. "Careful! If it really works, it will take you *anywhere*. Egypt, the moon, wherever you tell it."

"What if it does? What's that got to do with my father?"

"Well, suppose it *is* magic. Why couldn't you tell it to take you to your father?"

"Oh!" Lucy's eyes traveled across the courtyard, watching the shifting pattern of ravens on the grass. "Oh, I see!"

"Wait!" said Oscar, grabbing her hand as it moved toward the hole in the talisman. "I just thought of something. What if your father isn't in the courtyard? Suppose he's flying about somewhere in the clouds."

"She'll fall to her death," said the King, who had been listening with interest.

"I know he's in the courtyard," said Lucy. She didn't know, but saying she did made her feel brave. She pushed her finger through the hole and said, "Take me to my father!"

Nothing happened. "It doesn't work," said Lucy.

Oscar gave a sigh. "I suppose it was a long shot."

"Now just a minute," said the King. "I know a few things about magic, and that object looks magical enough to me. How did you say it worked, sir?" he asked Oscar.

"You put your finger through the hole and say where you want to go."

"Well, that isn't exactly what the Lady Lucy did. Or, more precisely, that isn't exactly what the Lady Lucy *said*."

Oscar and Lucy looked at each other. "I told it to take me to my father," said Lucy.

"But that's not a *place*," said Oscar, and from the look he gave her, Lucy knew he was thinking the exact same thing she was. "Go ahead!" he said, nodding.

Lucy put her finger through the hole again. "Take me to the place where my father is!" she said.

Instantly, it was as if a strong hand had jerked her arm and pulled her headfirst through the traveling talisman. It was like diving into water—all around her the air fizzed. She was upside down. She was falling.

Just before she slammed into the ground she thought of cereal being shaken out of a box.

She landed on her left side. Something under her knees was thrashing about, trying to extricate itself from her legs. She rolled to one side. "There he goes!" she heard Oscar shout.

"Watch him!" she shrieked as she leaped to her feet.

But none of the others were fast enough. By the time they reached Lucy's side, no one was sure which raven was her father.

"Try again," said Oscar. "Only this time don't let him get away.

So she tried again. "Take me to where my father is," she said, and this time the traveling talisman tossed her onto her back. She could feel a raven caught under her shoulder. Its body twisted under her weight. "Get the potion!" she gasped.

Oscar was feeling in his pockets. "I haven't got it." He turned to the Queen. "I think I gave it to you, Your Majesty."

"But I don't have it," said the Queen, surprised.

"Hurry!" said Lucy. Either she was going to crush her father to death, or somehow he would twist just far enough to bite her or tear at her with his talons.

"I gave it to you, and you used it to change Lucy back into herself," said Oscar.

"But I haven't got it now," said the Queen.

"Maybe you set it down somewhere."

"I suppose I must have."

"Oh!" cried Lucy, rolling away. "I can't lie here anymore. He's going to rip a piece out of my back!" The raven was struggling to stand up. Its wing was dragging on the ground. "Where is the potion?" said Lucy.

"Look out!" Oscar shouted.

Lucy's head turned in time to see a streak of black racing toward them across the grass. It was a cat.

"It's Tom!" cried Oscar.

"No!" Lucy screamed as the cat leaped at her father. Then Oscar pushed her aside and dove forward, grabbing Tom by the hindquarters. He dragged Tom backward, and Tom turned belly up, clawing with his back feet. Oscar let go with a bellow.

"Bertram! Do something!" shrieked the Queen.

Now Tom was tearing into Lucy's father. Though her father was fighting back, he was clearly losing the battle. "Stop it! Stop it!" Lucy screamed.

"Tom!" shouted the King. "I command you to stop!"

But Tom didn't stop. He had Lucy's father pinned to the ground. His teeth were sinking into the raven's neck. "Stop! Stop!" Lucy sobbed.

She didn't see the King raise his staff in the air. She barely heard him as he shouted what must have been intended to be the most expeditious spell possible:

"Evil cat—never more!
Go back to what you were before!"

And Tom, the cat, became Tom, the boy—a catlike boy who crouched on all fours. He let the raven's limp body drop to the ground. "I had to do it, Your Majesty," he said. "I couldn't let him punish you."

# CHAPTER TWENTY-THREE
## THE WRONG ENDING

He's not *quite* dead," said the Queen, leaning over the limp black thing that was Lucy's father.

"He's alive, Lucy!" said Oscar.

The answer to the question that Lucy had been too scared to ask didn't relieve her fear. It only numbed it a bit, like Novocain at the dentist's office.

Tom had drunk the last of the potion. That was how he had changed himself into a cat. He was admitting all this to the King, who was interrogating him and threatening him with a stick. Tom had been certain that Lucy's father would punish the King. That was what sorcerers did. They punished other sorcerers for something called *abuse of power* by stripping them of their magical abilities, by taking away their familiars. "I was only tryin' to protect you, Your Majesty!" Tom whimpered.

"Liar!" the King roared. "If I had my powers, I'd change you into the rat you are and throw you to the cats!"

Now the King was banishing Tom again. Perhaps this time it would work, Lucy thought as she watched Tom leave the courtyard.

It's just a story, she reminded herself. A story with characters who could surprise you, who could catch you off-guard. Anything could happen in a story. You could lose everything, she thought, looking at Oscar. A king could steal your life, your family. A cat could kill your father.

The King laid his hand on Lucy's shoulder. "There is still hope, my dear," he said, his voice gentle. "If your father wakes—he may be able to change himself back to human form. His injuries will vanish in the course of the transformation."

But the Queen was shaking her head. "He won't wake. He's too badly hurt. And I'm afraid there isn't much time."

Lucy couldn't help herself. She began to cry.

"Don't, Lucy. Please don't," said Oscar. "Your father will be all right."

"He's dying!"

"He's not going to die. What kind of a story would that be? It wouldn't make any sense!"

"Bad things happen all the time in stories," argued Lucy, her voice thick with tears. "People die—like Snow White's mother, and Cinderella's mother, *and* her father."

"Bad things do happen in stories. But the stories have to end right. It isn't right for your father to die."

"But your parents are dead!" Lucy cried, careless of how she made Oscar feel. "You'll never see them again, all because of a few sentences you wrote. That isn't right either. If it can happen to you, why can't it happen to me?"

If her words hurt him, Oscar didn't show it. "It won't happen because we won't let it happen," he said. "There's got to be something we can do."

"Like *what*?"

"Well—maybe we can get more potion." Oscar looked at the King, but the King shook his head.

"I don't see how," he said.

"Aren't there any other magicians around?" said Oscar.

The King shook his head.

"Did your father have any more of that potion, dear?" asked the Queen, putting her arm around Lucy's shoulders.

"I don't think so—just that bottle," said Lucy. She thought of tidying the attic with her mother, arranging papers on the worktable, sweeping broken glass from the floor. She hadn't seen any other potion then. She thought of her father, showing her how the potion worked. Even then she hadn't seen anything but that one little blue bottle. And Walter—Oscar—had come bounding across the table and knocked it to the floor. She remembered pushing spilled potion back into the bottle, watching the potion drip between the floorboards. "Oh!" she cried. "I know! I know where to find more potion!"

"Where?" said Oscar.

But Lucy was already pulling the traveling talisman from her neck. "There isn't time to explain. Watch over my father. I'll be back in a minute." She put her finger through the pentagon-shaped hole and said, "Take me to the attic of The Brick."

This time the sensation of falling lasted longer and the fizziness seemed to penetrate her skin and bones. Lucy had barely enough time to wonder whether it was because she was traveling farther—between worlds—

before she crashed like a meteorite onto the attic worktable. Papers and paraphernalia—some of it scientific, some of it magical, and much of it glass—went flying. Lucy rolled over and fell off the table.

She lay on the floor, watching the streaks of dusty sunlight from the window, listening to her own breathing, and wondering whether she had broken any bones. Her ear hurt; when she touched it, her hand came away sticky with blood.

No time to worry about that now. She must find the potion. She stood up and stepped carefully across the floor, her feet crunching on glass. When she thought she was in the right place, she crouched down. Her eyes traveled methodically across the floor, moving from crack to crack. She couldn't see anything between the wide floorboards. What if the potion had soaked into the wood? What if it had evaporated?

Then her eyes moved on and she saw a sparkle of blue. "There!" she said out loud. Only a drop, but a drop of potion was all she needed. That and something to put it in. Her hand picked up an unbroken test tube. She looked about for something she could use to coax the potion out of the crack. There was a pencil on the table—too large. She grabbed a pair of scissors, using one of the blades to reach into the crack. "Almost got it," she murmured. But the potion wouldn't stick to the scissors. She used them to pry up a long, slender splinter of wood from the floor. She bent the wood so that she could push it under the liquid.

"Careful," she whispered. The potion quivered like a drop of dew on a twig. "There!" she said as she dropped the splinter into the test tube.

And then she heard her mother. "Hello?" Her mother's voice sounded timid, frightened. "Who's there?"

Frantically, Lucy looked around for something—anything—with which to stopper the test tube. Her eyes swept across the worktable. She saw her father's mouse—his familiar, curled up in the sawdust at the bottom of its cage. Then she saw a neat stack of papers; she grabbed the top sheet and ripped off a piece. She crumpled it and stuffed it into the top of the test tube.

"Lucy?"

Too late! She whirled around to see her mother peering at her from the trapdoor entrance to the attic. Her mother's face looked mistrustful, as if she thought Lucy was a shadow or a trick of light.

"Mom . . ."

"Lucy!" Her mother was all the way up the stairs now. "Lucy! Is it really you?"

"Mom!"

Lucy almost fell over as her mother grabbed her and hugged her. "It's you! It's really you! Oh, I've been so worried!" her mother cried.

"Mom, please —"

"You're bleeding!"

"I'm okay, Mom."

"I thought you were dead!" Tears were streaming down her mother's face. "Where have you been? We've been so worried—oh! I've got to call Helen and Byron. And Ray Jensen—he's had the state police looking for you. Where have you been all these weeks?"

Weeks! Lucy wasn't sure just how long she had been a bird, but she felt certain it hadn't been weeks. Her mother entrapped her in another hug, and Lucy struggled to free herself. "Mom—it's about Dad—"

"Your father! Have you seen him?" Her mother leaned back to look at her. "Where is he?"

"Mom, I've got to go to him!" said Lucy, pulling away.

"Lucy—what's wrong? Where have you been all this time? Where is your father?"

Maybe dead by now, thought Lucy. "I'll explain everything as soon as I can," she said. "But there isn't time now. You just have to trust me. I'll be back."

"What do you mean?"

That was the last thing Lucy heard her mother say, because she had already put her finger through the hole in the talisman once again. "Take me to the place where my father is," she said.

The very next thing she said was "I've got it!" and then "Oh, no!" because she had landed on top of her father again.

"Quick, Lucy," said Oscar, helping her up and taking the test tube.

"Is he—is he still . . ."

"He's still alive, dear." The Queen's hands were cradling the raven's head. Its wing was twisted at an odd angle.

"I was stupid," said Lucy, her vision blurring as tears filled her eyes. "I told the traveling talisman to take me to where my father was. I crushed him."

Oscar was already digging the crumpled paper out of the test tube. "He'll be fine, Lucy."

"I tried to hurry. But my mother saw me."

"You weren't even gone a minute," said Oscar.

So time did run differently in the two worlds, thought Lucy. Then Oscar handed her the test tube and she drew out the wooden splinter. The drop of potion was still clinging to it.

For a second she worried. What if the lifeless bird lying on the ground wasn't her father after all? She touched the potion to the bird's wing. "I hope —" she started to say, and then she was knocked aside because what had been air was now filled up by her father, ever so much larger than the raven he had been, alive and whole and unbroken, blinking up at her and saying, "What the heck?" And the ending that had seemed so wrong only a short time before became the right ending after all.

# CHAPTER TWENTY-FOUR

## KINGS AND QUEENS

O scar was having a hard time grasping the fact that something good had happened at last.

He was sitting on one side of a long table in the palace's enormous banquet hall. Lucy and her father were sitting on the other side of the table; Tom's captains sat at a table across the room. King Bertram and Queen Leona were sitting at their own royal table on a dais at the end of the hall. Everyone was eating scrambled eggs; that was all there was to eat, according to the Queen, who had invited everyone to a feast in celebration of their finding Lucy's father.

Lucy was telling her father about their adventures— about writing in *The Book of Story Beginnings,* about coming to Cat'n'berd Island, about getting thrown off Captain Mack's ship, and then about the King and the terrible scene at the well. "Oscar turned me into a pigeon, Dad," she said.

An echo of the panic Oscar had felt came back to him—his fear of the King, watching Lucy fly away, then realizing his horrible mistake. "I didn't mean to," he said. But Lucy's father was smiling, enjoying the story.

Now Lucy was describing how Captain Mack had captured her. "She brought me to the palace and sold me to the Queen. So I was here when Oscar and Tom arrived with all the cats."

Tom and all the cats. Again Oscar felt the echoing panic. He hadn't known where Lucy was! And she was talking so cheerfully now, as if she had forgotten how terrified she herself had been only an hour ago. She might just as well have been describing an exciting story she had read in a book. Then again, thought Oscar, it *was* a story—a story with a beginning, a middle, and an end. Now that the end had come at last, what was there to be afraid of anymore?

Lucy was showing her father the traveling talisman. "We used it to find you when you were a raven, Dad, and we didn't know which raven. I kept landing on top of you."

"Don't think I didn't notice!" said her father,

laughing. A picture flashed in Oscar's mind like a flickering lamp: Ma's face, her eyes crinkled in a smile as he told her a funny story about something he and Earl had done.

"I used the traveling talisman to go home, Dad," said Lucy.

*Home,* thought Oscar. Like all important words, it was simple but powerful, capable of turning his mind toward thoughts he had been avoiding for days. What would it be like to go home? To talk to Ma the way Lucy was talking to her father? *There was a sea, right in front of our house, Ma. I climbed in the boat and . . .* Oscar felt alone all of a sudden, as if the table separating him from Lucy and her father were water and they were standing on a distant shore. They could go home and he could not.

"Home!" Lucy exclaimed just then. Oscar stared at her. Had she read his thoughts?

"Dad—we've got to go home right away!" she said. "Mom doesn't know what's happened to us. I saw her when I used the traveling talisman to go back for the potion. We've been gone for weeks and weeks."

"Has it really been that long?" said her father.

"I think time goes more slowly in this world," said Lucy. "A minute here could be a day or even a week back home."

Again the word *home.* And now the word *time,* just as powerful. It was years, not miles, that separated Oscar from the place he belonged.

"If that's true, your mother must be worried," said Lucy's father. "I suppose I ought to zip home and tell her we're safe and sound." He was studying the traveling talisman, turning it over and over in his hand. "I read about this thing in Lavonne's notes. Her description of the metallic composition sounded so interesting that I tried making it. Are you sure it really works?"

"Well, yes. But it hurts. It practically threw me down on the attic table," said Lucy. And then, "Dad!" Her voice grew alarmed as her father put his finger through the hole in the talisman.

"Not to worry," he told her. "If what you say is right, I'll be back in less than a minute."

"Can't we go with you?" said Lucy.

"If I recall correctly, the talisman works for only one person at a time."

"What if Mom's not home?"

"I'll do what you did," said her father. "Take me to where Jean is," he added, and then he was gone.

"Oh!" Lucy rolled her eyes. "I wish he would think things through once in a while! He doesn't even know what my mother's doing right now. What if she's driving the car? What if he crashes down on top of her and they have an accident?"

"It'll be all right," Oscar said quickly.

"Do you really think so?" Lucy asked.

To his own surprise, Oscar did. Why was he so sure that Lucy's story would end happily? Why couldn't he be sure of his own story?

"I just want to go home," said Lucy.

So do I, thought Oscar. He might even have said so, too, if something hadn't drawn his attention away. It was the Queen's voice, rising shrilly above the low rumble of conversation in the banquet hall. "You've said you're sorry, Bertram, but you can't possibly be sorry enough!" she cried. "All my birds are dead."

"For heaven's sake, Leona —they're not all dead. What do you call these obnoxious creatures?" The King waved his hand around the banquet hall, which, like every other room in the palace, was filled from floor to ceiling with stacks of bird cages.

"Oh, honestly! Are they fighting again?" said Lucy.

It seemed they were. Oscar couldn't hear what King Bertram was saying. He was muttering, shaking his fork in the air for emphasis. The look on the Queen's face made Oscar think of Ma, when Pa would go on and on, ranting about one thing or another.

"It's my fault," Oscar murmured.

"Why?" said Lucy.

"It's as if they can't do anything but fight," Oscar said. "Because of the beginning I gave them. The King likes cats and the Queen likes birds. They're so different they can't get along." He could remember the words of his story beginning as if they were right in front of him: *And just as cats and birds never get along, so it was that the King and Queen never got along. And everyone in the country suffered as a result.*

He looked across the room at Tom's captains. Some were looking nervously toward the royal table. Some were talking in low, worried voices to each other. Others simply looked glum, sitting with their heads in their hands.

"I suppose *The Book of Story Beginnings* is writing the rest of the story right now," said Lucy.

"It's doing a pretty rotten job of it." Oscar was thinking of the King and Queen's story, of course. But he was thinking about his own story as well. *The boat carried me to an island, Ma. And then a crazy sort of King changed me into a cat.*

There was a crash just then as the Queen threw a plate at the King.

"Why doesn't she just forgive him?" said Lucy. "He's said he's sorry."

"He can say he's sorry a thousand times and she'll never forgive him," said Oscar. "That's what the story is about."

"If she loves him, she ought to forgive him," said Lucy.

"Maybe she doesn't love him."

"Of course she loves him! He's the King. She's the Queen. Kings and queens in fairy tales always love each other," Lucy argued.

"What makes you think this is a fairy tale?" Oscar asked curiously.

"It's just like a fairy tale. Everybody's doing silly things that don't make any sense. It's like the king in 'Sleeping Beauty' ordering everybody to burn their spindles, and everybody does it, just like that. Or in 'Cinderella,' when every maiden in the land has to try on a shoe, just because the prince says so. Only here it's a king changing people into cats and a queen locking up all the birds and nobody questioning it."

Oscar looked at Tom's captains. With every crash, they cowered deeper into their chairs. Lucy was right: they were fairy-tale subjects, at the mercy of the King and Queen. *Not a very pretty situation,* he thought. He had given all of them a bad beginning, not just the King and Queen. The bad beginning had led to a terrible middle, and he supposed it would all lead to a terrible end. A fury as sudden and strong as a tornado rose up in Oscar. What kind of story was it, where a person's fate was determined by a cat eating a canary, by an unforgiving queen, and by a king so full of rage he turned people into cats?

Dimly, he heard Lucy's voice. "She does love him," she was saying. "She has to love him. Otherwise it doesn't make any sense. You're the one who said stories have to have the right ending. You were right about my father. I didn't believe you, but he was fine in the end. It's the same with your story about the King and Queen. There's only one right ending."

*My* story, thought Oscar. It *was* his story now, in a way he had never expected or wanted. For all Lucy's talk of the right ending, of a happy ending for the King and Queen, Oscar couldn't see how it would make up for what had happened to him. How could it make up for losing his family, for losing everything he loved?

No. If there really was a right ending to his story, he couldn't see it.

# CHAPTER TWENTY-FIVE
## THE BIRD TRADERS

Oscar looked so upset that Lucy had the uncomfortable feeling she had said the wrong thing. The feeling didn't last long. We're going home, she thought with rising joy. "I wish my father would come back," she said.

Before Oscar could respond, however, a shout rose above the King and Queen's bickering voices. "Beggin' your pardon!" a voice called.

Looking toward the royal table, Lucy saw a girl jumping up and down in front of the King and Queen. She was waving her arms for attention, and her long yellow braids were swinging like ropes. Lucy remembered (rather foggily, because the memory came from the time when she was a pigeon) that the girl's name was Cora.

"Beggin' your pardon, Your Majesties!" shouted Cora.

"What is it?" said the Queen, stopping midscold and glaring like a hawk.

"If you please, Your Majesty—there's folks here. Bird traders, they call themselves."

"Bird traders? I don't want to sell any of my birds," said the Queen.

"Put the whole lot of them up for sale!" roared the King.

"They ain't here to buy birds, sire, just to sell 'em. They got a whole flock of 'em."

"We want no more birds here unless they're plucked and ready to parboil!" growled the King, and the Queen gave him a stabbing glance.

"Send them in directly, Cora!" she said.

As Cora trotted obediently toward the far end of the banquet hall, Lucy heard an odd noise. It sounded like the wail of an approaching siren. As the noise grew louder, she detected smaller, squeaking overtones, as if someone were pulling along a wagon with loose wheels. Then the noise stumbled into the room. It was Captain Mack and Jarvis, loaded down with cages full of squeaking, shrieking seagulls. Behind them, a wailing Phoebe bobbed along in Millie's arms.

"What are they doing here?" said Oscar.

As the visitors traipsed forward, the Queen gave a cry of surprise. She shoved her chair back and hurried around the royal table. She leaned down from the dais and whisked Phoebe from Millie's arms. "My little lark! My sweet child! Whatever is the matter?" she exclaimed as she bustled back to her seat.

"The baby's a bit tired, Your Majesty," said Millie, trailing behind.

"She doesn't look tired. Perhaps she's hungry."

"Beggin' your pardon, Your Majesty, but she ain't hungry," said Captain Mack, climbing up on the dais herself. She set down her load of cages with a clatter. "She's been eatin' like a whale since the day she was born, and today wasn't no different. It's these birds have got her riled. We took this lot of gulls on board the *Rosalie* just this mornin'. Found 'em flappin' about the docks. Caught 'em straightaway. Poor little mite there crawled over and put her hand in a cage. Nearly had her pinkie taken off by one of these feisty fellows!"

"Oh, no!" The Queen looked horrified.

"No harm done. But the kid's terrified of birds somethin' awful now," said the captain.

"Those naughty birds!" said the Queen, switching into baby talk. "Seagulls are nasty, bullying creatures, aren't they, my pet? Naughty, naughty birdies!"

Captain Mack cleared her throat. "About these birds, Your Majesty. We been busy as can be all day, feedin' 'em the best food to be found. We was sure you'd want to buy 'em."

"The birds are mine already. They escaped from the palace this morning," said the Queen.

Captain Mack looked caught off-guard, but Millie quickly stepped in. "That's just what we figured, Your Majesty. We knew you'd be pleased to have 'em returned to you."

"Thought there might be a reward, Your Majesty," added Captain Mack.

"A reward," murmured the Queen.

"Compensation like—for the care of the birds," said the captain.

The Queen, preoccupied with Phoebe, barely looked up. "Cora—fetch twenty silvers from the treasury."

"Twenty silvers!" Captain Mack protested. "We got a dozen birds here! We missed the outgoin' tide on account of 'em."

"Twenty golds, then!"

At this the King, his voice full of disbelief, burst out, "Am I to understand, Leona, that you are going to pay this woman twenty gold coins for your own birds?"

"Fetch the money, Cora!" the Queen commanded.

"If you please, Your Majesty, there is no money. I gave you the last of it yesterday."

"No money?" said the Queen.

"No money! What's happened to the money?" blustered the King.

"Stop fussing, Bertram. Take this child while I find something to give these people for their trouble." The Queen thrust Phoebe into the King's arms and began to search her pockets, scattering birdseed on the floor. At last she looked about and seized a jewel-encrusted gold cup from the table. "Take this," she said.

"Ouch!" said the King just then, and Captain Mack thrust the cup inside her jacket as if she thought the King would take it back.

"Ouch!" said the King again, and Lucy saw that Phoebe was tugging on his beard.

"Look at that! She likes you, Bertram!" said the Queen.

"Take her!" said the King.

"Get your sister, Millie, and we'll be on our way," said the captain.

"No!" said the Queen, seizing Phoebe from the King's arms. Unfortunately, Phoebe didn't let go of the beard, and the King was yanked into an embrace with the Queen. With Phoebe sandwiched between them, Lucy thought they looked like an old-fashioned family portrait, all frowns.

"I don't want you to take her!" cried the Queen.

"We got a ship to sail back home, Your Majesty. It don't make no money sittin' in the harbor. We've stayed longer than we should've already."

"No!" The Queen drew away from Captain Mack. "Bertram! Do something!"

"Do! What can I do?" The King was trying to disentangle his beard from Phoebe's fists.

"Let me keep her. What do you want?" the Queen asked Captain Mack. "There's more gold cups. You can have all of them!"

"I ain't sellin' my own niece!"

"But I want her!" said the Queen, bursting into tears.

"Now, Leona. Don't cry." The King put his arms around the Queen.

"I can't help it!" she sobbed. "She's such a beautiful baby."

"Stop, Leona!" he begged her. "I can't bear to see you cry!"

He *does* care about her, thought Lucy. And then it struck her. "They aren't fighting anymore," she said.

"What?" said Oscar.

"Look! They're not fighting anymore." An idea was unfolding in Lucy's mind. "It's just like your brother Morris getting the croup!" she said.

"What are you talking about?" said Oscar.

"Don't you remember what we talked about in the rowboat? Your ma and pa had that big fight, and your pa moved out. But he came back in the middle of the night because Morris was sick."

"What does that have to do with anything?" said Oscar.

"*I never heard anybody making up.* That's just what you said about your ma and pa. But they must have made up. Or if they didn't, it's because the fight never really mattered in the first place. It didn't matter because Morris having the croup and almost dying was more important."

"I still don't see—"

"Oh!" said Lucy in exasperation. "Just look at the King and Queen. They haven't made up their quarrel, but all the same, they're not fighting anymore. They're not fighting because they care more about Phoebe, just like your ma and pa cared about Morris!"

Just then Captain Mack's voice rang out. "She ain't your baby! So give her back!"

"But she can't take her away," said Lucy, alarmed to see that the scene on the dais had become a scuffle.

The captain was shouting and trying to tug Phoebe away from the Queen. The Queen was crying and trying to hold on. "Captain Mack!" Lucy shouted.

The captain didn't hear.

"Captain Mack!" Lucy stood up and yelled as loud as she could.

This time the captain stopped shouting and looked at her. The Queen stopped crying and looked as well. Everyone was staring at her. Lucy could feel her face getting hot.

"What is it?" said Captain Mack.

"You musn't take Phoebe," said Lucy.

"Who says?" The captain was squinting at Lucy. Then recognition dawned on her face as her eyes alighted on Oscar. "Why, it's Billy Boy!" she exclaimed.

"Lucy, what are you doing?" whispered Oscar.

"I'm trying to give your story a happy ending," Lucy murmured. Then she called out, "I believe you are in need of a nurse for Phoebe, Captain Mack. Someone to take care of her while you're at sea!"

"A nurse?" said the Queen.

Lucy moved toward the dais. "Phoebe's an orphan," she explained. "Captain Mack was boarding her in town, but now she hasn't got a place to keep her. . . ."

"How d'you know about that?" said the captain.

"An orphan!" The Queen's eyes widened.

"I treat her like my own child," said Captain Mack.

"Bertram, we could adopt her!"

"Phoebe's my own kin! Nobody's goin' to adopt her!" said the captain.

"Oh, Auntie!" cried Millie. "Please let her be adopted! I can stay with her."

"We can make her the Royal Ward, Bertram. She'll have her very own nursery, and a nanny."

"I could be the nanny!" Millie said eagerly.

"Hold on!" said Captain Mack. "You can't just take a baby from its family. It ain't right. And as for you, Missy," she said to Millie, "last I heard, you was to be captain after me. It's always been my dream to have you take over when I'm gone."

"But I don't want to be a ship's captain!" cried Millie. "I want to be a lady!"

"And here you are hankerin' to be a nanny!" Captain Mack scoffed.

"I'd be a nanny at the palace! That's just like being a lady!"

"I'll not have it, Millie! Get your sister. We're goin'."

"Captain Mack!" called Lucy.

"What is it?" said the captain.

"You could ask for a ship."

"A ship! I already got a ship!"

"But you want a bigger one," said Lucy. "You want a ship with three masts!"

"If it's a ship you want, you'll have it!" said the Queen. "There's a whole fleet down at the harbor. You can have your pick of them."

Lucy thought she saw the captain's eyes flicker with interest.

"You can't just give away a ship!" said the King.

"You don't need them all, Bertram!"

"Never heard of such a thing! A king trading a ship for a baby!"

"Honestly, Bertram!" The Queen stamped her foot. "We're the King and Queen! We can do as we wish! And here is a baby—a child we can call our own!" The Queen burst into tears again.

The King took Phoebe from her arms. "My dear! I would give the entire fleet to make you happy! Surely you know that!"

"I didn't know it!"

"Well, it's true!" The King shifted his head sideways as Phoebe grasped his beard.

"If that's a real offer, I'll take it! You can have the baby," said Captain Mack.

"Oh, Auntie!" cried Millie. "You mean I can be a lady?"

"A glorified nanny," Captain Mack snorted. "And when you get tired of it, Missy, don't be surprised to hear me say I told you so."

"Oh, Auntie! Thank you!" Millie threw her arms about the captain.

"Oh, Bertram!" said the Queen, gazing at Phoebe. "Look at our beautiful baby!"

*A happy ending,* thought Lucy, and she looked around for Oscar.

# CHAPTER TWENTY-SIX

## A SHIP'S CAT

Oscar caught only a glimpse of Lucy's face, just enough to see that it was flushed with triumph. Then the air in front of him exploded with a loud crack. A flash of red and green sparks showered down on the table. Oscar coughed and leaped back as blueberry-colored smoke billowed out of nothing. He rubbed his stinging eyes and looked up to see Lucy's father standing on the table. He was holding a small branch in his hand. There was a white mouse on his shoulder. "That worked well!" he said, grinning. Then he noticed that he was standing on a tray of cold omelets. He stepped out of them and knocked over a jug of wine.

"Ah! Our honored guest returns!" the King's voice

boomed from the dais. "Welcome, sir! Welcome to our celebration!"

Lucy's father bowed, then climbed down from the table.

"We are pleased to present the new Royal Ward, Princess Phoebe," said the King, sparking a delighted smile from the Queen. "Not to mention our new Admiral of the Royal Fleet." The King gave an imperial wave in Captain Mack's direction.

"And me, sire! Lady Millie!" clamored Millie.

Lucy's father gave a pleasant nod toward the dais, then murmured, "Will someone please tell me what's going on?"

"We finished Oscar's story about the King and Queen, Dad," said Lucy.

"And the one about the ship of orphans," said Oscar.

"You're right! I hadn't even thought of that!" said Lucy, looking pleased. "And now that we've found you, Dad, that's three stories ended."

Oscar wished that Lucy would remember the last story, but she didn't. "We can go home now, Dad!" she said.

"Home!" said her father. "I promised your mother we would hurry back. You were absolutely right about time, Lucy. We've been missing almost six weeks. We've been on the news, in the papers . . ."

"How will we get home?" said Lucy.

*Home,* thought Oscar, and he didn't even hear the answer to her question. He could hear a baby crying. For a moment, he thought of Morris, howling in the middle of the night. But it was only Phoebe.

"What is it, darling?" said the Queen.

"If you please, Your Majesty. The baby's just tired is all," said Millie.

"The kid needs a nap, that's what," said Captain Mack. "Though how she'll ever get one here I don't know, what with all the squawkin' and screechin'."

The Queen looked concerned. "You think my birds will keep her awake?"

"Oh, I reckon she'll get used to the noise eventually. Just let her cry awhile. She'll go to sleep soon enough," said Captain Mack.

The Queen looked shocked by this suggestion. "I don't want her to cry!" she said.

"No child ever died of cryin'. It'll toughen 'er up— you'll see!"

"Indeed, I will not see!" said the Queen, looking indignant. "The birds will simply have to go. Bertram! I want to let my birds out. You've got to do something about the cats."

"What's that?" said the King, straining to hear over Phoebe's cries.

"The cats! You'll have to change them back into people. Then I can let the birds out of their cages, and it will be quiet, and this poor, exhausted child can go to sleep."

"I can't change them back. I told you—I've lost all my powers."

"What are we to do?" said the Queen.

I know what to do, thought Oscar. And perhaps because it had been a long time since he had known exactly what to do, he felt a little cheered. "Sir," he said to Lucy's father, "do you suppose you could undo the King's spell?"

"Me?" Lucy's father raised his eyebrows.

"You're a magician, Dad," said Lucy.

"Maybe the King could tell you what to do," said Oscar.

"Let's ask him," said Lucy.

The King was agreeable to Oscar's suggestion, and a short time later, they found themselves in the throne room. The vast army of cats, still somewhat battle-fatigued, were scattered about in various states of repose.

The King was giving instructions to Lucy's father. "What you need, sir, is an undoing spell. Which is to say that you must do everything backward. First off, consider your magic wand." The King held up the small branch that Lucy's father had brought back from The Brick. "For an ordinary spell, you've got to hold it in the proper direction, with the end that was originally farther from the root of the tree pointing away from you. For an undoing spell, you simply turn the wand around, like so. Next, you must ask for exactly what you *don't* want, all the while acting as if you don't care about the outcome. (That's because in ordinary spell-making, you *do* care.)" The King handed the wand to Lucy's father. "The spell should rhyme, of course," he added.

"Right." Lucy's father paused to think. "I've got it, I think. Now watch out, everyone. If I'm not mistaken, it's going to get a lot more crowded in here." He raised the wand, yawned deliberately, then spoke in a lackadaisical voice:

> "Keep your tails, keep your paws;
>   Keep your whiskers; keep your claws;
>   Stay as you are, cats everywhere.
>   If you'd rather be human—I don't care."

Instantly, the room swelled with the sound of hundreds of people gasping out loud. From all sides there were cries of "What?" and "Where am I?" and "What's going on?" There were men, women, and children everywhere, turning in confusion and bumping into one another.

"Why, it's the King's palace!" said a man standing near Oscar.

"And there's the King and Queen," said a woman standing next to the man.

"Say! Look at the baby," said the woman.

Now the King was climbing up on his throne. He stood on the seat. "My people!" he shouted above the hubbub. At the sound of his voice, everyone in the room fell into obedient silence. (Just like fairy-tale subjects *would* do, thought Oscar.) "We welcome you to our palace on this great and glorious day," said the King. "On this most remarkable day, which we hereby decree shall henceforth be considered the birthday of our adopted child"—at this, the Queen climbed up on her throne, next to the King. He took Phoebe from her arms and hoisted her into the air—"we present our new Royal Ward, Princess Phoebe!"

The crowd cheered. "You've done it, Dad!" Lucy exclaimed. She looked at Oscar. "It feels just like reading the end of a book, doesn't it?" she said.

More like writing it, thought Oscar. It was funny. He wasn't exactly sure he liked the ending of his story, even though he had played a hand in making it happen. It seemed like a silly sort of ending. He had the same urge to revise that he had sometimes when he wrote in his journal. Only in this case, he didn't know what he would have written instead.

"Now we can go home," said Lucy. "Can we use the traveling talisman, Dad?"

"Not exactly," said her father. "But I think I have an idea. I'll need a quiet sort of place."

"What about the ravens' courtyard?"

Oscar followed Lucy and her father out of the crowded throne room. Did they expect him to come home with them?

"I'm going to try to make a traveling circle," said Lucy's father as they entered the courtyard.

"What's that?" said Lucy.

A voice from behind them cut short the answer to her question. "Sir! Oh, sir!" Whirling around, Oscar saw that it was Tom.

"Where did he come from?" said Lucy. "I thought the King banished him."

Tom hurried forward and dropped to his knees before Lucy's father. "Please, sir! Don't leave me like this!" he cried.

"I don't understand," said Lucy's father.

"Please, sir! I'm nobody as a boy. Change me back into a cat!"

"No!" said Oscar. "You want to be a cat so you can be the King's familiar! You want to be in charge again. You liked having all that power." It seemed to Oscar that Tom was to blame for everything. If it hadn't been for Tom, the King and Queen wouldn't have quarreled. The King wouldn't have changed everyone into cats. He wouldn't have changed *me* into a cat, thought Oscar.

"No, sir!" said Tom, and when Oscar glared at him, he added, "I ain't saying it wasn't great while it lasted. I—I was important. I won't deny likin' it—bein' the King's cat, that is."

He turned his attention to Lucy's father again. "But I think, sir, that I'd be all right if I was just about anybody's cat. I was talkin' to that red-headed girl with the baby."

"Millie?" said Lucy.

"That's her. She was talkin' about ships. She don't like 'em much. Says there's all sorts of rats and mice that you can't do much about. But I could—don't you see? I could do somethin' about the rats and mice."

"You'd like to become a ship's cat, is that it?" said Lucy's father.

"Yes, sir."

"How do we know you won't go back to the King?" said Oscar.

"I won't!" Tom looked hurt.

"Oh, Oscar," said Lucy. "He says he won't."

"I don't trust him. He's nothing but a scoundrel."

"I ain't a scoundrel!" Tom protested.

"Are we really supposed to believe that you won't attack the Queen's birds again?" Oscar was startled by how sharp his own voice sounded—like a father admonishing a child. Then he had the absurd thought that in a way, Tom *was* his child. After all, if it hadn't been for his story beginning, Tom wouldn't even exist.

"I'll be honest with you, sir. I'll try my best to keep away from the Queen's birds. But a cat's a cat, and I can't say for sure what I'll do," said Tom, and Oscar had a queer feeling all of a sudden. He felt as if he were talking to a real person—a boy whom fate had dealt a hard blow, a boy whose only real fault was wanting more than his story seemed willing to give.

There was a long silence before Oscar realized that everyone—Tom included—was waiting for him to make a decision. "I suppose it *is* up to the birds to keep out of harm's way," he said, and any reluctance he had about saying it vanished when he saw the look of gratitude on Tom's face.

Then Lucy's father raised his tree-branch wand.

"This boy here
  wants pointed ears
  and whiskers and a tail
  A ship's cat's what he'd like to be—
  familiar to no one
  and completely free.
  Make it so—and let him sail!"

There was a sleek black shape on the ground. It flicked its tail and veered away from a snapping raven. Tom bounded across the courtyard and disappeared into the palace.

"I suppose he couldn't help it," said Oscar, watching him go. "He had to do what he did."

"What do you mean?" said Lucy.

"Because he was a character in a story. Stories *use* people," said Oscar.

Lucy was quiet. Oscar knew her well enough now to see that she was thinking. Right before she had something important to say, she always closed her mouth, holding her breath for a moment before she spoke. "I think it's the other way around," she said. "People use stories. After all, people have to have some sort of say in things. The King banished Tom, but Tom chose a different ending."

Oscar hadn't thought of it that way before. "Do you think he'll really become a ship's cat?" he wondered.

"If I were one of those rats, I'd watch out!" said Lucy's father with a smile. Then he took his wand and drew it across the grass of the courtyard. Ravens scattered in all directions as he moved in a circle, chanting:

"Outside the circle, here we stand.
Inside the circle are other lands—
Other lands where we would go;
Take us there, when we say so."

A pale green circle, wide as a wagon wheel, glimmered on the dark ground. There was nothing of particular interest inside the circle, only grass.

"Is that it? How does it work?" asked Lucy.

"As far as I know, just like the traveling talisman. You jump in and tell it where you want to go. The only difference is that more than one person can use it. The circle stays behind after you jump. I'll close it up after you two and use the traveling talisman myself. Now, who wants to go first?"

"I'll go," Lucy volunteered. "What do I say when I step in? Home?"

"I can't say *home*." The words blurted out of Oscar before he could stop them.

Lucy looked at him.

He shrugged. "I can't *go* home," he said, trying to use an ordinary sort of voice.

He must have failed, because he could see that Lucy understood at last. "Oh, Oscar!" she said, her face crumpling with concern. She turned to her father and pointed to the traveling circle. "Dad, can this thing take Oscar back home?"

Oscar's breath caught in his throat. Why hadn't he thought of that? He remembered a book of Ma's he had read once—all about a time machine that could take people from one time to another.

Lucy's father looked pensive. "I'm not exactly sure. I suppose it's possible," he said.

"It *has* to be possible," said Lucy, as if by speaking with such certainty she could make it so.

But it might *not* be possible, thought Oscar. In fact, Lucy's father was looking at him the way Pa did sometimes, when he was sizing you up to decide whether you were old enough to be told the truth about something.

"Can it take him home?" said Lucy.

Her father hesitated. "The truth is, I don't know," he said. "Everything I know about traveling talismans and traveling circles comes from reading Aunt Lavonne's notes. Unfortunately, she didn't have a lot to say about time travel. I'd be afraid to have you just jump into that circle without knowing more about what to expect, Oscar."

"I see." Oscar's heart was pounding. He concentrated on the dull rhythm, thinking of soldiers marching across hard ground.

"On the other hand, there may be more to learn from that book Lavonne found," Lucy's father said. "We might find the answer we need there."

"I know we will!" said Lucy.

"Would you mind coming home with us while I do a little research, Oscar?" her father asked.

"I don't mind." Oscar forced himself to smile. It wasn't even that hard, he discovered, not with Lucy looking so enthusiastic. Maybe he could go home after all.

"Wonderful!" said Lucy's father. "Now, Lucy, jump. Right into the circle. And I'd suggest something a little more precise than the word *home*. You don't want to find yourself tumbling down the roof of The Brick!"

# CHAPTER TWENTY-SEVEN

## THINKING ABOUT TIME

Lucy came down with a thud on her chosen destination, the front lawn of The Brick. She lay on her back, smiling up at the sight of a pale blue sky brushed with pink clouds. She could hear birds singing, hundreds of them. But only ordinary sorts of birds, she thought. They were singing because it was morning. The birds at home always sang in the morning.

She had barely stood up when she saw Oscar drop out of nowhere, making a belly-flop landing on the grass. She nearly laughed. "Is that what I looked like when I used the traveling talisman?" she said.

"Is this what it felt like?" Oscar groaned.

"Lucy? Is that you?"

Turning around, Lucy saw her mother running toward them. She caught Lucy up in a hug. "I thought you'd never come! And you, Oscar! Or should I say *Earl Norby*!" She laughed and hugged him as well. "Where's your father, Lucy?"

"He'll be here. He's closing up the traveling circle."

"Traveling *what*?"

Lucy was in the middle of explaining about the traveling circle when her father came crashing down near one of the cement urns. "Shel!" cried her mother as she ran over to help him up.

"What an *awful* way to travel!" said her father.

"Whatever took you so long? Byron and Helen called a half hour ago to find out if you were back yet."

"Do they know where we've been?" asked Lucy.

"No. I told them last night that I had talked to your father on the phone," said her mother. "They wanted to know where you had been, Shel, and I said Texas."

"Texas!"

"It was the first thing that jumped into my mind. Helen called Ray Jensen, and now everyone wants to know what you were *doing* in Texas. I invented something as best I could, but you're going to have to help me patch up the story, Shel."

"We *could* tell the truth," said Lucy's father.

"As if anyone would believe it! Now come inside,

everyone!" Lucy's mother put one arm around Lucy and one around Oscar. "I'll make us some breakfast. And I want to hear all about your adventures!"

As they sat around the table in the kitchen, Lucy kept quiet mostly, listening to Oscar. His face came alive as he talked to her mother. "And then, while we were surrounded by thousands of *cats,* I decided it would be a good idea to change Lucy into a *pigeon*!" he said. Her mother laughed. Oscar laughed as well, and Lucy suddenly had a picture in her mind of Oscar telling his own mother about their adventures. Ma would laugh and laugh.

I'll miss him, thought Lucy, and for a moment, her happiness was muddied by sadness. When her father sent Oscar back in time, she would have to say good-bye. She had the absurd thought of sending letters back and forth in time. Her letters to Oscar would get to him before she was even born. And as for Oscar's letters to her—well, he would probably be dead by the time she read them. It was unsettling to think about time in that way.

She looked at her father. He was just sitting there, drinking coffee with too much sugar the way he always did. He looked perfectly ordinary, perfectly at home, as if he'd never been away at all. As if he hadn't just been wielding a magic wand. It was then that Lucy noticed something missing. "Dad!" she exclaimed, interrupting Oscar in the middle of a sentence. "Where's your mouse?"

Her father set his coffee down. "Good question, Lucy. It has a very interesting answer."

"What happened to him?"

"Well, I had just closed up the traveling circle behind Oscar, when all of a sudden, the mouse leaped off my shoulder and went streaking across the courtyard. Of course, I went after him. But would you believe it? Somebody else went after him as well."

"Who?" said Lucy.

"A certain black cat."

"Tom!" said Oscar. "Did he catch him?"

"He's fast, that Tom. But not fast enough. The mouse made it to the wall of the palace. Just in time, he darted into a hole between the stones."

"What did Tom do?"

"Sort of sauntered off, as if he didn't much care."

"I bet he did care!" said Oscar. "Of all the sneaky things to do!"

"What about the mouse?" asked Lucy.

"I couldn't coax him out. So I left him there."

"Can you perform magic without him?"

"Another good question, Lucy. I'm afraid the answer is no. I tried before I came home. I felt rather silly, actually, pointing that wand, trying to turn one of those ravens into a rat. Luckily, I still had the traveling talisman. And luckily, it still worked."

"But what about Oscar going home? How can you send him back to 1914?" said Lucy.

"There's still the traveling talisman," Oscar said quickly. "Maybe I can use that to go back in time."

They both looked at Lucy's father.

"We can give it a try," he said. "That book of Lavonne's might tell us how to go about it."

Lucy was glad to see Oscar look relieved. But somehow she couldn't help feeling a little disappointed. She thought about her story beginning: *Once upon a time, there was a girl whose father was a magician.* She had wanted her father to turn lead into gold! What other marvelous things might he have done? "It's too bad about your familiar, Dad," she said. "Wouldn't you like to be a magician?"

"Oh, I don't know," said her father as he stirred yet more sugar into his coffee. "If you want my opinion, I don't think I was a very good one. Look at all the trouble I caused."

"Well, you made one good thing happen," said Lucy's mother. She reached across the table and squeezed Oscar's hand. "You found Oscar!"

*   *   *

The story Lucy's mother and father concocted for Aunt Helen, Uncle Byron, and Sheriff Jensen later that morning was an elaborate one. Lucy was barely able to follow the string of glib lies her parents invented. Oscar was introduced to everyone as a distant cousin—a descendent of the original Oscar Martin who had disappeared in 1914. According to Lucy's father, the original Oscar hadn't died. He had gone to Texas and later started a family. Her father claimed to have gone down to Texas to meet the modern-day Oscar, an orphan who was the last surviving descendent of the original Oscar. As Lucy's father was traveling to Texas, the modern-day Oscar had somehow found *his* way up to Iowa. Lucy's mother described how Oscar had pretended to be Earl Norby, then convinced Lucy that she should run away to Texas to find her father.

Lucy's personal opinion was that the story was a lot more complicated and even less believable than what had really happened. All the same, it seemed to satisfy Aunt Helen, who at last put an end to Sheriff Jensen's probing questions by putting her arm around Oscar and saying, "Just think if Lavonne could be here now! How happy she'd be to see her brother's grandson, even if all her talk about magic did turn out to be nonsense!"

*   *   *

The day after they came home was a Saturday. It was also a very important day in the town of Martin, for it was Earl Norby's birthday. "The church is having a party," Aunt Helen told them. "The whole town will show up. Maybe you folks will want to come, too."

They drove to the party in the station wagon, and Oscar marveled at their *automobile* as it rolled down the highway into town. "It's so quiet—like a magic carpet," he said. He poked his head out the window to watch the buildings on Main Street drift by. "Sunderlund's Store used to be there!" he said, pointing to a vacant lot with a couple of tractors in it. "And the livery was there," he added, pointing to the Prairie Cafe. "*This* hasn't changed," he said as they pulled up outside the church.

Oscar had come down to breakfast dressed in his clothes from 1914, but they had found him something more modern so as not to attract attention at the birthday party. All the same, whispers rippled through the crowd gathered at the picnic tables set up in the yard behind the church. Yet Oscar didn't seem to notice that everyone was gawking. His eyes were searching for someone. "Look! There's Earl!" he said, moving forward.

"Over here, Jean!" called Aunt Helen, waving to them from a table laden with food.

So Lucy and her parents went one way, and Oscar went the other, and pretty soon the party went back to being a party. Almost everybody knew Lucy's father, and he kept turning to her mother to introduce her to yet another childhood friend. Lucy watched them. Her mother was laughing as her father told a funny story to someone. She moved closer to him and he put his arm around her. It's another happy ending, thought Lucy. Her father was home, and for the first time, it seemed to her that her family might really belong in The Brick after all.

She looked around for Oscar, finding him where he had been sitting ever since they arrived, on a lawn chair next to Earl Norby. Oscar leaned forward. Lucy was too far away to hear what he said. Whatever it was, it made Earl throw back his head and laugh.

Oscar would go home, too, thought Lucy. He would travel back through time to be friends with Earl again. He would find his family, and his story would have a happy ending, too.

Just then a voice spoke close to her ear. "Seems your cousin has a pal."

Lucy looked around and saw Sheriff Jensen. "Cousin?" she said in surprise. Then she remembered that as far as Sheriff Jensen knew, Oscar was her distant cousin. She followed his gaze across the church lawn to where Earl was tracing a curve in the air with his cane, illustrating a story he was telling. Oscar interrupted Earl, giving him a friendly shove, and they both broke into laughter.

"You'd think they were old friends," said Sheriff Jensen. "Kind of strange, isn't it?"

"It sure is," Lucy murmured.

That night, when Lucy was trying to go to sleep, thoughts about time crept into her mind again.

"Talking like old friends," Sheriff Jensen had said at the picnic. Well, of course, they *were* old friends, Oscar and Earl—torn apart when they were teenagers. But if Oscar went back to his own time, their friendship wouldn't end abruptly. They would grow up together. Lucy could imagine them graduating from high school. Maybe Oscar would be the best man at Earl's wedding. Or maybe they would quarrel about something and go their separate ways. There was no way to tell. The only sure thing was that their future would be different.

But in this case, the future was already the past. And that was the problem.

It took some concentrating to figure it out. By writing in *The Book of Story Beginnings,* Oscar had set in motion a long chain of events that began with his own disappearance. But just suppose Oscar were to go back to a time before he had written his story beginnings. Having come back to the past from the future, Oscar would know not to write them. As a result, he wouldn't disappear. Aunt Lavonne wouldn't spend her entire life trying to find out what had happened to him. And I wouldn't even think of looking for *The Book of Story Beginnings,* thought Lucy. It wouldn't even be in the smokehouse for me to find.

One after another, Lucy thought of all the things that would never happen if Oscar went back in time. It was as if she were adding china cups to a precariously tall stack; suddenly, she thought of something that sent all the cups crashing. If Oscar went back in time and warned himself not to write in *The Book of Story Beginnings,* then he wouldn't be here now. But if he wasn't here now, how could he go back in time to warn himself?

Lucy got out of bed. Pushing open the door to the hall, she listened for a moment to the murmur of voices from her parents' room. Then she went to Oscar's room. His door was closed. He had been very quiet after supper, going up to bed even before it was dark outside. But there was a slit of light under the door. Lucy hesitated, then knocked.

"Who is it?"

"It's me. Can I come in?"

Oscar opened the door. His desk lamp was turned on, and Lucy saw his composition books in a neat pile within its circle of light. One of the books was open.

"What are you doing?" she asked.

"Trying to write." Oscar crossed the room to the chair. He threw his leg over it and sat backward, facing Lucy. He rested his arms and his chin on the back of the chair.

Lucy sat down on the edge of the bed. "I've been thinking about time," she said. She described her thoughts about how everything had already happened one way, and how it would have to happen another way when he went home. "It doesn't make any sense," she concluded.

"You're right," said Oscar when she was finished. "It doesn't make any sense. And I'm not going home."

"What?" Lucy stared at him.

"I thought of everything you just said, too. Then I talked to your father."

"What did he say?"

"He said he was pretty sure the traveling talisman could send me home."

"Then you should go!" said Lucy.

"I *can't*." Oscar's voice was firm.

"But why?"

"Because I don't know what will happen if I do!" Oscar raised his head and looked past Lucy, into the dark corner behind her. "When I was talking to Earl today, he told me how he met his wife at college. I never thought Earl would go to college. He and I were going to travel after high school. We talked about going to Mexico or Canada, even Europe maybe. Well, what if I went back and we did that? What if Earl never went to college? What if he never met his wife?"

Oscar gave a sigh. "Don't you see? If one thing changes, other things change, too. Who knows? Maybe *you* would never have been born if I went back in time."

"Of course I'd be born!"

"How do you know?"

"Because I'm *here*! I *was* born," said Lucy, scowling. It was frustrating to have to defend something as obvious as her own existence, and even more frustrating to feel that her defense might not be adequate.

"The point is that you might *not* be. It depends on how time works, which is something nobody knows for sure. Your father says that some people—scholars, I guess—think only the present is real. The past and the future don't even exist. That isn't much help, as far as I can tell. And some people say that the future and the present are made up of a lot of different worlds.

Each world comes out of a different set of circumstances that might have happened in the past. So, depending on the circumstances, you might exist in one or more worlds—"

"But what does all that mean?" Lucy interrupted.

"It means that nobody knows for sure what will happen if somebody goes back in time," said Oscar. "Anyway, that's why I'm not going back."

"But that's not right!" Lucy practically spat the words out. How could Oscar sit there so calmly and say something so wrong? She thought of what he had said about stories needing to end happily. It was as if Oscar were being cheated. "It isn't fair. I'll talk to my father," she told him.

"No! I've already talked to him. And it's not his decision. It's *mine*." Oscar's desk chair was the kind that swiveled, and he turned it now so that his back was to her. "I want to write in my journal," he said without looking around, and Lucy knew he wanted her to go.

But it *isn't* fair, she thought. Hot tears burned in her eyes as she closed Oscar's door behind her. "It isn't fair," she whispered. "He's got to go home."

# Chapter Twenty-eight
## Choosing

One morning at breakfast, a few weeks after the birthday party, Lucy's father made an announcement. "I'm going to take a teaching position at the community college this fall."

"I thought you didn't want to teach chemistry anymore," said Lucy.

"Well, it's only two classes in chemistry, and I'm much more excited about the other class I'll be teaching. It's on the history of science—the history of alchemy, actually. That book of Lavonne's is going to form the basis of my lectures," said her father. "Besides, we'll need the extra money. Your mother has decided she's going to start writing again."

"I want to try writing some short stories," said Lucy's mother.

"Really?" said Oscar, looking up from the cereal box he had been reading.

Lucy saw her parents glance at each other. Oscar hadn't talked much since the day of Earl's birthday party. This was the first time he had expressed interest in something.

"I know you like to write, Oscar," said Lucy's mother, smiling at him. "Maybe we can share ideas."

Ideas for stories, thought Lucy. As if they hadn't already had enough stories for a lifetime. She thought of *The Book of Story Beginnings*. It was up in the attic now. "Locked up safe and sound," her father had promised her mother, though Lucy suspected that he took it out for examination every once in a while. He was curious about what he called its "unique metaphysical properties."

Lucy wondered if Oscar was thinking about *The Book of Story Beginnings*. She knew he wouldn't tell her even if she were to ask. Along with not talking to her parents much, he had stopped talking to *her* as well. In fact, she hardly ever saw him these days. Sometimes he shut himself up in his room. But on most days, he left the house after breakfast and didn't come back until supper. Where he went he didn't say, and when Lucy dared to ask, he said, "Just around." He seemed to be a different sort of person now. He was still polite—Oscar was always polite—but it felt like nothing more than good manners. He had become closed off, secretive with his thoughts.

Sometimes Lucy thought she knew what Oscar was thinking and feeling. "He's sad," she told her father. "He misses his family. How can he bear to be here with us?"

"Give him time," said her father.

Because she had nothing else to do but wait for summer to end and school to begin, Lucy began to play her violin. She practiced each day in the music parlor, spending more time and effort than she ever had before. The sonata she was learning was difficult, full of scales that went up and up like the stairs in the Statue of Liberty, and complicated by so many trills there didn't seem to be enough room for her fingers to play them. One afternoon she grew frustrated. Halfway through the sonata, her fingers slipped into an easy piece she hadn't played in ages, a fiddle tune. She played it again, it sounded so pretty. It's just the sort of thing Ma would play, she thought.

Then she tried to work out the melody of "Billy Boy," playing it over and over, experimenting with little trills, sliding her fingers gypsy-style up and down the strings, making the violin "sing like a soprano," which was what her old teacher always used to say, until at last the violin really was singing, and Lucy felt a rush of pleasure like gold showering down on her.

Suddenly, a movement from the doorway made her stop. Her violin bow scraped into a sour note.

It was Oscar.

Lucy didn't know what to say. "This is your ma's violin," she said at last, holding it out to him.

"I see," said Oscar, but he didn't move to take the violin.

It hurt not knowing what Oscar was thinking, like having him close a door, leaving her outside. "You play well," he said. He turned and went out the front door. Lucy watched him from the window as he crossed the lawn and disappeared down the road to town.

That night Oscar didn't come home for supper.

"Ray called," said Lucy's father as they sat down at the kitchen table. "He took Oscar around in the patrol car this afternoon. Oscar's having supper over at Ray's house tonight."

"Sheriff Jensen!" Lucy said in astonishment.

"That's right."

"What's he doing with *him*?"

"Having fun, I suppose," said her father. "Oscar and Ray have kind of hit it off."

"Ray's been very kind," said her mother. "It's been a hard adjustment for Oscar. I'm sure he'll make friends at school, but right now, he must feel pretty alone."

Alone! If Oscar felt alone it was because he hadn't done anything but *be* alone. I'm alone, thought Lucy. I know what it's like to be alone. It stung her to learn that Oscar had sought company elsewhere.

After supper she waited for him on the front porch. She pretended to read a book at first. Then the sun sank in the sky and it grew dark, and she gave up pretending. The mosquitoes began to attack, and she swatted at them for a while, feeling sorry for herself and angry at the mosquitoes, or angry at something less easy to target than a mosquito. At last she went inside and got the bug spray.

When she came back, Sheriff Jensen's car was pulling away. Oscar waved goodbye, his tall form caught for a moment in Sheriff Jensen's headlights. He looked oddly modern in a T-shirt and a pair of cutoffs.

Lucy sat down on the steps and pumped repellent into her hand, slapping it on her arms and legs. She didn't look up as Oscar came toward her.

"That smells awful," he commented. "What is it?"

"It keeps mosquitoes away."

"That and all your friends. Ma used to make us use citronella. I thought that smelled bad." Oscar took the bottle and sat down.

"That's probably enough," Lucy said finally. The sight of Oscar splashing half a bottle of bug spray on his arms made her feel braver than usual, and she dared to ask a question. "What were you doing with Sheriff Jensen?" She didn't mean for her question to sound like an accusation, but somehow it did.

Oscar didn't seem to notice. "I don't know," he said. He leaned forward, resting his elbows on his knees. "He's a funny guy. I guess he makes me think of my pa."

"Your pa!"

"Well, sure. My pa was really funny sometimes. We'd go off and do things together, like fishing—even working in the barn, or hard jobs like chopping ice. He was always making me laugh—well, not always, I guess. Sometimes he made me madder than a hornet. But when we did have a good time . . ." Oscar paused, looking out into space. "Ray just makes me laugh," he added. "A fellow needs to laugh—that's all."

Of course! Feeling so alone and sad, Oscar needed to laugh. Lucy's heart melted a little. "Do you—do you miss your ma and pa?" she asked.

"Sure," said Oscar.

Lucy waited for him to say more. She watched the tiny lights of the fireflies. They moved questioningly through the darkness, as if they were making a map of the night air.

"Do you ever think about them, Lucy?" said Oscar.

"Who?" Lucy thought Oscar meant his mother and father.

"The King and Queen, Captain Mack and Millie, all of them."

"Oh!" Lucy had to shift her thinking. "I don't know. Sometimes, I guess."

"Do you suppose they're still there, wherever *there* is, going on with their lives?"

"I don't know," said Lucy. "Maybe they're like people in a story. They have a beginning, a middle, and an end, and that's it."

"Maybe," said Oscar. "But don't you think there are some stories that are more alive than that? When you put certain books back on the shelf, don't you feel as if the people inside are going on with their lives after the story is over?"

Lucy felt that way about most of the books she loved.

"The King was a little bit like my pa," said Oscar. "My pa had a temper like that. He'd go along pleasant as anything, and then something would set him off. He was always sorry about it afterward, I think." Oscar looked at Lucy. "I guess you think everybody reminds me of my pa," he said with a wry smile.

Lucy had thought that, but she didn't say so.

"The Queen made me think of my ma. Ma was always playing music, just like the Queen was always painting. Pa was proud of her, but he'd get mad all the same." Oscar was quiet a moment, then added, "Do you suppose they ever would have made up their quarrel if it hadn't been for Phoebe?"

"They did love each other," said Lucy. "But I think they needed Phoebe. They were so different from each other; they needed something in common."

"That isn't fair," said Oscar. "They shouldn't have to depend on a child to make things right between them." He sounded bitter.

"Maybe Phoebe's only part of it. What I mean is, it helps to have something in common, but she can't be everything for them. They need to choose to be happy." Lucy was thinking of her own parents. In the past, she had often felt as if she were the one holding them together. But it wasn't me at all, she realized suddenly. People have to decide for themselves to be happy.

"When I was out tonight with Ray, it was wonderful," said Oscar. "His car can go so fast. There's a siren louder than a train whistle! And a crystal set, right in the car!"

"A *what*?"

"I guess you call it a radio," said Oscar. "Ray played some music—loud, drumming music. He called it *rock-and-roll*. He turned on the siren and we went down the dirt road in back of the Lee farm as fast as anything, dust flying behind us. Down one hill and up another—I could feel myself lifting off the seat. . . ." Oscar looked at Lucy. "You see? It's not much for you. But for me, it's as if—well, how would you feel if you got to travel into the future? To see things you never even imagined!" He looked away again, and his voice grew tortured. "Right then, I was actually *happy* that I wrote what I did in *The Book of Story Beginnings*."

He went on before Lucy could respond. "Pa didn't think much of me wanting to be a writer," he said. "I couldn't even talk about it with him. But Ma knew what I wanted. I wanted to go out and see things. I wanted—well, a writer's got to have something to write about. I wasn't going to waste my life here. " Oscar waved his hand across the horizon, and Lucy imagined the way things might have looked to him so long ago. *Long, dull roads that went on forever before they came to anywhere that was somewhere.* That was what he had written in his story beginning.

"I felt like Pa was never going to let me leave home," said Oscar. "He wanted me to take over the farm when he got old. Sometimes I heard them arguing about it. Ma telling Pa to leave me alone about it. And Pa telling her to—" Oscar paused. "I just hated it when they fought. Sometimes I wanted to run away. That's why I wrote that story beginning."

"But you didn't mean for things to turn out the way they did."

"No." Oscar's voice was empty and sad. "I didn't."

"You can't be unhappy forever," said Lucy. "Your parents wouldn't want—"

"But to be *glad* for what I did! It's like being glad I murdered them."

"But you didn't murder them! They went on with their lives. They chose to be happy. They had to, even if they never forgot you, or never stopped missing you," said Lucy. She was shivering, not because she was cold, but because she always shivered when she tried to say something important. "You're just choosing," she said. "You're choosing to be happy about what's happened."

Though Oscar didn't say anything, Lucy could feel him listening. "The happiest endings—I think they're endings that feel like beginnings," she said, still shivering. She was thinking of the King and Queen. She was thinking of her own parents. "We're your family now, Oscar," she said. "You should choose us."

Oscar gave her a quiet look—the kind of look he might have given his own sister, she thought. A great sigh left him, like a ghost departing. He put his head down on his arms, and Lucy followed his gaze, looking out across the plains, at the four-lane highway that couldn't have been there in 1914, at a bright point of light, a jet moving across the background of stars. Meanwhile, all around in the darkness the endlessly patient song of the crickets went on, like a clock keeping time through the night, through all the nights in all the years.

Lucy thought she could feel what Oscar was thinking. He's choosing *now,* she thought to herself. He's choosing *this* ending, *this* beginning.

They sat there together for a long time, until at last Lucy's mother came to the screen door and told them it was time to come in. And they went in, and the door closed behind them, and all the Martins were home at last.